IDLE TALK

Voorkamer Stories (?)

To Robert
with love from
Mary-Anne   Oct 2000.

THE ANNIVERSARY EDITION OF HERMAN CHARLES BOSMAN

Planning began in late 1997 – the fiftieth anniversary of Bosman's first collection in book form, Mafeking Road *– to re-edit his works in their original, unabridged and uncensored texts. The project should be completed by 2005 – the centenary of his birth.*

GENERAL EDITORS:
STEPHEN GRAY AND CRAIG MACKENZIE

Already published in this edition:

MAFEKING ROAD AND OTHER STORIES
WILLEMSDORP
COLD STONE JUG

Herman Charles Bosman

IDLE TALK

Voorkamer Stories (I)

The Anniversary Edition

Edited by Craig MacKenzie

HUMAN & ROUSSEAU

Cape Town Pretoria Johannesburg

HERMAN CHARLES Bosman was born near Cape Town in 1905, but spent most of his life in the Transvaal. In 1926 he was posted as a novice teacher to a farm school in the Marico District. His spell at the school was cut short when, during a vacation to the family home in Johannesburg, he shot and killed his stepbrother. Initially sentenced to hang, his sentence was commuted to life imprisonment and he was eventually paroled in 1930, having served four years.

After a period working as a journalist in London, he returned to South Africa in 1940 and was thereafter employed on various magazines and newspapers. *Jacaranda in the Night,* a novel, and a collection of Oom Schalk Lourens stories, *Mafeking Road,* both appeared in 1947. His gaol memoir, *Cold Stone Jug,* followed in 1949. A year later he returned to the Marico, the region that had made him famous, in a series of sketches written weekly for *The Forum* under the rubric 'In die Voorkamer.' At the time he was a proofreader on the *Sunday Express* and working on *Willemsdorp* (already published in the anniversary edition).

Some of the Voorkamer sketches have appeared in earlier volumes – *Jurie Steyn's Post Office* and *A Bekkersdal Marathon* (both 1971) – but they are printed here for the first time in the sequence in which they originally appeared, thus allowing Bosman's intricate thematic patterning to be rediscovered. And, when the second part appears as the companion volume to this one, the sequence will also have been published in its entirety in book form for the first time.

Contents

Introduction

I N APRIL, 1950, just eighteen months before his death, Herman Charles Bosman embarked on one of his most ambitious projects: a series of 2 000-word stories written to a weekly deadline for Johannesburg's *The Forum*. It is testimony to his manic creative drive that he was able to produce eighty of these pieces in all, over a period of eighteen months without a single break, until his sudden death by heart failure in October, 1951.

The series appeared under the rubric 'In die Voorkamer', and was clearly intended to provide a comic counterpoint to the more sober 'forum' of political commentary and opinion-pieces that constituted the staple of this liberal-left weekly. Apart from a summary of the news, *The Forum* featured articles by leading political figures, journalists and academics – including Jordan K. Ngubane (a regular columnist) and such outside luminaries as Bertrand Russell – and had been launched to challenge, as Alan Paton said, "the whole Malanite creed, with its isolationism and its racial exclusiveness, not by British jingoism, but by a broader kind of South Africanism" (qtd. in *New Nation,* December, 1979).

Bosman had made earlier appearances in *The Forum* with three Oom Schalk stories in late 1949 and early 1950, but these merely paved the way for what would be the lengthy – albeit abruptly halted – Voorkamer series. The first story in the sequence, "The Budget" (15 April, 1950), was accompanied by a short note: "This is the first of a series of humorous sketches... by the well-known South African writer, Herman Charles Bosman. Mr Bosman's personae are a set of Bushveld neighbours who foregather in a voorkamer which doubles as local post office."

That the stories soon began to make their mark is attested to by Bosman's photograph gracing the cover of *The Forum* three episodes later. And in the issue of 3 November, 1950, Bosman was reintroduced to the readership, alongside another picture of him, in a passage paraphrasing South Africa's literary giant of the time: "Roy Campbell wrote in an article on South African literature, the other day, that he saw a great future for Herman Charles Bosman. Campbell sensed a genius who could make the platteland live as few others had succeeded in doing; whose subtle humour, knowledge of human nature, and gift of expression would one day win him fame among South African writers." The author of that note was in all likelihood *The Forum*'s co-editor Lily Rabkin, who took personal charge of the literary pages, and who was all too soon to be called upon once again to record her appreciation of Bosman in those pages upon his sudden death.

It is typical of Bosman that he chose to locate the "broader kind of South Africanism" referred to by Paton in a narrow, backveld setting. In the bushveld meeting-place of Jurie Steyn's voorkamer, also the Drogevlei post office, local farmers gather under the pretext of waiting for the Government lorry bearing their letters and empty milk-cans from Bekkersdal. Usually prompted by At Naudé, they offer their weekly Marico perspective on topical subjects.

The pattern of the pieces is typically a desultory, meandering conversation sparked off by an item of news (a marathon dancing competition, atomic testing, the appointment of General Douglas MacArthur to the supreme command in South Korea, a race classification mix-up), an event in the district (the return of a pretty girl from finishing-school in the Cape, the annual school concert, a stranger arriving on the Government lorry), or a perennial topic (ghosts, white ants, bank managers). Various voices, almost entirely in direct or reported speech, take up the thread of chat, usually turning it in a different direction and often having fun needling or duping one of the present company.

The pieces are more accurately described as 'conversation pieces' or 'sketches' rather than 'short stories' in that they are often less formal and seldom have a strong narrative line. Like Bosman's famous Oom Schalk Lourens stories, however, the Voorkamer pieces are firmly rooted in the medium of the spoken word. The sequence can in fact be seen to be a further development of Bosman's preoccupation with oral narrative modes, his fascination with *telling* stories. This time, in the place of a single storyteller figure through whom the entire narrative is filtered, we have a set of speakers – the habitués of Jurie Steyn's voorkamer.

Apart from Jurie Steyn himself, puffed up with his new role as postmaster, we usually encounter Gysbert van Tonder, cattle-smuggler and hostile neighbour of Jurie's; Chris Welman, the Dopper from the Eastern Cape who prides himself on his singing abilities, and who was once a 'white labourer' digging foundations in Johannesburg; At Naudé, avid radio-listener and the chief purveyor of news; young 'Meneer' Vermaak, the earnest schoolmaster who is remorselessly baited by the others; Johnny Coen, the most romantically inclined of the backveld rustics; and Oupa Sarel Bekker, their elder statesman who bears a distinct resemblance to Schalk Lourens. Conveying all of this to the reader is an anonymous narrator, memorably described by Gillian Siebert as "a transparent minutes secretary of the eternal, inconclusive voorkamer debates" (*New Nation,* June, 1972).

These Marico denizens are situated a generation after Oom Schalk Lourens and his Boer War comrades in the 1920s. The unbounded liberties of frontier life have gradually been fenced in by outside agencies – legislating bodies in Pretoria, border police patrols, the Land Bank. The ox-wagon and mule-cart of Oom Schalk's day have been supplanted by the Government lorry that runs between Bekkersdal and Groblersdal, delivering visitors and gossip from the outside world into the heart of the Marico. (Bekkersdal, we learn near the end of the sequence, is named after Oupa Bekker's grandfather; both it and Groblersdal have been relocated by Bosman to the Dwarsberg and are not to be confused with the present-day places. Jurie Steyn's post office, however, is modelled on the one run by Jurie Bekker [*sic*] on the Nietverdiend–Ramoutsa road, photographed by David Goldblatt in a ruined state in the 1960s. And Ottoshoop, where Johnny Coen once worked as a shunter, is an actual siding just south of Zeerust.)

At Naudé's 'wireless' also brings the outside world to the reluctant farmers' doorstep, and resist though they might (indeed, they cussedly ignore At Naudé's recycled bulletins), their world, with all the glamour of the open veld life, is steadily and irrevocably being encroached upon. Where the 'rooinek' in *Mafeking Road* came with a laden ox-wagon and the desire to settle, people pass in and out of this world on a regular basis; there are even seasonal tourists. The lure of the big cities is proving irresistible: Johnny Coen pines for a Marico lass who has gone to the bad in Johannesburg; Chris Welman's son, Tobie, has spent some years at a reform school there; their representative in Pretoria visits them only at election time… This is becoming a forgotten world, containing people increasingly marginalised by developments elsewhere. Impoverished and abandoned, but obstinately resisting the inevitable, these farmers gather to pit their homely wisdom against all innovations. Indeed, a great deal of the humour of the pieces lies in the way these wiseacres attempt to fit such novelties into their limited frames of reference.

They joke about it constantly, but the harsh reality of their isolation and poverty is only superficially masked by their laughter. At times it cannot be disguised. Witness the pathos in the description, in "School Concert", of the family whose grandfather has to stay behind in the tent on the kerkplein when the others attend Nagmaal, because there are not enough shoes to go around. And the description of the men decked out in their best attire ("Home from Finishing-school") to impress the returning damsel is simultaneously funny and pathetic.

Oom Schalk's romantic world may be fading away, but now we have Oupa Bekker to recall that era for us with his stories about how news was conveyed "in the old days", how the freebooting republics of Goshen (which they pronounce Goosen), Stellaland and Ohrigstad (of which he was apparently Finance Minister) were run, and what the Transvaal was like in the days when Potchefstroom was its capital. Where Schalk Lourens had oracular status in this society, however, Oupa Bekker is more of a deaf and doddery museum-piece. Like Schalk, he can still catch his listeners out with a twist in the narrative, but whereas Schalk had a ready circle agape for the unexpected, Oupa Bekker's interlocutors resist his increasingly demented tales of "die ou dae", and head him off on more than one occasion.

These farmers are disillusioned and disgruntled, and they no longer want to hear Oupa Bekker's tales of better times. Their alienation from the soil is particularly in evidence in "Local Colour", in which a writer coming to the district for local lore and folk-wisdom leaves dismayed at the farmers' unrelenting literalness and lack of interest in the hazy wonders of nature. The story humorously registers their deracination: there is no romance left, it seems, just a harsh, grinding struggle for survival. Bosman's self-irony is present in this story as well, in the figure of the writer looking for the kind of rural romance about which only leisured city-dwellers have illusions. It is also present in the portraits of the young schoolmasters Charlie Rossouw and Vermaak, sent out, as Bosman himself once was, to educate the rustics – and receiving an education from them instead.

Oupa Bekker and At Naudé are rivals for the attention of the voorkamer audience, as they represent two different, and opposed, epistemological modes. The German critic Walter Benjamin's distinction between 'knowledge' and 'information' is apt here. In the slow, measured pace of Oupa Bekker's world, news came in the form of people passing through the district, and there was time to digest that news, comment on it and cast it into a form of *knowledge*. By contrast, At Naudé and his radio bring disembodied bits of *information* to the voorkamer regulars, for which they usually have little use.

Perversely, Bosman often has Oupa Bekker winning this battle. Unlike

At Naudé, Oupa Bekker still heeds Schalk Lourens's dicta concerning the telling of a tale: how fast to go, when to mention certain details and what to leave out. At Naudé's news is like the modern world itself that threatens this isolated region: fragmented, diverse and discordant, it brings little solace to the marginalised men in the voorkamer and they often wilfully misunderstand At Naudé as a form of retribution. Scornfully pushing aside his information about "stone-throwings in Johannesburg locations and about how many new kinds of bombs the Russians had got", they are more interested in whether it "was true that the ouderling at Pilanesberg really forgot himself in the way that Jurie Steyn's wife had heard about from a kraal Mtosa at the kitchen door... Now, there was news for you" ("News Story").

Bosman situates Jurie Steyn's voorkamer at the boundary between the old and the new. This is suggested by the room itself: it is simultaneously an old-world waiting room, where guests are served coffee while passing the time of day in leisurely loquacity, and an actual post office, rather poorly equipped but nevertheless the sorting-house of information and communication. Jurie Steyn may loyally hang his stamps to dry on the wall when the leaky roof lets in the rain, and he may take great pride in his brass scales and new wire-netting, but once modern developments reach the Marico in earnest, he too will be superseded. The institution of Jurie Steyn's post office is on the brink of passing away, and with it the last vestiges of its old-world charm.

The Voorkamer stories have a fascination all their own. On a technical level, Bosman's shift from a single storyteller to multiple narrators can be seen as a further development of his fascination with storytelling. Working with the unwieldy logistics of the conversation format must have proved more of a challenge to him than continuing to produce the trusty old monologue: it required more skill at juggling the voices of the collocutors, while still maintaining an overall narrative thrust.

No story in this sequence is without its sparkle and charm, but a different strategy is called for on the part of the reader. After all, each is an occasional newspaper column, written to beguile and amuse the readers of the very day. Rather than looking for the gradual building towards a climactic ending, where the various threads of the narrative converge, the reader should perhaps learn to relish the individual moments of brilliance – the quirky, unpredictable turns that naturally arise out of unscripted human discourse. Witnessing the interaction of the characters and their gradual unfoldings as individuals is therefore a chief source of pleasure.

As we come to know them as regulars, we can predict their reactions to any given topic and even anticipate with glee the inevitable clashes of sensibilities and opinions. Jurie Steyn is usually stolidly prosaic, Gysbert van Tonder adversarial and belligerent, Chris Welman contrary and occasionally brusque. At Naudé wants to offer them all a contemporary insight, while Oupa Bekker attempts to keep the historical perspective meaningful. For his part, the schoolmaster earnestly corrects them all by the book, often missing the point, while the rival youngster in the group, Johnny Coen, is constitutionally naïve but also frequently their peacemaker.

Selections of the Voorkamer pieces have appeared in book form, but the sequence has never been reproduced in its entirety. Lionel Abrahams's two editions of Voorkamer stories – *Jurie Steyn's Post Office* and *A Bekkersdal Marathon* (both 1971) – reprinted only half of the eighty pieces (to be precise, thirty-nine out of seventy-nine – or eighty if one counts "School Concert" as two episodes), and in substantially re-arranged order. In his Compiler's Foreword to *Jurie Steyn's Post Office* Abrahams explained that his criterion for selection for his stories was that "after nineteen years [they] still yield pleasure enough to justify their preservation in book form." The rearrangement of the pieces across two volumes he justified as follows: "It might have been desirable to have retained the order in which the pieces originally appeared; but six of them, embodying linked episodes of the 'romance' involving Pauline Gerber... are scattered across the middle of the series. So it has been necessary to rearrange the order for the sake of containing the Pauline Gerber 'novella' entire in this first volume."

The Pauline Gerber episodes were not presented there in their entirety, however. "Dreams of Rain" is one of several omissions, and it contains a key instalment: the rejection of Johnny Coen by Pauline Gerber and his subsequent disillusionment. Interestingly, it appears as a minute (but none the less significant) interpolation into the larger topic of this particular story (rain, and the farmers' dreams about it), and was perhaps therefore overlooked. But this demonstrates something essential about Bosman's modus operandi: his skilful *co-presentation* of the various narrative motifs that together are woven into the larger tapestry upon which he was working. So clustering the stories, and rearranging their running order, ironically merely fragments and distorts this larger design.

The other point is that the Pauline Gerber episodes, although major, constitute only one of the many threads that are woven through the sequence. Abrahams's reshuffling has meant that most of these have been lost. Re-editing the sequence in its entirety, and in order, allows readers to take up these threads once more. In this way we learn, for instance, about two of schoolmaster Vermaak's early predecessors, both dismissed by the Transvaal Education Department, before Vermaak himself appears on the scene. Their behaviour evidently earned the displeasure of the Dwarsberg community, and so young Vermaak is never entirely able to reverse the disfavour with which education is perceived in the region.

We gather also the reasons for the enmity between Jurie Steyn and Gysbert van Tonder early on (a land dispute, referred to in "The Budget"), and therefore understand their rivalry in later stories a little better. We see, too, that the resentment that gradually builds up between Jurie Steyn and young Vermaak is a consequence of Jurie Steyn's wife's suspected partiality for the learned schoolmaster; the developing intrigue of their affair goes to explain the many scornful comments Jurie Steyn makes about Vermaak and mere "book learning." This triangle is then complicated by Alida van Niekerk, the doting daughter of the family with whom Vermaak is boarding. Similarly, we understand better the innuendo in "The Coffee that Tasted like Tar", when the farmers begin to suspect that Jurie Steyn may be being poisoned; and we also click at last when his wife makes her jealous aside in "School Concert" about that Alida. But the person whose favours Vermaak has *really* been soliciting remains skilfully hidden from view until the cliffhanger ending of this part of the cycle. (To be continued in Part II.)

Likewise, the infatuation of the chronic bolter, Johnny Coen, with Minnie Nienaber is revealed only obliquely (in "Psycho-analysis"), as is his rescue mission to Johannesburg. But the aftermath of this is not resolved, and then only as if by accident, until "Play within a Play", a whole sixteen weeks later. Other flickers of motif are almost subliminal: Gysbert van Tonder's apprehension over others being about to think that he may have a touch of the tar; the progress of At Naudé who, having worked his way up from being a bywoner, especially prizes radio learning, then becomes fed up with the SABC, reverts to the daily printed press, then resumes hamming... Such delicate threads are only for the connoisseur to detect. For this is the warp (the series of weekly incidents) and woof (the serial of continuing events) of the intricate Voorkamer stories, where nuance is all, now once again available to Bosman's readers exactly as he originally intended.

In their day the Abrahams volumes certainly served their purpose of introducing new readers to the missing Voorkamer part of Bosman's oeuvre. But now, some fifty years on, perhaps the readers of a later generation should bear in mind some other factors which contribute to a full enjoyment of the true sequence. Whereas Bosman's previous work is less time-bound, here the content is linked to a calendar, specifically that of 1950. When the readers of *The Forum* were taking their copies out on to the stoep or balcony once again with spring in the great world, it was also "Springtime in the Marico." Political watersheds – to give only one example – like the passage of the infamous Population Registration Act, do not go unremarked upon, as in the scathing satire of the "Birth Certificate" episode of 12 August, which aptly connected up to *The Forum*'s editorial matter.

But by and large Bosman stresses the interconnectedness of all South African life – that is his whole point. School holidays occur in town and country alike, and the end of year wind-up with Christmas preparations and the New Year service in the Marico, played out in a carefully constructed reality, touched and amused everyone.

Here then is the first half of Bosman's Voorkamer enterprise – the tale that unfolded week by week from 15 April to 22 December, 1950 – fittingly opened and closed by none other than the inimitable Dominee Welthagen himself.

And now read on.

Craig MacKenzie
Johannesburg, 1999

The Budget

WE WERE sitting in Jurie Steyn's voorkamer at Drogevlei, waiting for the Government lorry from Bekkersdal, that brought us our letters and empty milk-cans. Jurie Steyn's voorkamer had served as the Drogevlei post office for some years, and Jurie Steyn was postmaster. His complaint was that the post office didn't pay. It didn't pay him, he said, to be called away from his lands every time somebody came in for a penny stamp. What was more, Gysbert van Tonder could walk right into his voorkamer whenever he liked, and without knocking. Gysbert was Jurie Steyn's neighbour, and Jurie had naturally not been on friendly terms with him since the time Gysbert van Tonder got a justice of the peace and a land-surveyor and a policeman riding a skimmel horse to explain to Jurie Steyn on what side of the vlei the boundary fence ran.

What gave Jurie Steyn some measure of satisfaction, he said, was the fact that his post office couldn't pay the Government, either.

"Maybe it will pay better now," At Naudé said. "Now that you can charge more for the stamps, I mean."

At Naudé had a wireless, and was therefore always first with the news. Moreover, At Naudé made that remark with a slight sneer.

Now, Jurie Steyn is funny in that way. He doesn't mind what he himself says about his post office. But he doesn't care much for the ill-informed kind of comment that he sometimes gets from people who don't know how exacting a postmaster's duties are. I can still remember some of the things Jurie Steyn said to a stranger who dropped in one day for a half-crown postal order, when Jurie had been busy with the cream separator. The stranger spoke of the buttermilk smudges on the postal order, which made the ink run in a blue blotch when he tried to fill it in. It was then that Jurie Steyn asked the stranger if he thought Marico buttermilk wasn't good enough for him, and what he thought he could get for half a crown. Jurie Steyn also started coming from behind the counter, so that he could explain better to the stranger what a man could get in the Bushveld for considerably less than half a crown. Unfortunately, the stranger couldn't wait to hear. He said that he had left his engine running when he came into the post office.

From that it would appear that he was not such a complete stranger to the ways of the Groot Marico.

With regard to At Naudé's remark now, however, we could see that

Jurie Steyn would have preferred to let it pass. He took out a thick book with black covers and started ticking off lists with a pencil in an important sort of a way. But all the time we could sense the bitterness against At Naudé that was welling up inside him. When the pencil-point broke, Jurie Steyn couldn't stand it any more.

"Anyway, At," he said, "even twopence a half-ounce is cheaper than getting a Mchopi runner to carry a letter in a long stick with a cleft in the end. But, of course, you wouldn't understand about things like progress."

Jurie Steyn shouldn't have said that. Immediately three or four of us wanted to start talking at the same time.

"Cheaper, maybe," Johnny Coen said, "but not better, or quicker – or – or – *cleaner* – " Johnny Coen almost choked with laughter. He thought he was being very clever.

Meanwhile, Chris Welman was trying to tell a story we had heard from him often before about a letter that was posted at Christmas time in Volksrust and arrived at its destination, Magoeba's Kloof, twenty-eight years later, and on Dingaan's Day.

"If a native runner took twenty-eight years to get from Volksrust to Magoeba's Kloof," Chris Welman said, "we would have known that he didn't run much. He must at least have stopped once or twice at huts along the way for kaffir beer."

Meanwhile, Oupa Sarel Bekker, who was one of the oldest inhabitants of the Marico and had known Bekkersdal before it was even a properly measured-out farm, started taking part in the conversation. But because Oupa Bekker was slightly deaf, and a bit queer in the head through advancing years, he thought we were saying that Jurie Steyn had been running along the main road, carrying a letter in a cleft stick. Accordingly, Oupa Bekker warned Jurie Steyn to be careful of mambas. The kloof was full of brown mambas at that time of year, Oupa Bekker said.

"All the same, in the days of the Republics you would not get a white man doing a thing like that," Oupa Bekker went on, shaking his head. "Not even in the Republic of Goosen. And not even after the Republic of Goosen's Minister of Finance had lost all the State revenues in an unfortunate game of poker that he had been invited to take part in at the Mafeking Hotel. And there was quite a big surplus, too, that year, which the Minister of Finance kept tucked away in an inside pocket right through the poker game, and which he could still remember having had on him when he went into the bar. Although he could never remember what happened to that surplus afterwards. The Minister of Finance never went

18

back to Goosen, of course. He stayed on in Mafeking. When I saw him again he was offering to help carry people's luggage from the Zeederberg coach station to the hotel."

Oupa Bekker was getting ready to say a lot more, when Jurie Steyn interrupted him, demanding to know what all that had got to do with his post office.

"I said that even when things were very bad in the old days, you would still never see a white postmaster running in the sun with a letter in a cleft stick," Oupa Bekker explained, adding, "like a Mchopi."

Jurie Steyn's wife did not want any unpleasantness. So she came and sat on the riempies bench next to Oupa Bekker and made it clear to him, in a friendly sort of way, what the discussion was all about.

"You see, Oupa," Jurie Steyn's wife said finally, after a pause for breath, "that's just what we have been *saying*. We've been saying that in the old days, before they had proper post offices, people used to send letters with Mchopi runners."

"But that's what I've been saying also," Oupa Bekker persisted. "I say, why doesn't Jurie rather go in his mule-cart?"

Jurie Steyn's wife gave it up after that. Especially when Jurie Steyn himself walked over to where Oupa Bekker was sitting.

"You know, Oupa," Jurie said, talking very quietly, "you have been an ouderling for many years, and we all respect you in the Groot Marico. We also respect your grey hairs. But you must not lose that respect through – through talking about things that you don't understand."

Oupa Bekker tightened his grip on his tamboetie-wood walking-stick.

"Now if you had spoken to me like that in the Republican days, Jurie Steyn," the old man said, in a cracked voice. "In the Republic of Stella-land, for instance – "

"You and your republics, Oupa," Jurie Steyn said, giving up the argument and turning back to the counter. "Goosen, Stellaland, Lydenburg – I suppose you were also in the Ohrigstad Republic?"

Oupa Bekker sat up very stiffly on the riempies bench, then.

"In the Ohrigstad Republic," he declared, and in his eyes there gleamed for a moment a light as from a great past, "in the Republic of Ohrigstad I had the honour to be the Minister of Finance."

"Honour," Jurie Steyn repeated, sarcastically, but yet not speaking loud enough for Oupa Bekker to hear. "I wonder how *he* lost the money in the State's skatkis. Playing snakes and ladders, I suppose."

All the same, there were those of us who were much interested in Oupa

Bekker's statement. Johnny Coen moved his chair closer to Oupa Bekker, then. Even though Ohrigstad had been only a small republic, and hadn't lasted very long, still there was something about the sound of the words "Minister of Finance" that could not but awaken in us a sense of awe.

"I hope you deposited the State revenues in the Reserve Bank, in a proper manner," At Naudé said, winking at us, but impressed all the same.

"There was no Reserve Bank in those days," Oupa Bekker said, "or any other kind of banks either, in the Republic of Ohrigstad. No, I just kept the national treasury in a stocking under my mattress. It was the safest place, of course."

Johnny Coen put the next question.

"What was the most difficult part of being Finance Minister, Oupa?" he asked. "I suppose it was making the budget balance?"

"Money was the hardest thing," Oupa Bekker said, sighing.

"It still is," Chris Welman interjected. "You don't need to have been a Finance Minister, either, to know that."

"But, of course, it wasn't as bad as today," Oupa Bekker went on. "Being Minister of Finance, I mean. For instance, we didn't need to worry about finding money for education, because there just wasn't any, of course."

Jurie Steyn coughed in a significant kind of way, then, but Oupa Bekker ignored him.

"I don't think," he went on, "that we would have stood for education in the Ohrigstad Republic. We knew we were better off without it. And then there was no need to spend money on railways and harbours, because there weren't any, either. Or hospitals. We lived a healthy life in those days, except maybe for lions. And if you died from a lion, there wasn't much of you left over that could be *taken* to a hospital. Of course, we had to spend a good bit of money on defence, in those days. Gunpowder and lead, and oil to make the springs of our Ou-Sannas work more smoothly. You see, we were expecting trouble any day from Paul Kruger and the Doppers. But it was hard for me to know how to work out a popular budget, especially as there were only seventeen income-tax payers in the whole of the Republic. I thought of imposing a tax on the President's state coach, even. I found that that suggestion was very popular with the income-tax paying group. But you have no idea how much it annoyed the President.

"I imposed all sorts of taxes afterwards, which nobody would have to pay. These taxes didn't bring in much in the way of money, of course. But they were very popular, all the same. And I can still remember how popular my budget was, the year I put a very heavy tax on opium. I had heard somewhere about an opium tax. Naturally, of course, I did not expect this tax to bring in a penny. But I knew how glad the burghers of the Ohrigstad Republic would be, each one of them, to think that there was a tax that they escaped. In the end I had to repeal the tax on opium, however. That was when one of our seventeen income-tax payers threatened to emigrate to the Cape. This income-tax payer had a yellowish complexion and sloping eyes, and ran the only laundry in the Ohrigstad Republic."

Oupa Bekker was still talking about the measures he introduced to counteract inflation in the early days of the Republic of Ohrigstad, when the lorry from Bekkersdal arrived in a cloud of dust. The next few minutes were taken up with a hurried sorting of letters and packages, all of which proceeded to the background noises of clanking milk-cans. Oupa Bekker left when the lorry arrived, since he was expecting neither correspondence nor a milk-can. The lorry-driver and his assistant seated themselves on the riempies bench which the old man had vacated. Jurie Steyn's wife brought them in coffee.

"You know," Jurie Steyn said to Chris Welman, in between putting sealing wax on a letter he was getting ready for the mailbag. "I often wonder what is going to happen to Oupa Bekker – such an old man and all, and still such a liar. All that Finance Minister rubbish of his. How they ever appointed him an ouderling in the church, I don't know. For one thing, I mean, he couldn't have been *born*, at the time of the Ohrigstad Republic." Jurie reflected for a few moments. "Or could he?"

"I don't know," Chris Welman answered truthfully.

A little later the lorry-driver and his assistant departed. We heard them putting water in the radiator. Some time afterwards we heard them starting up the engine, noisily, the driver swearing quite a lot to himself.

It was when the lorry had already started to move off that Jurie Steyn remembered about the registered letter on which he had put the seals. He grabbed up the letter and was over the counter in a single bound.

Chris Welman and I followed him to the door. We watched Jurie Steyn for a considerable distance, streaking along in the sun behind the lorry and shouting and waving the letter in front of him, and jumping over thorn-bushes.

"Just like a Mchopi runner," I heard Chris Welman say.

A Bekkersdal Marathon

AT NAUDÉ, who had a wireless set, came into Jurie Steyn's voorkamer, where we were sitting waiting for the railway lorry from Bekkersdal, and gave us the latest news. He said that the newest thing in Europe was that young people there were going in for non-stop dancing. It was called marathon dancing, At Naudé told us, and those young people were trying to break the record for who could remain on their feet longest, dancing.

We listened for a while to what At Naudé had to say, and then we suddenly remembered a marathon event that had taken place in the little dorp of Bekkersdal – almost in our midst, you could say. What was more, there were quite a number of us sitting in Jurie Steyn's post office, who had actually taken part in that non-stop affair, and without knowing that we were breaking records, and without expecting any sort of a prize for it, either.

We discussed that affair at considerable length and from all angles, and we were still talking about it when the lorry came. And we agreed that it had been in several respects an unusual occurrence. We also agreed that it was questionable if we could have carried off things so successfully that day, if it had not been for Billy Robertse.

You see, our organist at Bekkersdal was Billy Robertse. He had once been a sailor and had come to the Bushveld some years before, travelling on foot. His belongings, fastened in a red handkerchief, were slung over his shoulder on a stick. Billy Robertse was journeying in that fashion for the sake of his health. He suffered from an unfortunate complaint for which he had at regular intervals to drink something out of a black bottle that he always carried handy in his jacket pocket.

Billy Robertse would even keep that bottle beside him in the organist's gallery in case of a sudden attack. And if the hymn the predikant gave out had many verses, you could be sure that about halfway through Billy Robertse would bring the bottle up to his mouth, leaning sideways towards what was in it. And he would put several extra twirls into the second part of the hymn.

When he first applied for the position of organist in the Bekkersdal church, Billy Robertse told the meeting of deacons that he had learnt to play the organ in a cathedral in Northern Europe. Several deacons felt, then, that they could not favour his application. They said that the cathedral sounded too Papist, the way Billy Robertse described it, with a dome 300 feet high and with marble apostles. But it was lucky for Billy Robertse that he was able to mention, at the following combined meeting of elders and deacons, that he had also played the piano in a South American dance hall, of which the manager was a Presbyterian. He asked the meeting to overlook his unfortunate past, saying that he had had a hard life, and anybody could make mistakes. In any case, he had never cared much for the Romish atmosphere of the cathedral, he said, and had been happier in the dance hall.

In the end, Billy Robertse got the appointment. But in his sermons for several Sundays after that the predikant, Dominee Welthagen, spoke very strongly against the evils of dance halls. He described those places of awful sin in such burning words that at least one young man went to see Billy Robertse, privately, with a view to taking lessons in playing the piano.

But Billy Robertse was a good musician. And he took a deep interest in his work. And he said that when he sat down on the organist's stool behind the pulpit, and his fingers were flying over the keyboards, and he was pulling out the stops, and his feet were pressing down the notes that sent the deep bass notes through the pipes – then he felt that he could play all day, he said.

I don't suppose he guessed that he would one day be put to the test, however.

It all happened through Dominee Welthagen one Sunday morning going into a trance in the pulpit. And we did not realise that he was in a trance. It was an illness that overtook him in a strange and sudden fashion.

At each service the predikant, after reading a passage from the Bible, would lean forward with his hand on the pulpit rail and give out the number of the hymn we had to sing. For years his manner of conducting the service had been exactly the same. He would say, for instance: "We will now sing Psalm 82, verses 1 to 4." Then he would allow his head to sink forward on to his chest and he would remain rigid, as though in prayer, until the last notes of the hymn died away in the church.

Now, on that particular morning, just after he had announced the number of the psalm, without mentioning what verses, Dominee Welthagen again took a firm grip on the pulpit rail and allowed his head to sink forward on to his breast. We did not realise that he had fallen into a trance of a peculiar character that kept his body standing upright while his mind was a blank. We learnt that only later.

In the meantime, while the organ was playing the opening bars, we began to realise that Dominee Welthagen had not indicated how many verses we had to sing. But he would discover his mistake, we thought, after we had been singing for a few minutes.

All the same, one or two of the younger members of the congregation did titter, slightly, when they took up their hymn-books. For Dominee Welthagen had given out Psalm 119. And everybody knows that Psalm 119 has 176 verses.

This was a church service that will never be forgotten in Bekkersdal.

We sang the first verse and then the second and then the third. When we got to about the sixth verse and the minister still gave no sign that it would be the last, we assumed that he wished us to sing the first eight verses. For, if you open your hymn-book, you'll see that Psalm 119 is divided into sets of eight verses, each ending with the word "Pouse."

We ended the last notes of verse eight with more than an ordinary number of turns and twirls, confident that at any moment Dominee Welthagen would raise his head and let us know that we could sing "Amen."

It was when the organ started up very slowly and solemnly with the music for verse nine that a real feeling of disquiet overcame the congregation. But, of course, we gave no sign of what went on in our minds. We held Dominee Welthagen in too much veneration.

Nevertheless, I would rather not say too much about our feelings, when verse followed verse and Pouse succeeded Pouse, and still Dominee Welthagen made no sign that we had sung long enough, or that there was anything unusual in what he was demanding of us.

After they had recovered from their first surprise, the members of the church council conducted themselves in a most exemplary manner. Elders and deacons tiptoed up and down the aisles, whispering words of reassurance to such members of the congregation, men as well as women, who gave signs of wanting to panic.

At one stage it looked as though we were going to have trouble from the organist. That was when Billy Robertse, at the end of the 34th verse, held up his black bottle and signalled quietly to the elders to indicate that his medicine was finished. At the end of the 35th verse he made signals of a less quiet character, and again at the end of the 36th verse. That was when Elder Landsman tiptoed out of the church and went round to the konsistorie, where the Nagmaal wine was kept. When Elder Landsman came back into the church he had a long black bottle half hidden under his manel. He took the bottle up to the organist's gallery, still walking on tiptoe.

At verse 61 there was almost a breakdown. That was when a message came from the back of the organ, where Koster Claassen and the assistant verger, whose task it was to turn the handle that kept the organ supplied with wind, were in a state near to exhaustion. So it was Deacon Cronjé's turn to go tiptoeing out of the church. Deacon Cronjé was head-warder at the local gaol. When he came back it was with three burly native convicts in striped jerseys, who also went through the church on tiptoe. They arrived just in time to take over the handle from Koster Claassen and the assistant verger.

At verse 98 the organist again started making signals about his medicine. Once more Elder Landsman went round to the konsistorie. This time he was accompanied by another elder and a deacon, and they stayed away somewhat longer than the time when Elder Landsman had gone on his own. On their return the deacon bumped into a small hymn-book table at the back of the church. Perhaps it was because the deacon was a fat, red-faced man, and not used to tiptoeing.

At verse 124 the organist signalled again, and the same three members of the church council filed out to the konsistorie, the deacon walking in front this time.

It was about then that the pastor of the Full Gospel Apostolic Faith Church, about whom Dominee Welthagen had in the past used almost as strong language as about the Pope, came up to the front gate of the church to see what was afoot. He lived near our church and, having heard the same hymn tune being played over and over for about eight hours, he was a very amazed man. Then he saw the door of the konsistorie open, and two elders and a deacon coming out, walking on tiptoe – they having apparently forgotten that they were not in church, then. When the pastor saw one of the elders hiding a black bottle under his manel, a look of understanding came over his features. The pastor walked off, shaking his head.

At verse 152 the organist signalled again. This time Elder Landsman and the other elder went out alone. The deacon stayed behind on the deacon's bench, apparently in deep thought. The organist signalled again, for the last time, at verse 169. So you can imagine how many visits the two elders made to the konsistorie altogether.

The last verse came, and the last line of the last verse. This time it had to be "Amen." Nothing could stop it. I would rather not describe the state that the congregation was in. And by then the three native convicts, red stripes and all, were, in the Bakhatla tongue, threatening mutiny. "Aa-m-e-e-n" came from what sounded like less than a score of voices, hoarse with singing.

The organ music ceased.

Maybe it was the sudden silence that at last brought Dominee Welt-hagen out of his long trance. He raised his head and looked slowly about him. His gaze travelled over his congregation and then, looking at the windows, he saw that it was night. We understood right away what was going on in Dominee Welthagen's mind. He thought he had just come into the pulpit, and that this was the beginning of the evening service. We realised that, during all the time we had been singing, the predikant had been in a state of unconsciousness.

Once again Dominee Welthagen took a firm grip of the pulpit rail. His head again started drooping forward on to his breast. But before he went into a trance for the second time, he gave out the hymn for the evening service. "We will," Dominee Welthagen announced, "sing Psalm 119."

Psycho-analysis

"KOOS NIENABER got a letter from his daughter, Minnie, last week," Jurie Steyn announced to several of us sitting in his voorkamer that served as the Drogevlei post office. "It's two years now that she has been working in an office in Johannesburg. You wouldn't think it. Two years… "

"What was in the letter?" At Naudé asked, coming to the point.

"Well," Jurie Steyn began, "Minnie says that… "

Jurie Steyn was quick to sense our amusement.

"If that's how you carry on," he announced, "I won't tell you anything. I know what you are all thinking, laughing in that silly way. Well, just let one of you try and be postmaster, like me, in between milking and ploughing and getting the wrong statements from the creamery and the pigs rooting up the sweet-potatoes – not to talk about the calving season, even – and then see how much time you'll have left over for steaming open and reading other people's letters."

Johnny Coen, who was young and was more than a little interested in Minnie Nienaber, hastened to set Jurie Steyn's mind at rest.

"You know, we make the same sort of joke about every postmaster in the Bushveld," Johnny Coen said. "We don't mean anything by it. It's a very old joke. Now, if we were living in Johannesburg, like Minnie Nienaber, we might perhaps be able to think out some newer sort of things to say – "

"What we would say," At Naudé interrupted – At Naudé always being up-to-date, since he has a wireless and reads a newspaper every week – "What we would say is that you sublet your post office as a hideout for the Jeppe gang."

Naturally, we did not know what the Jeppe gang was. At Naudé took quite a long time to explain. When he had finished, Oupa Bekker, who is the oldest inhabitant of the Marico Bushveld, said that there seemed to him to be something spirited about the Jeppe gang, which reminded him a lot of his own youth in the Pilanesberg area of the Waterberg District. Oupa Bekker said that he had several times, lately, thought of visiting his youngest grand-daughter in Johannesburg. Maybe they could teach him a few things in Johannesburg, he said. And maybe, also, he could teach *them* a thing or two.

But all this talk was getting us away from Minnie Nienaber's letter. And once again it was Johnny Coen that brought the subject round to Jurie Steyn's first remark.

"It must be that Koos Nienaber told you what was in his daughter's letter," Johnny Coen said. "Koos Nienaber must have come round here and told you. Otherwise you would never have known, I mean. You couldn't *possibly* have known."

That was what had happened, Jurie Steyn acknowledged. He went on to say that he was grateful to Johnny Coen for not harbouring those unworthy suspicions against him that were sometimes entertained by people living in the Groot Marico who did not have Johnny Coen's advantages of education and worldly experience. We knew that he just said that to flatter Johnny Coen, who had once been a railway shunter at Ottoshoop.

Thereupon Jurie Steyn acquainted us in detail with the contents of Minnie Nienaber's letter, as retailed to him by her father, Koos Nienaber.

"Koos said that Minnie has been," Jurie Steyn said, "has been – well, just a minute – oh, yes, here it is – I got old Koos Nienaber to write it down for me – she's been psycho – psycho-analysed. Here it is, written down and all – 'sielsontleding.'"

I won't deny that we were all much impressed. It was something that we had never heard of before. Jurie Steyn saw the effect his statement had made on us.

"Yes," he repeated, sure of himself – and more sure of the word, too, now – "yes, in the gold-mining city of Johannesburg, Minnie Nienaber got psycho-analysed."

After a few moments of silence, Gysbert van Tonder made himself heard. Gysbert often spoke out of his turn, that way.

"Well, it's not the first time a thing like that happened to a girl living in Johannesburg on her own," Gysbert said. "One thing, the door of her parents' home will always remain open for her. But I am surprised at old Koos Nienaber mentioning it to you. He's usually so proud."

I noticed that Johnny Coen looked crestfallen for a moment, until Jurie Steyn made haste to explain that it didn't mean that at all.

According to what Koos Nienaber told him – Jurie Steyn said – it had become fashionable in Johannesburg for people to go and be attended to by a new sort of doctor, who didn't worry about how sick your body was, but saw to it that he got your mind right. This kind of doctor could straighten out anything that was wrong with your *mind*, Jurie Steyn explained. And you didn't have to be sick, even, to go along and get yourself treated by a doctor like that. It was a very fashionable thing to do, Jurie Steyn added. Johnny Coen looked relieved.

"According to what Koos Nienaber told me," Jurie Steyn said, "this new kind of doctor doesn't test your heart any more, by listening through that rubber tube thing. Instead, he just asks you what you dreamt last night. And then he works it all out with a dream-book. But it's not just an ordinary dream-book that says if you dreamt last night of a herd of cattle it means that there is a grave peril ahead for some person that you haven't met yet… "

"Well, I dreamt a couple of nights ago that I was driving a lot of Afrikander cattle across the Bechuanaland Protectorate border," Fritz Pretorius said. "Just like I have often done, on a night when there isn't much of a moon. Only, what was funny about my dream was that I dreamt I was smuggling cattle *into* the Protectorate, instead of out of it. Can you imagine a Marico farmer doing a foolish thing like that? I suppose this dream means I am going mad, or something."

After At Naudé had said how surprised he was that Fritz Pretorius should have to be told in a dream what everybody knew about him in any case – and after Fritz Pretorius's invitation to At Naudé to come and repeat that remark outside the post office had come to nothing – Jurie Steyn went on to explain further about what that new kind of treatment was that Minnie Nienaber was receiving from a new kind of doctor in Johannesburg, and that she had no need for.

"It's not the ordinary kind of dream-book, like that Napoleon dream-book on which my wife set so much store before we got married," Jurie Steyn continued, "but it's a dream-book written by professors. Minnie has been getting all sorts of fears, lately. Just silly sorts of fears, her father says. Nothing to worry about. I suppose anybody from the Groot Marico who has stayed in Johannesburg as long as Minnie Nienaber has done would get frightened in the same way. Only, what puzzles me is that it took her so long to start getting frightened… "

"Maybe she has also begun to listen in to the wireless, like At Naudé," Chris Welman said. "Maybe she has also started hearing things about the Jeppe gang. It's queer that she wasn't frightened, like that, when she first went there. But I could have told her that Johannesburg was no place for a young girl. Why, you should have seen the Angus bull they awarded the Challenge Trophy to, the year I went down to the Agricultural Show with my Shorthorns. And they even tried to chase my fat cow, Vleisfontein III, out of the show grounds. They said they thought it was some animal that had strayed in from across the railway line."

Thereupon At Naudé told us about a Rand Agricultural Show that *he* had attended. That was the year in which his Afrikander bull Doornboom IV, which he had fed on lucerne and turnips throughout the winter, was awarded the silver medal. An agricultural magazine even took a photograph of himself and of Doornboom IV, At Naudé said. But unfortunately, through some mistake that the printer made, the wrong words were printed under At Naudé's photograph. Instead of being called "Proud Owner", At Naudé was called "Silver Medal Pedigree Bull." He complained to the magazine about it, afterwards, At Naudé said, but the editor just wrote back to say that none of his readers had noticed anything wrong.

"That just shows you," At Naudé said to us – and even though it had happened a long time ago, he still sounded quite indignant – "and they couldn't possibly have thought that I looked like Doornboom IV, because that was the year I shaved off my moustache."

What annoyed him most of all, At Naudé added, was that it stated under his photograph that he had been fed on lucerne and turnips for the whole winter.

"It's very funny," Jurie Steyn said, just then, "but all this talk of yours fits in with what Minnie Nienaber said in her letter. That was the reason why, in the end, she decided to go along and get herself psycho-analysed. I mean, there was nothing wrong with her, of course. They say you have got to have nothing wrong with you, before you can get psycho-analysed. This new kind of doctor can't do anything for you if there is something the matter with you – "

"I don't know of any doctor that can do anything for you when there is something the matter with you," Oupa Bekker interrupted. "The last time I went to see a doctor was during the rinderpest. The doctor said I must wear a piece of leopard skin behind my left ear. That would keep the rinderpest away from my oxen, he said, and it would at the same time cure me of my rheumatism. The doctor only said that after he had thrown the bones for the second time. The first time he threw the bones the doctor said – "

But by that time we were all laughing very loudly. We didn't mean *that* kind of a doctor, we said to Oupa Bekker. We did not mean a Mshangaan witch-doctor. We meant a white doctor, who had been to a university, and all that.

Oupa Bekker was silent for a few moments.

"Perhaps you are right," he said at last. "Because all my cattle died of the rinderpest. Mind you, I have never had rheumatism since that time. Perhaps all that that witch-doctor *could* cure was rheumatism. From what Jurie Steyn tells us, I can see he was just old-fashioned. It seems that a doctor is of no use today, unless he can cure nothing at all. But I still say I don't think much of that doctor that threw the bones upward of fifty years ago. For I was more concerned about my cattle's rinderpest than about my own ailment. All the same, if you want a cure for rheumatism – there it is. A piece of leopard skin tied behind your left ear. The skin from just an ordinary piece of leopard."

With all this talk, it was quite a while before Jurie Steyn could get a word in. But what he had to say, then, was quite interesting.

"You don't seem to realise it," Jurie Steyn said, "but you have been talking all this while about Minnie Nienaber's symptoms. The reason why she went to get herself psycho-analysed, I mean. It was about those awful dreams she has been having of late. Chris Welman has mentioned his prize cow that got chased out of the Rand Show, and At Naudé has told us about his silver-medal bull, and Oupa Bekker has reminded us of the old days, when this part of the Marico was all leopard country. Well, that was Minnie Nienaber's trouble. That was why she went to that new kind of doctor. She had the most awful dreams – Koos Nienaber tells me. She dreamt of being ordered to leave places – night clubs, and so on, Koos Nienaber says. And she also used to dream regularly of being chased by wild bulls. And of being chased by Natal Indians with long sugar-cane knives. And latterly she had nightmares almost every night, through dreaming that she was being chased by a leopard. That was why, in the end, she went to have herself psycho-analysed."

We discussed Minnie Nienaber's troubles at some length. And we ended up by saying that we would like to know where the Afrikaner people would be today, if our women could run to a new sort of doctor, every time they dreamt of being chased by a wild animal. If Louis Trichardt's wife dreamt that she was being chased by a rhinoceros, we said, then she would jolly well have to escape from that rhinoceros in her dream. She would not be able to come to her husband with her dream-troubles next day, seeing that he already had so many Voortrekker problems on his mind.

Indeed, the whole discussion would have ended in quite a sensible and commonplace sort of fashion, were it not for the strange way in which Johnny Coen reacted.

"You know, Oupa Bekker," Johnny Coen said, "you spoke about going to Johannesburg. Well, you can come with me, if you like. I know you aren't really going to join the Jeppe gang. But I am going to look for Minnie Nienaber. Dreams and all that – I know it's just a lot of nonsense. But I feel somehow – I *know* that Minnie needs me."

Secret Agent

THE STRANGER who arrived on the Government lorry from Bekkersdal told us that his name was Losper. He was having a look round that part of the Marico, he said, and he did not expect to stay more than a few days. He was dressed in city clothes and carried a leather briefcase. But because he did not wear pointed black shoes and did not say how sad it was that Flip Prinsloo should have died so suddenly at the age of sixty-eight, of snakebite, we knew that he was not a life insurance agent. Furthermore, because he did not once seek to steer the conversation round to the sinful practices of some people who offered a man a quite substantial bribe when he was just carrying out his duty, we also knew that the stranger was not a plain-clothes man who had been sent round to investigate the increase in cattle-smuggling over the Conventie-lyn. Quite a number of us breathed more easily, then.

Nevertheless, we were naturally intrigued to know what Meneer Losper had come there for. But with the exception of Gysbert van Tonder – who did not have much manners since the time he had accompanied a couple of Americans on safari to the lower reaches of the Limpopo – we were all too polite to ask a man straight out what his business was, and then explain to him how he could do it better.

That trip with the two Americans influenced Gysbert van Tonder's mind, all right. For he came back talking very loudly. And he bought a waistcoat at the Indian store especially so that he could carry a cigar in it. And he spoke of himself as Gysbert O. van Tonder. And he once also slapped Dominee Welthagen on the back to express his appreciation of the Nagmaal sermon Dominee Welthagen had delivered on the Holy Patriarchs and the Prophets.

When Gysbert van Tonder came back from that journey, we understood how right the Voortrekker, Hendrik Potgieter, had been over a hundred years ago, when he said that the parts around the lower end of the Limpopo were no fit place for a white man.

We asked Gysbert van Tonder how that part of the country affected the two Americans. And he said he did not think it affected them *much*. But it was a queer sort of area, all round, Gysbert explained. And there was a lot of that back-slapping business, too. He said he could still remember how one of the Americans slapped Chief Umfutusu on the back and how Chief Umfutusu, in his turn, slapped the American on the ear with a clay pot full of greenish drink that the chief was holding in his hand at the time.

The American was very pleased about it, Gysbert van Tonder said, and he devoted a lot of space to it in his diary. The American classed Chief Umfutusu's action as among the less understood tribal customs that had to do with welcoming distinguished white travellers. Later on, when Gysbert van Tonder and the Americans came to a Mshangaan village that was having some trouble with hut tax, the American who kept the diary was able to write a lot more about what he called an obscure African ritual that that tribe observed in welcoming a superior order of stranger. For that whole Mshangaan village, men, women and children, had rushed out and pelted Gysbert and the two Americans with wet cow-dung.

In his diary the American compared this incident with the ceremonial greeting that a tribe of Bavendas once accorded the explorer Stanley, when they threw him backwards into a dam – to show respect, as Stanley explained, afterwards.

Well anyway, here was this stranger, Losper, a middle-aged man with a suitcase, sitting in the post office and asking Jurie Steyn if he could put him up in a spare room for a few days, while he had a look round.

"I'll pay the same rates as I paid in the boarding-house in Zeerust," Meneer Losper said. "Not that I think you might overcharge me, of course, but I am only allowed a fixed sum by the department for accommodation and travelling expenses."

"Look here, Neef Losper," Jurie Steyn said, "you didn't tell me your first name, so I can only call you Neef Losper – "

"My first name is Org," the stranger said.

"Well, then, Neef Org," Jurie Steyn went on. "From the way you talk I can see that you are unacquainted with the customs of the Groot Marico. In the first place, I am a postmaster and a farmer. I don't know which is the worst job, what with money orders and the blue-tongue. I have got to put axle-grease on my mule-cart and sealing wax on the mailbag. And sometimes I get mixed up. Any man in my position would. One day I'll paste a revenue stamp on my off-mule and I'll brand a half-moon and a bar on the Bekkersdal mailbag. Then there will be trouble. There will be trouble with my off-mule, I mean. The post office won't notice any difference. But my off-mule is funny, that way. He'll pull the mule-cart, all right. But then everything has got to be the way *he* wants it. He won't have people laughing at him because he's got a revenue stamp stuck on his behind. I sometimes think that my off-mule *knows* that a shilling revenue stamp is what you put on a piece of paper after you've told a Justice of the Peace a lot of lies – "

"Not lies," Gysbert van Tonder interjected.

"A lot of lies," Jurie Steyn went on, "about another man's cattle straying into a person's lucerne lands while that person was taking his sick child to Zeerust – "

Gysbert van Tonder, who was Jurie Steyn's neighbour, half rose out of his riempies chair, then, and made some sneering remarks about Jurie Steyn and his off-mule. He said he never had much time for either of them. And he said he would not like to describe the way his lucerne lands looked after Jurie Steyn's cattle had finished straying over them. He said he would not like to use that expression, because there was a stranger present.

Meneer Losper seemed interested, then, and sat well forward to listen. And it looked as though Gysbert van Tonder would have said the words, too. Only, At Naudé, who has a wireless to which he listens in regularly, put a stop to the argument. He said that this was a respectable voorkamer, with family portraits on the wall.

"And there's Jurie Steyn's wife in the kitchen, too," At Naudé said. "You can't use the same sort of language here as in the Volksraad, where there are all men."

Actually, Jurie Steyn's wife had gone out of the kitchen, about then. Ever since that young schoolmaster with the black hair parted in the middle had come to Bekkersdal, Jurie Steyn's wife had taken a good deal of interest in education matters. Consequently, when the stranger, Org Losper, said he was from the department, Jurie Steyn's wife thought right away – judging from his shifty appearance – that he might be a school inspector. And so sent a message to the young schoolmaster to warn him in time, so that he could put away the saws and hammers that he used for the private fretwork that he did in front of the class while the children were writing compositions.

In the meantime, Jurie Steyn was getting to the point.

"So you can't expect me to be running a boarding-house as well as everything else, Neef Org," he was saying. "But all the same, you are welcome to stay. And you can stay as long as you like. Only, you must not offer again to pay. If you had known more about these parts, you would also have known that the Groot Marico has got a very fine reputation for hospitality. When you come and stay with a man he gets insulted if you offer him money. But I shall be glad to invite you into my home as a member of my own family."

Then Org Losper said that that was exactly what he didn't want, any more. And he was firm about it, too.

"When you're a member of the family, you can't say no to anything," he explained. "In the Pilanesberg I tore my best trousers on the wire. I was helping, as a member of the family, to round up the donkeys for the water-cart. At Nietverdiend a Large White bit a piece out of my second-best trousers and my leg. That was when I was a member of the family and was helping to carry buckets of swill to the pig troughs. The farmer said the Large White was just being playful that day. Well, maybe the Large White thought I was also a member of the family – *his* family, I mean. At Abjaterskop I nearly fell into a disused mineshaft on a farm there. Then I was a member of the family, assisting to throw a dead bull down the shaft. The bull had died of anthrax and I was helping to pull him by one haunch and I was walking backwards and when I jumped away from the opening of the mineshaft it was almost too late.

"I can also tell you what happened to me in the Dwarsberge when I was also a member of the family. And also about what happened when I was a member of the family at Derdepoort. I did not know that that family was having a misunderstanding with the family next door about water rights. And it was when I was opening a water furrow with a shovel that a load of buckshot went through my hat. As a member of the family, I was standing ankle-deep in the mud at the time, and so I couldn't run

34

very fast. So you see, when I say I would rather pay, it is not that I am ignorant of the very fine tradition that the Marico has for the friendly and bountiful entertainment that it accords the stranger. But I do not wish to presume further on your kindness. If I have much more Bushveld hospitality I might never see my wife and children again. It's all very well being a member of somebody else's family. But I have a duty to my *own* family. I want to get back to them alive."

Johnny Coen remarked that next time Gysbert van Tonder had an American tourist on his hands, he need not take him to the Limpopo, but could just show him around the Marico farms.

It was then that Gysbert van Tonder asked Org Losper straight out what his business was. And, to our surprise, the stranger was very frank about it.

"It is a new job that has been made for me by the Department of Defence," Org Losper said. "There wasn't that post before. You see, I worked very hard at the last elections, getting people's names taken off the electoral roll. You have no idea how many names I got taken off. I even got some of our candidate's supporters crossed off. But you know how it is, we all make mistakes. It is a very secret post. It is a top Defence secret. I am under oath not to disclose anything about it. But I am free to tell you that I am making certain investigations on behalf of the Department of Defence. I am trying to find out *whether something has been seen here.* But, of course, the post has been made for me, if you understand what I mean."

We said we understood, all right. And we also knew that, since he was under oath about it, the nature of Org Losper's investigations in the Groot Marico would leak out sooner or later.

As it happened, we found out within the next couple of days. A Mahalapi who worked for Adriaan Geel told us. And then we realised how difficult Org Losper's work was. And we no longer envied him his Government job – even though it had been especially created for him.

If you know the Mtosas, you'll understand why Org Losper's job was so hard. For instance, there was only one member of the whole Mtosa tribe who had ever had any close contact with white men. And he had unfortunately grown up among Trekboers, whose last piece of crockery that they had brought with them from the Cape had got broken almost a generation earlier.

We felt that the Department of Defence could have made an easier job for Org Losper than to send him round asking those questions of the Mtosas, they who did not even know what ordinary kitchen saucers were, leave alone flying ones.

Bull-calf

THE GOVERNMENT lorry from Bekkersdal was late. Jurie Steyn had several times come from behind his post office counter and had stood at the front door, gazing in the direction of the poort.

"How am I going to get through the milking?" he asked in an aggrieved tone, cupping a hand over his eyes some more and staring across the kameeldorings. "I've had these mailbags ready and everything since early this morning – before the cattle went out of the kraal, even."

Johnny Coen looked at the untidy bundles on the counter and his lip curled.

"Next time you make up the mailbags in the kraal, you should perhaps wait until the cattle have gone out," Johnny Coen said. "Then they wouldn't walk over the mailbags... Or was it pigs?"

To our surprise, Jurie Steyn did not take offence.

"I really do believe, sometimes," he replied, thoughtfully, "that it would be better if I did go and do my post office work in the stable. I get no peace here, in the voorkamer. It is that Duusman. He's been chewing the mailbags again. It's a habit I despise in him. But that's the worst of rearing a bull-calf by hand. I've sometimes thought I'll just *give* Duusman the voorkamer and I'll move into the stable. That's at least one place that Duusman never goes into, anyway. He won't be seen in a stable – not him. He's much too stuck-up."

Gysbert van Tonder said that that showed you how intelligent a hand-raised bull-calf like Duusman could be. To be able to tell the difference between Jurie Steyn's voorkamer and a stable. Many a human being would hardly know the difference, even. Not at first glance, that was, Gysbert explained.

Now, although he was always saying things to Duusman's detriment, Jurie Steyn was secretly very proud of his hansbul, and he really thought that Duusman was different from any other bull-calf in the Marico that had been brought up by hand. And so Jurie Steyn felt not a little flattered at Gysbert van Tonder's remark.

"I won't say Duusman hasn't got brains," Jurie Steyn acknowledged, modestly, "if only he'll use them in the right way."

We could not help feeling that, with those words, Jurie Steyn would like us to think that he himself had brains – just because he had brought Duusman up by hand.

In the meantime, Oupa Bekker had been nodding his head up and down.

"It's all very well rearing a calf or a goat or a sheep by hand," he announced, "but you mustn't also *educate* him. The moment a bull-calf gets educated above his station in life, he's got no more respect for you. He doesn't seem to understand that, just because you're older than he is, you must know more."

"I wouldn't say that's always the case, Oupa," Johnny Coen said. "I mean, it's not just only age. There are also other things that broaden the mind – like travel, say."

We knew, of course, that Johnny Coen was referring to the time he was working on the railways at Ottoshoop.

"Well, I wouldn't object if Duusman took it into his head to travel a bit," Jurie Steyn asserted. "It would do him good. He'll soon find out that it's not every hand-raised bull-calf that has got as good a home as he has. And he's so inconsiderate. After he's been loafing about the vlei all morning, Duusman will never think of wiping the clay from between his hooves before he comes walking into the voorkamer for his dish of kaboe-mealies. That's a hand-raised bull-calf all over. But it's my wife that spoilt him, of course. I knew right from the start that no good could come from her feeding him in the voorkamer. 'Give Duusman his lunch in the kitchen, Truitjie,' I used to say to my wife from the very beginning. 'Then, later on, when he's more grown up, he'll be used to coming round to the back door for his meals. If Duusman gets into the habit of walking in at the front door he'll start having ideas about himself before he's much older. You watch if I'm not right.' But she wouldn't listen to me. Now you see what's happening. I'm only looking forward to the day when Duusman will have grown so wide and fat that he won't be able to come in through the door of the voorkamer any more."

That was the moment when Oupa Bekker giggled. It was a disturbing sort of sound. Oupa Bekker was, after all, somebody aged and respected. Except when he said silly things – such as when he said that he could make quite a good living even if mealies were only ten shillings a bag, never mind the new price of twenty-four shillings. Then we knew that he was just aged.

And the way Oupa Bekker giggled now was not pleasant. Even At Naudé looked unhappy. And At Naudé had a wireless set and had heard some queer noises coming over it in his time – and not merely as a result of his not having been properly tuned in, by any means. There was the time, for instance, when he invited several of us to come and listen in to what he informed us was an opera being broadcast, and right through, at intervals, At Naudé said, "Yes, I know what you kêrels think. You think it's the atmospherics."

"What I want to say is," Oupa Bekker remarked, after his laughter had set over into coughing and Chris Welman had slapped – some of us thought punched – the old man vigorously on the back, "if you think that will be the end of your trouble with a bull-calf that you've reared by hand – "

Oupa Bekker gave signs of wanting to laugh again. But he stopped himself in time. That was when he saw Chris Welman, with a determined look in his eye, making a move to get out of his chair for the second time.

Oupa Bekker pulled himself together, then.

Before that, I had noticed a strained look on Chris Welman's face. He did not seem to be himself, somehow. Chris Welman seemed to be taking it much too seriously, this nonsense that was being talked about Jurie Steyn's bull-calf.

"You say your wife has spoilt Duusman, Jurie?" Oupa Bekker asked.

"Completely," Jurie Steyn admitted.

Oupa Bekker looked thoughtful.

"But you don't think," he asked, "that you might also perhaps have had a hand in spoiling him? Think carefully, now."

"Well," Jurie said, somewhat reluctantly, "a little, maybe."

That seemed to be the sum of what Oupa Bekker wanted to know. In any case, he said nothing more. That made us all feel uncomfortable. It was a good deal worse than when he giggled in that annoying old-man sort of way, that was not much different from an old woman's giggle. But now he remained silent. And you couldn't go and thump an old man on his back just for keeping quiet. At least, in public you couldn't. Not when people were looking.

"Duusman chew?" Oupa Bekker asked.

"Chew – how do you mean, chew?" Jurie Steyn repeated. We could see he was hedging.

"Tobacco," Oupa Bekker insisted, firmly.

"Well," Jurie Steyn said, "he does come in every morning for a plug of Piet Retief rolled tobacco. It started as a joke, of course. But, all right, if you put it that way, Duusman does chew. But he spits most of it out again. I started him off on the habit. It seemed funny to me, the idea of a bull-calf chewing. But he's got into the habit, now. It seemed funny at the time, if you understand what I mean. But now, well, I think Duusman will burst the doorframe down if he doesn't get his chew every morning – "

"And you blame it on your wife," Oupa Bekker said. And he started laughing again. And even when his laughter went up into very high notes he did not bother to look round to see how Chris Welman was taking it.

It was almost as though Oupa Bekker knew that Chris Welman would not slam him on the back again, even if Oupa Bekker's laughter ended in his coughing his head off.

"You yourself can't stop chewing tobacco, no matter how hard you try – can you, now?" Oupa Bekker remarked to Jurie. "I know *I* can't. And all I've got left are a few top teeth that aren't near as good as yours or Duusman's."

When Jurie Steyn did not answer, Oupa Bekker said that he should send Duusman to the butcher's shop. But he did not think that Duusman would make even good butcher's meat, Oupa Bekker added.

Well, we all knew, of course, that if you had once reared a bull-calf by hand, you could never send him to the butcher's shop, even if the land company were foreclosing on you.

It was a relief to us all when the lorry arrived in dust and noise and with milk-cans and circulars from shopkeepers.

But we should have felt more surprised, somehow, when, along with the driver and his assistant, there also alighted from the lorry young Tobie, Chris Welman's son, who had gone to Johannesburg and whom we had not seen for several years.

Tobie Welman was slim and good-looking, and he walked with a light step, and his black hair was slicked back from his forehead, and a cigarette dangled from his lip.

And when Chris Welman walked out to meet Tobie, as though he had been expecting him, we wondered why he had not told us that his son was coming back. We would, after all, not have said anything about Tobie Welman having been in reform school.

Duusman forced his way into the voorkamer, about then, lowing. "Moo," Duusman said.

Local Colour

WE WERE talking about the book-writing man, Gabriel Penzhorn, who was in the Marico on a visit, wearing a white helmet above his spectacles and with a notebook and a fountain pen below his spectacles. He had come to the Marico to get local colour and atmosphere, he said, for his new South African novel. What was wrong with his last novel, it would seem, was that it did not have enough local colour and atmosphere in it.

So we told Penzhorn that the best place for him to get atmosphere in these parts was in that kloof other side Lobatse, where that gas came out from. Only last term the school-teacher had taken the children there, and he had explained to them about the wonders of Nature. We said to Gabriel Penzhorn that there was atmosphere for him, all right. In fact, the school-master had told the children that there was a whole gaseous envelope of it. Penzhorn could even collect some of it in a glass jar, with a piece of rubber tubing on it, like the schoolmaster had done.

And as for local colour, well, we said, there was that stretch of blue bush on this side of Abjaterskop, which we called the bloubos. It wasn't really blue, we said, but it only looked blue. All the same, it was the best piece of blue bush we had seen anywhere in the Northern Transvaal. The schoolmaster had brought a piece of that home with him also, we explained.

Gabriel Penzhorn made it clear, however, that that stretch of blue bush was not the sort of local colour he wanted at all. Nor was he much interested in the kind of atmosphere that he could go and collect in a bottle with a piece of rubber tubing, just from other side Lobatse.

From that we could see that Gabriel Penzhorn was particular. We did not blame him for it, of course. We realised that if it was things that a writer had to put into a book, then only the best could be good enough. Nevertheless, since most of us had been born in the Marico, and we took pride in our district, we could not help feeling just a little hurt.

"As far as I can see," Johnny Coen said to us one day in Jurie Steyn's post office, "what this book-writing man wants is not atmosphere, but stinks. Perhaps that's the sort of books he writes. I wonder. Have they got pictures in, does anybody know?"

But nobody knew.

"Well, if it's stinks that Penzhorn wants," Johnny Coen proceeded, "just let him go and stand on the siding at Ottoshoop when they open a truck of Bird Island guano. Phew! He won't even need a glass jar to collect that sort of atmosphere in. He can just hold his white helmet in his hand and let a few whiffs of guano atmosphere *float* into it. But if he puts a white helmetful of that kind of atmosphere into his next book, I think the police will have something to say."

Oupa Bekker looked reflective. At first we thought that he hadn't been following much of our conversation, since it was intellectual, having to do with books. We knew that Oupa Bekker had led more of an open-air sort of life, having lived in the Transvaal in the old days, when the Transvaal did not set much store on book learning. But to our surprise we found that Oupa Bekker could take part in a talk about culture as well as any of us. What was more, he did not give himself any airs on account of his having this accomplishment, either.

"Stinks?" Oupa Bekker enquired. "Stinks? Well, let me tell you. There never have been any stinks like the kind we had when we were running that tannery on the Molopo River in the rainy season, in the old days. We thought that the water of the Molopo that the flour-mill on the erf next to us didn't use for their water-wheel would be all right for us with our tannery. We didn't need running water. Just ordinary standing water was good enough for us. And when I say standing water, I mean standing. You have got no idea how it stood. And we didn't tan just plain ox-hides and sheepskins, but every kind of skin we could get. Tanning was our business, you understand. We tanned lion and zebra skins along with the elephant and rhinoceros hides. After a while the man who owned the flour-mill couldn't stand it any longer. So *he* moved higher up the river. And if I tell you that he was a Bulgarian and he couldn't stand it, that will possibly give you an idea of what that tannery smelt like. Then, one day, a farmer came from the Dwarsberge... Yes, they are still the same Dwarsberge, and they haven't changed much with the years. Only, today I can't see as far from the top of the Dwarsberge as I could when I was young. And they look different, also, somehow, with that little whitewashed house no longer in the poort, and with Lettie Gouws no longer standing at the front gate, in an apron with blue squares."

Oupa Bekker paused and sighed. But it was quite a light sigh, that was not so much regret for the past as a tribute to the sweetness of vanished youth.

"Anyway," Oupa Bekker continued, "this farmer from the Dwarsberge brought us a wagon-load of polecat skins. You can imagine what that stink was like. Even before we started tanning them, I mean. Above the smell of the tannery we could smell that load of muishond when the wagon was still fording the drift at Steekgrasvlei. Bill Knoetze – that was my partner – and I felt that this was going slightly too far, even though we were in the tanning business. At first we tried to laugh it off, in the way that we have in the Marico. We tried to pretend to the farmer from the Dwarsberge when he came into the office that we thought it was *he* that stank like that. And we asked him if he couldn't do something about

41

it. Like getting himself buried, say. But the farmer said no, it wasn't him. It was just his wagon. He made that statement after he had held out his hand for us to shake and Bill Knoetze, before taking the farmer's hand, had play-acted that he was going to faint. And it wasn't just all play-acting either. How he knew that there was something about his wagon, the farmer said, that was peculiar, was through his having passed mule-carts along the road. And he noticed that the mules shied.

"All the same, that was how we came to give up the first tanning business that had ever been set up along the Molopo. Bill Knoetze left after that wagon-load of polecat skins had been in the tanning fluid for about a fortnight. I left a week later. But just before that the Chief of the Mahalapis had come from T'lakieng to find out if we had koedoe leather that he wanted for veldskoens. And when he walked with us through the tannery the Chief of the Mahalapis sniffed the breeze several times, as though trying to make up his mind about something. In the end, the Chief said it would appear to him as though we had a flower garden somewhere near. And he asked could he take a bunch of asters back to his kraal with him for his youngest wife, who had been to mission school and liked such things. It was too dry at T'lakieng for geraniums, the Chief said."

Oupa Bekker was still talking when Gabriel Penzhorn walked into Jurie Steyn's voorkamer. He intended taking the lorry back to civilisation, Penzhorn explained to us. His stay in the Marico had been quite interesting, he said. He didn't say it with enthusiasm, however. And he added that he had not been able to write as many things in his notebook as he had hoped to.

"They all say the same thing," Gabriel Penzhorn proceeded. "I no sooner tell a farmer or his wife that I am a novelist and that I am looking for material to put into my next book, than he or she tells me – sometimes both of them together tell me – about the kind of book that they would write if *they* only had time; or if only they remembered to order some ink, next time they went to the Indian store at Ramoutsa."

He consulted his notes in a dispirited sort of way.

"Yes," Penzhorn went on, "the Indian store at Ramoutsa. Most of the farmers use also another word, I've noticed, in place of Indian. Now, what can one do with material like that? What I want to know are things about the veld. About the ways of the bush and the way the farmers think here… I've come to the conclusion that they don't think here."

At Naudé pulled Penzhorn up sharp, then. And he asked him, what with the white ants and galblaas, if he thought a farmer ever got time to think. And he asked him, with the controlled price of mealies 24s. a bag, instead of 24s 9d., as we had all expected, what he thought the Marico farmer had left to think *with*? By that time Fritz Pretorius was telling us, with a wild sort of laugh, about the last cheque he got from the creamery, and Hans van Tonder was saying things about those contour walls that the Agriculture Department man had suggested to stop soil erosion.

"The Agriculture Department man looks like a contour wall himself," Hans van Tonder said, "with those sticking up eyebrows."

Meanwhile, Jurie Steyn was stating, not in any spirit of bitterness, but just as a fact, the exact difference that the new increase in railway tariffs meant to the price of seven-and-a-half-inch piping.

Gabriel Penzhorn closed his notebook.

"I don't mean that sort of talk," he said. "Buying and selling. The low language of barter and the market-place. I can get that sort of talk from any produce merchant in Newtown. Or from any stockbroker I care to drop in on. But I don't care to. What I came here for was – "

That was the moment when Jurie Steyn's wife, having overheard part of our conversation, flounced in from the kitchen.

"And what about eggs?" she demanded. "If I showed you what I pay for bone-meal then you *would* have something to write in your little note-book. Why should there be all that difference between the retail price of eggs and the price I get? I tell you it's the middlem – "

"Veld lore," Gabriel Penzhorn interrupted, sounding quite savage, now. "That's what I came here for. But I can see you don't know what it is, or anything about it. I want to know about things like the red sky in the morning is the shepherd's warning. Morgen rood, plomp in die sloot. I want to know about how you can tell from the yellowing grass on the edge of a veld footpath that it is going to be an early winter. I want to know about when the tinktinkies fly low over the dam is it going to be a heavy downpour or a slow motreën. I want to know when the wren-war-bler – "

"I know if the tinktinkies fly low over my dam, the next thing they'll be doing is sitting high up eating my cling-peaches in the orchard," At Naudé said. "And if that canning factory at Welgevonden ever thinks I'm going to deal with them again… "

In the meantime, Jurie Steyn's wife was talking about the time she changed her Leghorns from mealies and skim milk to a standard ration. They went into a six-month moult, Jurie Steyn's wife said.

When the lorry from Groblersdal arrived Hans van Tonder was feeling in his pockets to show us an account he had got only the other day for cement. And Gabriel Penzhorn, in a voice that was almost pathetic, was saying something, over and over again, about the red sky at night.

The driver told us afterwards that on the way back in the lorry Gabriel Penzhorn made a certain remark to him. If we did not know otherwise, we might perhaps have thought that Gabriel Penzhorn had overheard some of the earlier part of our conversation in the voorkamer that morning.

"The Marico," Gabriel Penzhorn said to the lorry-driver, "stinks."

Ghost Trouble

THEY WERE having ghost trouble again in the Spelonksdrift area, Chris Welman said to us when we were sitting in Jurie Steyn's post office. The worst kind of ghost trouble, Chris Welman added.

We could guess what that meant.

Everybody knew, of course, that Spelonksdrift was swarming with ghosts, any time after midnight. The ghosts came out of the caves in the Dwarsberge nearby. During the day it was quite all right. Then even the most difficult spectres would go and lie down in the hollowed-out places at the foot of the koppie and try and get some rest. But after dark they would make their way to the drift, dragging chains and carrying on generally. That much we all knew. I mean, there was not even a Mtosa cattle-herd so ignorant as willingly to venture near the drift after nightfall.

When it came to having to do with ghosts, a Mtosa could be almost as educated as a white man.

Again, with regard to ghosts, we still remember the time when the new school-teacher, Charlie Rossouw, who was fresh from college, taught the Standard Five class, in the history lesson, about the Great Trek. He was talking about the Voortrekker leader, Lodewyk Loggenberg, and about the route his party took, and about the *Dagboek* that Lodewyk Loggenberg kept. The young school-teacher said that he did not want his class to think of history as just names of persons that they had to remember, but that the Voortrekkers belonged to their own nation, and were people like their own fathers, say, or – if that was too unpleasant a thought – perhaps like their uncles. Or maybe even like the second cousins of their aunts' half-sisters by marriage. That young school-teacher was very thorough in his way.

44

Then, drawing on the blackboard with a piece of chalk, Charlie Rossouw explained to the class that Lodewyk Loggenberg had passed through the Groot Marico with his wagons. "Perhaps the trek passed right in front of where this schoolhouse is today," the teacher said. "Maybe Lodewyk Loggenberg's long line of wagons, with voorryers and agter-ryers and with the Staats Bybel in the bok and with copper moulds from which to make candles six at a time after you fixed the wick in the middle, properly (I mean, you know the difference now between a form candle and a water candle: we did that last week) – maybe these Voortrekkers passed along right here, and the tracks that their wagon-wheels made over the veld were the beginning of what we today call the Government Road. Think of that. I wonder what Lodewyk Loggenberg wrote in his *Dagboek* when he went along this way towards Spelonksdrift? What he thought of this part of the country, I mean. That grand old Patriarch. Does anybody know what a Patriarch is?"

Practically every child in his Standard Five class put up his or her hand, then. No, they did not know what a Patriarch was. But they did know what Lodewyk Loggenberg wrote in his *Dagboek* about Spelonksdrift. And they told the schoolmaster. And the schoolmaster, because he was young and fresh from college, laughed in a lighthearted manner at the answers the pupils gave him. It was all the same answer, really. And it was only after Faans Grobler, who was chairman of our school commit-tee, had spoken earnestly to Charlie Rossouw about how serious a thing it was to laugh at a Standard Five pupil when he gave the right answer, that Charlie Rossouw went to Zeerust on a push bicycle over a weekend. Charlie Rossouw spent several hours in the public library at Zeerust. When he came back he was a changed man.

After that, he put in even more time than he had done in the Zeerust library in explaining to Standard Five – which was the top class – that he had not known, until then, that that particular passage about the haunted character of the Spelonksdrift appeared in Lodewyk Loggenberg's *Dag-boek*. He had never been taught that at university, Charlie Rossouw said. But it was clear enough, now, of course. He had read it in print. It gave him an insight into Lodewyk Loggenberg's mind that he did not have before, he acknowledged. But then, while he was at the teachers' college, he was not able to go into all those details about South African history. He had to study subjects like blackboard work and cardboard modelling and the theory of education and the depth of the Indian Ocean and the Scholastic Philosophers, including Archbishop Anselm and Thomas

Aquinas and Peter Lombard and Duns Scotus. And there was also Albertus Magnus, Charlie Rossouw said. So he should not be blamed for not knowing *everything* that Lodewyk Loggenberg wrote in his *Dagboek.* He had been so busy, night after night, trying to make out what Duns Scotus was trying to get at. But now that he had himself gone into the world a bit, the schoolmaster said, it seemed to him that there was quite a lot in common between Duns Scotus and Lodewyk Loggenberg. In his opinion, they would both of them have got pretty high marks for cardboard modelling.

Francina Smit, who was in Standard Five, and who was good at arithmetic, said afterwards that Charlie Rossouw made that remark with what she could only describe as a sneer.

All the same, Charlie Rossouw said to his class, even though it was true that Lodewyk Loggenberg *had* written those things about Spelonksdrift in his *Dagboek,* it would be best if the class kept quiet about it when the inspector came. He was sure that the school inspector would misunderstand an answer like that. He did not believe that the inspector knew Lodewyk Loggenberg's *Dagboek* very well. He even went so far as to doubt whether the school inspector knew much about Thomas Aquinas.

A little later, when Charlie Rossouw was sacked from the Education Department, we in the Groot Marico were pleased about it. There was just something about Charlie Rossouw that made us feel that he was getting too big for his boots. The next thing he would be telling his class was that the earth turns round the sun. Whereas you've only got to lie in the tamboekie grass on Abjaterskop towards evening and *watch*, and you'll see for yourself that it isn't so. All those astronomers and people like that — where would they be if they once lay on Abjaterskop in the setting sun, and shredded a plug of roll tobacco with a pocket knife, in the setting sun, and looked about them, and thought a little? Put an astronomer on top of Abjaterskop, in the setting sun, and with a plug of roll tobacco, and lying in the tamboekie grass, and where would he *be*?

Anyway, even though we who were sitting in Jurie Steyn's voorkamer that also served as the Drogevlei post office, were not astronomers, or anywhere near, we were nevertheless much impressed by Chris Welman's statement that they were having ghost trouble at Spelonksdrift. When it came to seeing a ghost you didn't need to be an astronomer and to have a telescope: a ghost was something that you could actually see best just with the naked eye.

Now, if the spirits of the dead were content to haunt only the drift after nightfall, then no harm could come to any human being. No human being was ever *there* after nightfall. It was when a pale apparition took to the road, and wandered through the poort to have a look round, that unfortunate incidents occurred.

If you were travelling along the Government Road at night and you saw a person walking – or riding on horseback, even – and you saw the moon shining through that person, then you would know, of course, that you had met a ghost. If there was no moon, then you would see the stars shining through the ghost. Or you might even see a withaak tree or a piece of road showing through the ghost.

Gysbert van Tonder once encountered an elderly ghost, riding a mule, right in the middle of the poort. And Gysbert van Tonder held long converse with the ghost, whom he took to be an elderly farmer that had come back from a dance at Nietverdiend – coming back so late because he was elderly. It was when Gysbert van Tonder recognised the mule that the elderly farmer was sitting on as old Koffiebek, that had belonged to his grandfather and that had died many years before of grass-belly, that Gysbert van Tonder grew to have doubts. What made him suspicious, Gysbert van Tonder said, was that he had never in his life seen Koffiebek standing so still, with a man sitting on his back, talking. During the whole conversation Koffiebek did not once try to bite a chunk out of his rider's leg. In the same moment Gysbert van Tonder realised that it was because there wasn't much of his rider for Koffiebek *to* bite.

"What made it all so queer," Gysbert van Tonder said, "was that I had been talking to the elderly farmer on the mule about a new comet that there was in the sky, then. And I had asked him if he thought it meant the end of the world, and he said he hoped not, because there were several things that he wanted to do still. And it didn't strike me that, all the time we were talking about the comet, the old farmer was sitting between me and the comet, and I was seeing the comet through the middle of his left lung. I could see his right lung, too, the way it swelled out when he breathed."

It was getting late, not only in Jurie Steyn's post office, but everywhere in the Marico, and the lorry from Bekkersdal had not yet arrived with our letters and milk-cans. They must be having trouble along the road, we said to each other.

And because of the line of conversation that Chris Welman had started we were glad when Jurie Steyn, on his return from the milking shed, lit the paraffin lamp in the voorkamer before it was properly dark.

Oupa Bekker had been very quiet, most of the evening. Several times he had looked out into the gathering dusk, shaking his head at it. But after Jurie Steyn had lit the oil-lamp, Oupa Bekker cheered up a good deal. Then he started telling us about the time when he encountered a ghost near Spelonksdrift, in the old days.

"I had lost my way in the dark," Oupa Bekker declared, "and so I thought that that stretch of water was just an ordinary crossing over the Molopo River. I had no idea that it was Spelonksdrift. So I pulled up at the edge of the stream to let my horse drink. Mind you, I should have known that it was Spelonksdrift just through my horse not having been at all thirsty. Indeed, afterwards it struck me that I had never before seen a horse with so little taste for water. All he did was to look slowly about him and shiver."

At Naudé asked Jurie Steyn's wife to turn the paraffin lamp up a bit higher, just about then. He said he was thinking of the lorry-driver. The lorry-driver would be able to see the light in Jurie Steyn's voorkamer from a long way off, if the lamp was turned up properly, At Naudé explained. It was queer how several of us, at that moment, started feeling concern for the lorry-driver. We all seemed to remember, at once, that he was a married man with five children. Jurie Steyn's wife did not have to turn much on the screw to make the lamp burn brighter. We men did it all for her. But then, of course, we Marico men are chivalrous that way.

In the meantime, Oupa Bekker had been drooling on in his old-man way of talking, with the result that when we were back in our seats again we found that we had missed the in-between part of his story. All we heard was the end part. We heard about his dispute with the ghost, that had ended in the ghost letting him have it across the chops with the back of his hand.

"So I went next day to see Dr Angus Stuart," Oupa Bekker continued. "In those days he was the only doctor between here and Rysmierbult. I didn't tell him anything about what had happened at Spelonksdrift. I just showed him my face, with those red marks on it... And do you know what? After he had had a good look at those marks through a magnifying glass, the doctor said that they could have been caused only by a ghost hitting me over the jaw with the back of a blue-flame hand."

That story started Johnny Coen off telling us about the time he was walking through the poort one night, with Dawie Ferreira who had once been a policeman at Newclare. And while he and Dawie Ferreira were walking through the poort, a Bechuana through whom they could see the Milky Way shining came up to them. In addition to having the Milky Way visible through his spine, the Bechuana was also carrying his head under his arm. But Dawie Ferreira, because he was a former policeman, knew

48

how to deal with that Bechuana, Johnny Coen said. He promptly asked him where his pass was for being on a public road at that time of night. You couldn't see the Bechuana for dust after that, Johnny Coen said. In fact, the dust that the Bechuana with his head under his arm raised on the Government Road of the Marico seemed to become part of, and to reach beyond, the Milky Way that shone through his milt and was also a road.

The lorry from Bekkersdal arrived very late. The driver looked per-turbed.

"We had big-end trouble at Spelonksdrift," the lorry-driver said, "and an old farmer riding a mule came up and gave me a lot of sauce. He acted as though he was a ghost, or something. As though I'd take notice of that sort of nonsense. *I saw through him, all right.* Then he sloshed me one across the jaw. When I tried to land him one back he was gone."

The lorry-driver had marks on his cheek that could have been caused by a back-hander from an elderly farmer riding a mule.

Oom Tobie's Sickness

FROM THE way he was muffled to the chin in a khaki overcoat and his wife's scarf in the heat of the day, we knew why Tobias Schutte was sitting on the riempies bench in Jurie Steyn's voorkamer. We knew that Tobias Schutte was going by lorry to Bekkersdal to get some more medical treatment. There was nobody in the Groot Marico who suffered as regularly and acutely from maladies – imaginary or otherwise – as did Tobias Schutte. For that reason he was known as "Iepekonders Oom Tobie" from this side of the Pilanesberg right to the Kalahari: a good way into the Kalahari, sometimes – the exact distance depending on how far the Klipkop Bushmen had to go into the desert to find msumas.

"You look to be in a pretty bad way again, Oom Tobie," Chris Welman said in a tone that Oom Tobie accepted as implying sympathy. Nobody else in the voorkamer took it up that way, however. To the rest of us, Chris Welman's remark was just a plain sneer. "What's it this time, Oom Tobie," he went on, "the miltsiek or St. Vitus's dance? But you got it while you were working, I'll bet."

"Just before I started working, to be exact," Oom Tobie replied. "I was just getting ready to plant in the first pole for the new cattle camp when the sickness overtook me. Of a sudden I came all over queer. So I just had to leave the whole job to the Cape Coloured man, Pieterse, and the

49

Bechuanas. The planting of the poles, the wiring, chasing away meerkats – I had to leave it all to them. They are at it now. I don't know what I'd do without Pieterse. I must give him an old pair of trousers again, one of these days. I've got a pair that are quite good still, except that they are worn out in the seat. It's queer how all my trousers get worn out like that, in the seat. The clothes you get today aren't what they used to be. I buy a new pair of trousers to wear when I go out on the lands, and before I know where I am they're frayed all thin, at the seat… "

"Was Pieterse – I mean, did Pieterse not look very surprised, sort of, at your being taken ill so suddenly, Oom Tobie?" Jurie Steyn asked, doing his best to keep a straight face.

"Well, no," Oom Tobie replied in all honesty. "When he helped me back on to the stoep from the place where we were going to put up the fence, Pieterse said he had felt for quite some days that I had this illness coming on. It wasn't so much anything he could see about me as what he *felt,* he said. And he could remember the exact time, too, when he first had that feeling. It was the afternoon when the poles and the rolls of barbed wire came from Ramoutsa. He didn't himself feel too good, either, that afternoon, he said. It was as though there was something unhealthy in the air. He's an extraordinary fellow, Pieterse. But that's because he's Cape Coloured, I suppose. I wouldn't be surprised if he's some part of him Slams, too. You know these Malays… "

Chris Welman asked Oom Tobie what he thought his illness was, this time. "Well, I know it can't be the horse-sickness," Oom Tobie said, "because I had the horse-sickness last year. And when you've had the horse-sickness once you don't get it again. You're salted."

The new school-teacher, Vermaak, who wasn't long out of college, and whom Jurie Steyn's wife seemed to think a lot of, on account of his education, then said that it was the first time he had ever heard of a human being getting horse-sickness.

Several of us, speaking at the same time, told the school-teacher that there were lots of things he had never heard of, and that a white man getting horse-sickness was what he now had an opportunity of getting instructed about. We told him that if he remained in the Groot Marico longer, and observed a little, he would no doubt learn things that would surprise him, yet.

The schoolmaster said that that had already happened to him. Just from looking around, he said.

"What I have got this time, now, is, I think, the blue-tongue," Oom

Tobie continued. "Mind you, I used to think that only sheep get the blue-tongue. When there is rain after a long drought – that is the worst time for the blue-tongue. And you know the dry spell was pretty long, here in the district, before these rains started. So I think it must be blue-tongue."

Gysbert van Tonder asked Oom Tobie to put his tongue out, so we could see. We all pretended to take a lot of interest in Oom Tobie's tongue, then. It was, of course, quite an ordinary-looking sort of tongue, perhaps somewhat on the thick side and with tobacco-juice stains in the cracks. Oom Tobie first protruded his tongue out straight in front of his face as far as it would go – a by no means inconsiderable distance. Then he let his tongue hang down on his chin, for a bit.

Oom Tobie was engaged in lifting his tongue up again, in the direction of his eyebrows, so that we could see the underneath part of it, when Jurie Steyn's wife came into the voorkamer from the kitchen. From her remarks, then, it was clear that she had not heard any of our previous conversation.

"I am ashamed of you, Oom Tobie," Jurie Steyn's wife announced, speaking very severely. "Sticking out your tongue at Mr Vermaak like that."

The schoolmaster was sharing the riempies bench with Oom Tobie.

Oom Tobie started to explain what it was all about. But because he forgot, in the excitement of the moment, to put his tongue back again, first, all he could utter was a sequence of somewhat peculiar noises.

"If you disagree with Mr Vermaak on any subject," Jurie Steyn's wife went on, "then you can at least discuss the matter with him in a respectable sort of way. To stick out your tongue at a man, and to *wobble* it, is no way to carry on a discussion, Oom Tobie. I can only hope that Mr Vermaak does not think *everybody* in the Bushveld is so unrefined."

By that time Oom Tobie had found his tongue again, however, in quite a literal way. And in a few simple sentences he was able to acquaint Jurie Steyn's wife with the facts of the situation. Oom Tobie might have made those sentences even simpler, perhaps. Only he happened, out of the corner of his eye, to catch a glimpse of Jurie Steyn behind the counter. And Oom Tobie was sick enough on account of the blue-tongue. He did not want to become still more of an invalid as a result of a misunderstanding with Jurie Steyn, who was known for his strength and ill-temper.

"But if it's the blue-tongue in sheep that I've got," Oom Tobie proceeded, hastily, "then it won't show first in my tongue, so much. You see it first in the limp sort of way my wool hangs. It was the same with the horse-sickness. The first sign of it was a feeling of stiffness just behind the fetlock. It was several days before I started getting the snuffles – "

Gysbert van Tonder interrupted Oom Tobie at that point.

"Tell us, Oom Tobie… " Gysbert van Tonder began, and as he spoke his glance travelled in the direction of young Vermaak, the school-teacher. We guessed what was going on in Gysbert van Tonder's mind. We felt the same way about it, too. You see, in the Marico we might per-haps laugh at Oom Tobie, and invent a nickname for him, and we didn't mind if the Klipkop tribe of Bushmen in the Kalahari also spoke of him by that nickname. Those things we could understand. But even when we laughed at Oom Tobie, we also had a respect for him. And we didn't like the idea that a stranger straight from university, like young Vermaak, wearing city clothes and all, should not give Oom Tobie his due. For that matter, the Klipkop Bushmen still gave Oom Tobie his due. And *they* did not wear city clothes. Not by a long chalk the Klipkop Bushmen didn't.

And what we were genuinely proud of Oom Tobie about was the fact that he had had more wild and domestic animal diseases than any man you could come across anywhere in Africa. At catch-weights and with no holds barred, we could put him, in his own line, against any sick man from Woodstock Beach to the Zambezi. And while we could laugh at him as much as we wanted, we did not like strangers to.

Consequently, when Gysbert van Tonder turned to Oom Tobie with a determined expression on his face, we knew what Gysbert was going to say. He was going to ask Oom Tobie, salted with horse-sickness and all, *really* to show his paces.

"Tell us," Gysbert van Tonder said, getting up from his chair and fold-ing his arms across his chest. "Tell us, Oom Tobie, about the time you had *snake*-sickness."

Thus encouraged, Oom Tobie told us, and with an elaborate amount of detail.

"But I wouldn't like to have to go through all that again," he ended up. "All the time I was suffering from snake disease I felt so *low*, if you understand what I mean. With my backside right on the ground, as it were."

Chris Welman coughed, then.

For Jurie Steyn's wife was still present, and it seemed as though Oom Tobie was perhaps getting a bit coarse. To our surprise, however, Jurie Steyn himself said that it was quite in order. When you were talking about snakes, it was only natural that you should talk about them as they were, he said. It would be ungodly to pretend that a snake was different from what we all knew a snake to be.

He spoke with a warmth that made us all feel uncomfortable.

"For that matter," Jurie Steyn added, with a sort of careful deliberation, "there is more than just one kind of snake right here in the Marico. There are *lots* of kinds."

I noticed that the young school-teacher looked down, when Jurie spoke like that. I also noticed that shortly afterwards Jurie Steyn's wife went back to the kitchen.

We were glad when Oom Tobie started talking about his illness again. It seemed to remove quite a lot of strain.

"Maybe it isn't the blue-tongue," Oom Tobie said, "because I felt it coming on even before the time that Pieterse spoke to me about it. I felt it after I had bought that barbed wire at the store at Ramoutsa. So I think maybe it's something I ate. I ate two bananas. They gave me those two bananas as a bonsella for all the wire I bought."

Shortly afterwards the Government lorry came. And I still remember what At Naudé, who reads the newspapers, said when Oom Tobie, all buttoned up in his coat and scarf, and with a cushion under his arm, climbed aboard the lorry.

"Oom Tobie looks like he's a Member of Parliament," At Naudé said, "fixed up for an all-night sitting."

Nevertheless, we were not too happy when, next time the lorry came, the driver told us what the doctor at Bekkersdal had told him was wrong with Oom Tobie. For it was a human disease, this time. And it would almost appear as though the Cape Coloured man, Pieterse, really was to some extent Slams. Moreover, we ourselves had been in somewhat close contact with Oom Tobie, and so we did not feel too comfortable about it.

It looked as though Oom Tobie had landed a winner, all right, and it was not impossible that the bonsella bananas had played a part in it.

All the same, it's queer how frightened everybody gets when you hear the word smallpox.

News Story

"THE WAY the world is today," At Naudé said, shaking his head, "I don't know what is going to happen."

From that it was clear that At Naudé had been hearing news over the wireless again that made him fear for the future of the country. We did not exactly sit up, then. We in the Dwarsberge knew that it was the wireless that made At Naudé that way. And he could tremble as much as he liked for the country's future or his own. There was never any change, either, in the kind of news he would bring us. Every time it was about stone-throwings in Johannesburg locations and about how many new kinds of bombs the Russians had got, and about how many people had gone to gaol for telling the Russians about still other kinds of bombs they could make. Although it did not look as though the Russians *needed* to be educated much in that line.

And we could never really understand why At Naudé listened at all. We hardly ever listened to *him*, for that matter. We would rather hear from Gysbert van Tonder if it was true that the ouderling at Pilanesberg really forgot himself in the way that Jurie Steyn's wife had heard about from a kraal Mtosa at the kitchen door. The Mtosa had come by to buy half-penny stamps to stick on his forehead for the yearly Ndlolo dance. Now, there was news for you. About the ouderling, I mean. And even to hear that the Ndlolo dance was being held soon again was at least something. And if it should turn out that what was being said about the Pilanesberg ouderling was not true, well, then, the same thing applied to a lot of what At Naudé heard over the wireless also.

"I don't know what is going to happen," At Naudé repeated, "the way the world is today. I just heard over the wireless – "

"That's how the news we got in the old days was better," Oupa Bekker said. "I mean in the real old days, when there was no wireless, and there was not the telegraph, either. The news you got then you could do something with. And you didn't have to go to the post office and get it from the newspaper. The post office is the curse of the Transvaal… "

Jurie Steyn said that Oupa Bekker was quite right, there. He himself would never have taken on the job of postmaster at Drogevlei if he had as much as guessed that there were four separate forms that he would have to fill in, each of them different, just for a simple five-shilling money order. It was so much brainier and neater, Jurie Steyn said, for people who wanted to send five shillings somewhere, if they would just wrap up a couple of half-crowns in a thick wad of brown paper and then post them in the ordinary way, like a letter. That was what the new red pillar-box in front of his door was *for*, Jurie Steyn explained. The authorities had gone to the expense of that red pillar-box in order to help the public. And yet you still found people coming in for postal orders and money orders. The other day a man even came in and asked could he telegraph some money, somewhere.

"I gave that man a piece of brown paper and showed him the pillar-box," Jurie Steyn said. "It seemed, until then, that he did not know what kind of progress we had been making here. I therefore asked him if I could show him some more ways in regard to how advanced the Groot Marico was getting. But he said, no, the indications I had already given him were plenty."

Jurie Steyn said that he thought it was handsome of the man to have spoken up for the Marico like that, seeing that he was quite a newcomer to these parts.

Because we never knew how long Jurie Steyn would be when once he got on the subject of his work, we were glad when Johnny Coen asked Oupa Bekker to explain some more to us about how they got news in the old days. We were all pleased, that is, except At Naudé, who had again tried to get in a remark but had got no further than to say that if we knew something we would all shiver in our veldskoens.

"How did we get news?" Oupa Bekker said, replying to another question of Johnny Coen's. "Well, you would be standing in the lands, say, and then one of the Bechuanas would point to a small cloud of dust in the poort, and you would walk across to the big tree by the dam, where the road bends, and the traveller would come past there, with two vos horses in front of his Cape-cart, and he would get off from the cart and shake hands and say he was Du Plessis. And you would say you were Bekker, and he would say, afterwards, that he couldn't stay the night on your farm, because he had to get to Tsalala's Kop. Well, there was *news*. You could talk about it for days. For weeks even. You have got no idea how often my wife and I discussed it. And we knew everything that there was to know about the man. We knew his name was Du Plessis."

At Naudé said, then, that he did not think much of that sort of news. People must have been a bit *simpel* in the head, in those old times that Oupa Bekker was talking about, if they thought anything about that sort of news. Why, if you compared it with what the radio announcer said, only yesterday…

Jurie Steyn's wife came in from the kitchen at that moment. There was a light of excitement in her eyes. And when she spoke it was to none of us in particular.

"It has just occurred to me," Jurie Steyn's wife said, "that is, if it's *true* what they are saying about the Pilanesberg ouderling, of course. Well, it has just struck me that, when he forgot himself in the way they say – provided that he *did* forget himself like that, mind you – well, perhaps the ouderling didn't know that anybody was looking."

That was a possibility that had not so far occurred to us, and we discussed it at some length. In between our talk At Naudé was blurting out something about the rays from a still newer kind of bomb that would kill you right in the middle of the veld and through fifty feet of concrete. So we said, of course, that the best thing to do would be to keep a pretty safe distance away from concrete, with those sort of rays about, if concrete was as dangerous as all that.

We were in no mood for foolishness. Oupa Bekker took this as an encouragement for him to go on.

"Or another day," Oupa Bekker continued, "you would again be standing in your lands, say, or sitting, even, if there was a long day of ploughing ahead, and you did not want to tire yourself out unnecessarily. You would be sitting on a stone in the shade of a tree, say, and you would think to yourself how lazy those Bechuanas look, going backwards and forwards, backwards and forwards, with the plough and the oxen, and you would get quite sleepy, say, thinki ng to yourself how lazy those Bechuanas are. If it wasn't for the oxen to keep them going, they wouldn't do any work at all, you might perhaps think.

"And then, without your in the least expecting it, you would again have news. And the news would find a stone for himself and come along and sit down right next to you. It would be the new veldkornet, say. And why nobody saw any dust in the poort, that time, was because the veldkornet didn't come along the road. And you would make a joke with him and say: 'I suppose that's why they call you a *veld*kornet, because you don't travel along the road, but you come by the *veld*langes.' And the veldkornet would laugh and ask you a few questions, and he would tell you that they had good rains at Derdepoort… Well, there was something that I could tell my wife over and over again, for weeks. It was news. For weeks I had that to think about. The visit of the veldkornet. In the old days it was real news."

We could see, from the way At Naudé was fidgeting in his chair, that he guessed we were just egging the old man on to talk in order to scoff at all the important European news that At Naudé regularly retailed to us, and that we were getting tired of.

After a while At Naudé could no longer contain himself.

"This second-childhood drivel that Oupa Bekker is talking," At Naudé announced, not looking at anybody in particular, but saying it to all of us, in the way Jurie Steyn's wife had spoken when she came out of the kitchen. "Well, I would actually sooner listen to scandal about the Pilanesberg ouderling. There is at least some sort of meaning to it. I am not being unfriendly to Oupa Bekker, of course. I know it's just that he's old. But it's also quite clear to me that he doesn't know what news *is*, at all."

Jurie Steyn said that it was at least as sensible as a man lying on the veld under fifty feet of concrete because of some rays. If a man were to lie under fifty feet of concrete he wouldn't be able to breathe, leave alone anything else.

In the meantime, Johnny Coen had been asking Oupa Bekker to tell us some more.

"On another day, say," Oupa Bekker went on, "you would not be in your lands at all, but you would be sitting on your front stoep, drinking coffee, say. And the Cape-cart with the two vos horses in front would be coming down the road again, but in the opposite direction, going *towards* the poort, this time. And you would not see much of Du Plessis's face, because his hat would be pulled over his eyes. And the veldkornet would be sitting on the Cape-cart next to him, say."

Oupa Bekker paused. He paused for quite a while, too, holding a lighted match cupped over his pipe as though he was out on the veld where there was wind, and puffing vigorously.

"And my wife and I would go on talking about it for years afterwards, say," Oupa Bekker went on. "For years after Du Plessis was hanged, I mean."

School Concert

THE PREPARATIONS for the annual school concert were in full swing.

In the Marico these school concerts were held in the second part of June, when the nights were pleasantly cool. It was too hot, in December, for recitations and singing and reading the Joernaal that carried playful references to the activities and idiosyncrasies of individual members of the Dwarsberg population. On a midsummer's night, in a little school building crowded to the doors with children and adults and with more adults leaning in through the windows and keeping out the air, the songs and the recitations sounded limp, somehow. Moreover, the personal references in the Joernaal did not sound quite as playful, then, as they were intended to be.

The institution of the Joernaal dated back to the time of the first Hollander schoolmaster in the Groot Marico. The Joernaal was a very popular feature of school concerts in Limburg, where he came from, the Hollander schoolmaster explained. For weeks beforehand the schoolmaster, assisted by some of the pupils in the upper class, would write down, in the funniest way they knew, odds and ends of things about people living in the neighbourhood. Why, they just about killed themselves laughing, while they were writing those things down in a classroom in old Limburg, the Hollander schoolmaster said, and then, at the concert, one of the pupils would read it all out. Oh, it was a real scream. You wouldn't mention people's names, of course, the Hollander schoolmaster went on to say. They would just *hint* at who they were. It was all done in a subtle sort of way, naturally, but it was also clear enough so that you couldn't possibly miss the allusion. And you knew straight away who was *meant*.

That was what the first Hollander schoolmaster in the Marico explained, oh, long ago, before the reading, at a school concert, of the first Joernaal.

Today, in the Dwarsberge, they still talk about that concert.

It would appear, somehow, that in drawing up the Joernaal, the Hollander schoolmaster had not been quite subtle enough. Or, maybe, what they would split their sides laughing at in Limburg would raise quite different sorts of emotions north of the railway line to Ottoshoop. That's the way it is with humour, of course. Anyway, while the head pupil was reading out the Joernaal – stuttering a bit now and again because he could sense what that silence on the part of a Bushveld audience meant – the Hollander schoolmaster had tears streaming down his cheeks, the way his laughter was convulsing him. Seated on the platform next to the pupil who was reading, the schoolmaster would reach into his pocket every so often for his handkerchief to wipe his eyes with. That made the audience freeze into a yet greater stillness.

A farmer's wife said afterwards that she felt she could just choke, then.

"If what was in that Joernaal were *jokes*, now," Koos Kirstein – who had been a prominent cattle-smuggler in his day – said, "well I can laugh at a joke with the best of them. I read the page of jokes at the back of the

Kerkbode regularly every month. But can anybody see anything to titter at in asking where I got the money from to buy that harmonium that my daughter plays hymns on? That came in the Joernaal."

Koos Kirstein asked that question of a church elder a few days after the school concert, and the elder said, no, there was nothing funny in it. Everybody in the Marico *knew* where Koos Kirstein got his money from, the elder said.

"And saying I am so well in with the police," Koos Kirstein continued. "Saying in the Joernaal that a policeman on border patrol went and hid behind my harmonium when a special plain-clothes inspector from Pretoria walked into my voorkamer unexpectedly. Why, the school-master just about doubled up laughing, when that bit was being read out."

Anyway, the reading of that first Joernaal at a Marico school concert never reached a proper end. When the proceedings terminated the head pupil still had a considerable number of unread foolscap sheets in his hand. And he was stuttering more than ever. For he had just finished the part about the Indian store at Ramoutsa refusing to give Giel Oosthuizen any more credit until he paid off something on last year's account.

Before that he had read out something about a crateful of muscovy ducks at the Zeerust market that Faans Lemmer had loaded on to his own wagon by mistake, and that he afterwards, still making the same error, unloaded into his own chicken pen – not noticing at the time the difference between the muscovy ducks and his own Australorps, as he afterwards explained to the market master.

The head pupil had also read out something about why Frikkie Snyman's grandfather had to stay behind in the tent on the kerkplein when the rest of the family went to the Nagmaal. It wasn't the rheumatics that kept Frikkie Snyman's grandfather away from the Communion service, the Joernaal said, but he stayed behind in the tent because he didn't have an extra pair of laced-up shop boots. It was when Frikkie Snyman's wife, Hanna, knelt in church at the end of a pew and her long skirt that had all flowers on came up over one ankle – the Joernaal said – that you realised how Frikkie Snyman's grandfather was sitting barefooted in the tent on the kerkplein.

That was about as far as the head pupil got with the reading of the Joernaal... And to this day they can still show you, in an old Marico schoolroom, the burnt corner of a blackboard from where the lamp fell on it when the audience turned the platform upside down on the Hollander schoolmaster. Nothing happened to the head pupil, however. He sensed what was coming and got away, in time, into the rafters. Unlike most head pupils, he had a quick mind.

All that happened very long ago, of course, as we were saying to each other in Jurie Steyn's post office. Today, the Marico was very different, we said to one another. Those old farmers didn't have the advantages that we enjoyed today, we said. There was no Afrikander Cattle Breeders' Society in those days, or even the Dwarsberge Hog Breeders' Society, and you would never see a front garden with irises in it – or a front garden at all, for that matter. And you couldn't order clothes from Johannesburg, just filling in your measurements, so that all your wife had to do was…

But it was when Jurie Steyn's wife explained what she had to do to the last serge suit that Jurie Steyn ordered by post, just giving his size, that we saw that this example that we mentioned did not perhaps reflect progress in the Marico in its best light.

From the way Jurie Steyn's wife spoke, it would seem that the easiest part of the alterations she had to make was cutting off the trouser turn-ups and inserting the material in the neck part of the jacket. "And then the suit still hung on Jurie like a sack," she concluded.

But Gysbert van Tonder said that she must not blame the Johannesburg store for it too much. There was something about the way Jurie Steyn was *built*, Gysbert van Tonder said. And we could not help noticing a certain nasty undertone in his voice, then, when he said that.

Johnny Coen smoothed the matter over very quickly, however. He had also had difficulties, ordering suits by post, he said. But he found it helped the Johannesburg store a lot if you sent a full-length photograph of yourself along with the order. They always returned the photograph. No, Johnny Coen said in reply to a question from At Naudé, he didn't know why that Johannesburg store sent the photographs back so promptly, under registered cover and all. And then, when he saw that At Naudé was laughing, Johnny Coen said that that firm could, perhaps, if it wanted to, keep all those photographs and frame them. But, all the same, he added, it would help the shop a lot if, next time Jurie Steyn ordered a suit by post, he also put in a full-length photograph of himself.

But all this talk was getting us away from what we had been saying about how more broad-minded the Groot Marico had become since the old days, due to progress. It was then that Koos Nienaber brought us back to what we were discussing.

"Where our forefathers in the Marico were different from the way we are today," Koos Nienaber said, "is because they hadn't learnt to laugh at themselves, yet. They took themselves much too seriously. Although they had to, I suppose, since it was all going to be put into history books. Or at least as much of it as could be put into history books. But we today are different. We wouldn't carry on in an undignified manner if, at the next concert, there should be something in the Joernaal to show up our little human weaknesses. We would laugh, I mean. Take Jurie Steyn and his serge suit, now. Well, we've got a sense of humour, today. I mean, Jurie Steyn would be the first to laugh at how funny he looks in that serge suit – "

"How do you mean I look funny in my new suit?" Jurie Steyn demanded.

At Naudé came in between the two of them, then, and made it clear to Jurie Steyn that Koos Nienaber had been saying those things merely by way of argument, and to prove his point. Koos Nienaber didn't mean that Jurie Steyn actually *looked* funny in his new suit, At Naudé explained.

"If he doesn't mean it, what does he want to say it for?" Jurie Steyn said, sounding only half convinced. "And, anyway, Koos Nienaber needn't talk. When he came round with the collection plate at the last Nagmaal, and he was wearing his new manel, I thought Koos Nienaber was an ourang-outang."

Nevertheless, we all acknowledged at the end that we were looking forward to the school concert. And there should be quite a lot of fun in having the Joernaal, we said. Seeing how today we had a sense of humour.

It was not only schoolchildren and their parents that came to attend the concert in that little school building of which the middle partition had been taken away to make it into one hall. For instance, there was Hendrik Prinsloo, who had come all the way from Vleispoort by Cape-cart, and had not meant to attend the concert at all, since he was on his way to Zeerust and was just passing that way, when some of the parents persuaded him, for the sake of his horses, to outspan under the thorn-trees on the school grounds by the side of the Government Road.

It was observed that Hendrik Prinsloo had a red face and that he mistook one of the swingle-bars for the step when he alighted from the Cape-cart. So – after they had looked to see what was under the seat of the Cape-cart – several of the farmers present counselled Hendrik Prinsloo to rest awhile by the roadside, seeing it was already getting on towards evening. They also sent a native over to At Naudé's house for glasses, instructing him to be as quick as he liked. And if At Naudé didn't have glasses, cups would do, one of the farmers added, thoughtfully. By the look of things it was going to be a good children's concert, they said.

Meanwhile the schoolroom was filling up quite nicely. There had been some talk, during the past few days, that a scientist from the Agricultural Research Institute, who was known to be in the neighbourhood, would distribute the school prizes at the concert and also give a little lecture on his favourite subject, which was correct winter grazing. Even that rumour did not keep people away, however. They had the good sense to guess that it was only a rumour, anyhow. Afterwards it was found out that it had been started by Chris Welman, because the schoolmaster had turned down Chris Welman's offer to sing "Boereseun", with actions, at the concert.

There was loud applause when young Vermaak, the schoolmaster, came on to the platform. His black hair was neatly parted in the middle and his city suit of blue serge looked very smart in the lamplight. You could hardly notice those darker patches on the jacket to which Jurie Steyn's wife drew attention, when she said that you could see where Alida van Niekerk had again been trying to clean the schoolmaster's suit with paraffin. Vermaak was boarding at the Van Niekerks', and Alida was their eldest daughter.

The schoolmaster said he was glad to see that there was such a considerable crowd there, tonight, including quite a number of fathers, whom he knew personally, who were looking in at the windows. There were still a few vacant seats for them inside, he said, if they would care to come in. But Gysbert van Tonder, speaking on behalf of those fathers, said no, they did not mind being self-sacrificing in that way. It was not right that the schoolroom should be cluttered up with a lot of fat, healthy men, over whose heads the smaller children would not be able to see properly. There was also a neighbour of theirs, from Vleispoort, Hendrik Prinsloo, who was resting a little. And they wanted to keep an eye on his Cape-cart, which was standing there all by itself in the dark. If the schoolmaster looked out of that nearest window he would be able to see that lonely Cape-cart, Gysbert van Tonder said.

Young Vermaak, who didn't know what was going on, seemed touched at this display of solicitude for a neighbour by just simple-hearted Bushveld farmers. Several of the wives of those farmers sniffed, however.

Three little boys carrying little riding whips and wearing little red jackets came on to the platform and the schoolmaster explained that they would sing a hunting song called "Jan Pohl", which had been translated from English by the great Afrikaans poet, Van Blerk Willemse. Everybody agreed that the translation was a far superior cultural work to the

62

original, the schoolmaster said. In fact you wouldn't recognise that it was the same song, even, if it wasn't for the tune. But that would also be put right shortly, the schoolmaster added. The celebrated Afrikaans composer, Frik Dinkelman, was going to get to work on it.

At Naudé said to the other fathers standing at the window that that man in the song, Jan Pohl, must be a bit queer in the head. "Wearing a red jacket and with a riding whip and a bugle to go and shoot a ribbok in the rante," At Naudé said.

Another father pointed out that that Jan Pohl didn't even have such a thing as a native walking along in front, through the tamboekie grass, where there was always a likelihood of mambas.

The next item on the programme was a group of boys and girls, in pairs, pirouetting about the platform to the music of "Pollie, Ons Gaan Pêrel Toe." Since many of the parents were Doppers, the schoolmaster took the trouble first to explain that what the children were doing wasn't really *dancing* at all. They were stepping about, quickly, sort of, in couples, kind of, to the measure of a polka in a manner of speaking. It was Volkspele, and had the approval of the Synod, the schoolmaster said. All the same, a few of the more earnest members of the audience kept their eyes down on the floor, while that was going on. They also refrained, in a quite stern manner, from beating time to the music with their feet.

For that reason it came as something of a relief when, at the end of the Volkspele, a number of children with wide blue collars trooped on to the stage. They were going to sing "Die Vaal se Bootman." It was really a Russian song, the schoolmaster explained. But the way the great Afrikaans poet Van Blerk Willemse had handled it, you wouldn't think it, at all. Maybe why it was such an outstanding translation, the schoolmaster said, was because Van Blerk Willemse didn't know any Russian, and didn't want to, either.

The song was a great success. The audience was still humming "Yo-ho-yo" to themselves a good way into the next item on the programme.

Meanwhile, the fathers outside the school building had deserted their places by the windows and had drifted in the direction of the Cape-cart to make sure that everything was still in order there. And they sat down on the ground as close as they could get to the Cape-cart, to make sure that things stayed in order. One of the fathers, still singing "Yo-ho-yo" even went and sat right on top of Hendrik Prinsloo's face, without noticing anything wrong. Hendrik Prinsloo didn't notice anything, either, at first, but when he did he made such a fuss, shouting "Elephants" and such-like, that At Naudé, who had remained at the schoolroom window, came running up to the Cape-cart, fearing the worst.

"Is that all?" At Naudé asked, when it was explained to him what had happened. "From the way Hendrik Prinsloo was carrying on, I thought some clumsy —— " he used a strong word, "some clumsy —— had kicked over the jar."

In the meantime Hendrik Prinsloo had risen to a half-sitting posture, with his hand up to his face. "Feel here, kêrels," he said. "The middle part of my face has suddenly gone all flat, and my jaw is all sideways. Just feel here."

The farmers around the Cape-cart were fortunately able – in between singing "Yo-ho-yo" – to set Hendrik Prinsloo's mind at rest. He was worrying about nothing at all, they assured him. His face had always been that way.

Nevertheless, Hendrik Prinsloo did not appear to be as grateful as he should have been for that explanation. He said quite a lot of things that we felt did not fit in with a school concert.

"The schoolmaster says the Joernaal is going to be read out shortly," At Naudé announced. "Well, I hope there is going to be nothing in it like the sort of things Hendrik Prinsloo is saying now. All the same, I wonder what there is going to be in the Joernaal – you know what I mean – funny stories about people we all know."

Gysbert van Tonder started telling us about a Joernaal he had once heard read out at a Nagelspruit school concert. A deputation of farmers saw the schoolmaster on to the Government lorry immediately afterwards, Gysbert van Tonder said. The schoolmaster's clothes and books they sent after him, carriage forward, next day.

"I wonder, though," At Naudé said, "will young Vermaak mention in the Joernaal about himself and – and – you know who I mean – that *will* be a laugh."

As it turned out, however, there was no mention of that in the Joernaal. Nor was there any reference, direct or indirect, to anybody else in the Marico, either. In compiling the Joernaal, all that the schoolmaster had done was to cut a whole lot of jokes out of back numbers of magazines and to include also some funny stories that had been popular in the Marico for many years, and for generations, even. And because there was nothing that you enjoy as much as hearing an old joke for the hundredth time, the Joernaal got the audience into a state of uproarious good humour.

It was all so *jolly* that Jurie Steyn's wife did not even say anything sarcastic when Alida van Niekerk went and picked up the schoolmaster's programme, that had dropped on to the floor, for him.

The concert in the schoolroom went on until quite late, and every-body said how successful it was. The concert at the Cape-cart, which nearly all the fathers joined in, afterwards, was perhaps even more suc-cessful, and lasted a good deal longer. And Chris Welman did get his chance, there, to sing "Boereseun", with actions.

And when Hendrik Prinsloo drove off eventually, in his Cape-cart, into the night, there was handshaking all round, and they cheered him, and everybody asked him to be sure and come round again to the next school concert, also.

Next day there was only the locked door of the old school building to show that it was the end of term.

And at the side of a footpath that a solitary child walked along to and from school lay fragments of a torn-up quarterly report.

Railway Deputation

BECAUSE IT was nearing the end of the Volksraad session, it was decided that a deputation of Dwarsberg farmers would go and call on the member when he got back to Pretoria. Over the generations it had developed into an institution – a deputation of farmers going to see the Volksraad mem-ber about a railway line through the Bushveld.

The promise of a railway line was an essential part of any election speech delivered north of Sephton's Nek. A candidate would no more con-template leaving that promise out of his speech than he would think of omitting the joke about the Cape Coloured man who went to sleep in the graveyard. For a candidate not to mention the railway line through the Bushveld would be just as much of a shock to his constituents as if the can-didate had forgotten to ask an ouderling to open the meeting with prayer.

But we never seemed to *get* that railway line, somehow.

"What's the good of a deputation, anyway?" Jurie Steyn asked. "When you think of what happened to the last deputation, I mean. Or take the deputation before that, when I was one of the delegates. Well, I'll say this much for our Volksraad member – he did take us to the bioscope, because we were strangers to Pretoria. And he spoke up for us, too, when a girl with yellow hair sitting in a glass compartment asked how far from the front we wanted to be. And our Volksraad member said not too near the front, because it was a film with shooting in it, and he didn't want anything to happen to us, seeing how we were his constituents."

Jurie Steyn said that the girl with yellow hair and a military-looking man in a red-and-gold uniform who opened the door for them – because they were friends of the Volksraad member, no doubt – laughed a good deal.

"I must say that our Volksraad member is very considerate that way," Jurie Steyn added. "It made us feel at home in the city, straight off, having that pretty girl and that high army man so friendly and everything. When we came out of the bioscope and they saw us again, the two of them started laughing right from the beginning, almost. That made us feel as though we *belonged*, if you understand what I mean."

Then Gysbert van Tonder told us about the time when he was a member of a railway-line deputation in Pretoria. And he said the same thing about how thoughtful the Volksraad member was in regard to giving the delegates pleasure.

"He took us to the merry-go-round," Gysbert van Tonder said. "To right in front of the merry-go-round, as far as his motor-car could go. And he told the man who collected the tickets that we were friends of his from the platteland and that the man must keep a look out to see that Oom Kasper Geel's beard didn't get tangled in the machinery that made the horses turn round and round. So everything was very friendly, straight away. You've got to admit that our Volksraad member has got a touch for that sort of thing. The man that our Volksraad member spoke to about us nearly fell off the merry-go-round himself, laughing."

We all said that we knew, of course, that a delegation that we sent from the Bushveld to Pretoria about the railway line could always be sure of a good time. Our Volksraad member never minded how much trouble he put himself to in the way of introducing the delegation to the best people, and providing the delegation with the classiest entertainments that the big city offered, and making the delegation feel really at *home* through the things he said about the delegation to persons standing around. Like the time he bought the delegates a packet of bananas and a tin of fish and he showed them where they could go and eat it.

"He went with us right up to the building," Gysbert van Tonder, who was one of the delegates on that occasion also, said. "In fact, he took us right in at the front door. There were koedoe and gemsbok and tsessebe horns all round the walls, just like in my voorkamer. But big – you've got no idea how big. And grand – all along the walls were glass cases and stuffed giraffes and medals with gold and brass flower-pots and things. It was the finest dining room you could ever imagine. And our Volksraad

66

member told the owner of the place that we were from his constituency and that he must look after us and that, above all, he mustn't keep us there. The owner, who was dressed all in blue, with a blue cap, laughed a lot, then, and so we were all as at home, there, as you please, and he showed us what staircase we had to go up by."

Gysbert van Tonder said that all they found to sit on, upstairs, was a tamboetie riempiesbank with a piece of string in front of it, that they had to unfasten, first. It was a comfortable enough riempiesbank, Gysbert said, but a bit on the oldfashioned side, he thought. On the left was a statue in white stone of a young woman without much clothes on who was bending forward with her arms folded, because of the cold. On the right was a stuffed hippopotamus.

Gysbert van Tonder said that the delegation felt that the Volksraad member had that time done them really proud – using his influence to provide them with elegant surroundings in which to eat their bananas and tinned fish, which they opened with a pocket knife.

But there was some sort of unfortunate misunderstanding about it afterwards, Gysbert van Tonder added. That was when another man wearing a blue suit and a blue cap came up and spoke to them. This man looked older than the owner and he was shorter and fatter. They took him to be the owner's father-in-law. And he spoke about the banana peels lying on the floor and about their sitting calm as you like on a historical riempiesbank that hadn't been in use for over a hundred and fifty years. But mostly the owner's father-in-law spoke about the fish oil that had got splashed on the behind part of the young woman without clothes on when the pocket knife slipped that the delegates had opened the tin with.

"And although we said to the owner's father-in-law that we were railway-line delegates from the Dwarsberge, it didn't seem to make much difference," Gysbert van Tonder finished up. "He said we weren't on the railway line now. I must say that I did feel afterwards that what the Volksraad member arranged for our happiness and comfort that time was a bit *too* stylish."

And Jurie Steyn said that after all that we still didn't get a railway-line, or anywhere near. All that happened, he remembered, was that the Government arranged for the weekly lorry through the Bushveld from Bekkersdal to be given a new coat of light-green paint.

Then Oupa Bekker started telling us about the first railway-line deputation from the Dwarsberge that ever went to Pretoria. He was a member of that deputation.

"The railway engine was quite different from what it's like today, of course," Oupa Bekker said. "It had a long thin chimney curving up from in front of it, I remember. And above the wheels it was all open and you could see right into the works and things. In the same way, I suppose, a Bushveld railway delegation in those days would have looked a lot different from the kind of deputation that will be going to Pretoria again at the end of the Volksraad session next month."

But he said that with the years the principle of the thing hadn't changed so you would notice.

"We had written to our Volksraad member to say we were coming, and what it was about," Oupa Bekker continued. "And when he received us he was most sympathetic. He received us in his hotel room and he had a bottle of brandy sent up and he said it had to be the best, because only that was good enough for us. He said that in his opinion steam had come to stay and he showed us a lot of coloured pictures of engines that he had cut out of children's papers. And he asked us would we rather have a condensing or a low-pressure engine.

"Afterwards a man with black side-whiskers and wearing a stiff collar came into the hotel room and the Volksraad member told us that he was a civil engineer and could help us a lot. The civil engineer started talking to us straight away about how important it was that we should have the right kind of printing on our railway timetables. We could see from that what a fine, full sort of mind the civil engineer had – a brain that took in everything. He also spoke about the kind of buns that we would sell in the station tea-rooms.

"Later on, with the brandy and the talk, the civil engineer got really friendly, and started calling us by our first names, and all. We saw then that, in spite of his full mind, there was a playful side to him, also. Indeed, after a while, the civil engineer got so playful that he brought out three little thimbles and a pea, that he had found in one of his pockets. And, just to sort of pass the time, he asked us to guess under which thimble the pea was hidden."

Oupa Bekker sighed.

"All the same," he remarked, "that Volksraad member was a real gentleman. There are not many like him today. When he saw us back to the coach station he was apologising all the way because the civil engineer had cleaned us out."

White Ant

JURIE STEYN was rubbing vigorously along the side of his counter with a rag soaked in paraffin. He was also saying things which, afterwards, in calmer moments, he would no doubt regret. When his wife came into the voorkamer with a tin of Cooper's dip, Jurie Steyn stopped using that sort of language and contented himself with observations of a general nature about the hardships of life in the Marico.

"All the same, they are very wonderful creatures, those little white ants," the schoolmaster remarked. "Among the books I brought here into the Marico, to read in my spare time, is a book called *The Life of the White Ant*. Actually, of course, the white ant is not a true ant at all. The right name for the white ant is isoptera – "

Jurie Steyn had another, and shorter, name for the white ant right on the tip of his tongue. And he started saying it, too. Only, he remembered his wife's presence, in time, and so he changed the word to something else.

"This isn't the first time the white ants got in behind your counter," At Naudé announced. "The last lot of stamps you sold me had little holes eaten all round the edges."

"That's just perforations," Jurie Steyn replied. "All postage stamps are that way. Next time you have got a postage stamp in your hand, just look at it carefully, and you'll see. There's a law about it, or something. In the department we talk of those little holes as perforations. It is what makes it possible for us, in the department, to tear stamps off easily, without having to use a scissors. Of course, it's not everybody that knows that."

At Naudé looked as much hurt as surprised.

"You mustn't think I am *so* ignorant, Jurie," he said severely. "Mind you, I am not saying that, perhaps, when this post office was first opened, and you were still new to affairs, and you couldn't be expected to *know* about perforations and things, coming to this job raw, from behind the plough – I'm not saying that you mightn't have cut the stamps loose with a scissors or a No. 3 pruning shears, even. At the start, mind you. And nobody would have blamed you for it, either. I mean, nobody ever has blamed you. We've all, in fact, admired the way you took to this work. I spoke to Gysbert van Tonder about it, too, more than once. Indeed, we both admired you. We spoke about how you stood behind that counter, with kraal manure in your hair, and all, just like you were Postmaster-General. Bold as brass, we said, too."

The subtle flattery in At Naudé's speech served to mollify Jurie Steyn. "You said all that about me?" he asked. "You did?"

"Yes," At Naudé proceeded smoothly. "And we also admired the neat way you learnt to handle the post office rubber stamp, Gysbert and I. We said you held on to it like it was a branding iron. And we noticed how you would whistle, too, just before bringing the rubber stamp down on a parcel, and how you would step aside afterwards, quickly, just as though you half expected the parcel to jump up and poke you in the short ribs. To tell you the truth, Jurie, we were *proud* of you."

Jurie Steyn was visibly touched. And so he said that he admitted he had been a bit arrogant in the way he had spoken to At Naudé about the perforations. The white ants had got amongst his postage stamps, Jurie Steyn acknowledged – once. But what they ate you could hardly notice, he said. They just chewed a little around the edges.

But Gysbert van Tonder said that, all the same, that was enough. His youngest daughter was a member of the Sunshine Children's Club of the church magazine in Cape Town, Gysbert said. And his youngest daughter wrote to Aunt Susann, who was the woman editor, to say that it was her birthday. And when Aunt Susann mentioned his youngest daughter's birthday in the Sunshine Club corner of the church magazine, Aunt Susann wrote that she was a little girl staying in the lonely African wilds. *Gramadoelas* was the word that Aunt Susann used, Gysbert van Tonder said. And all just because Aunt Susann had noticed the way that part of the springbok on the stamp on his youngest daughter's letter had been eaten off by white ants, Gysbert van Tonder said.

He added that his daughter had lost all interest in the Sunshine Children's Club, since then. It sounded so uncivilised, the way Aunt Susann wrote about her.

"As though we're living in a grass hut and a string of crocodiles around it, with their teeth showing," Gysbert van Tonder said. "As though it's all still konsessie farms and we haven't made improvements. And it's no use trying to explain to her, either, that she must just feel sorry for Aunt Susann for not knowing any better. You can't explain things like that to a child."

Nevertheless, while we all sympathised with Gysbert van Tonder, we had to concede that it was not in any way Jurie Steyn's fault. We had all had experience of white ants, and we knew that, mostly, when you came along with the paraffin and Cooper's dip, it was too late. By the time you saw those little tunnels, which the white ants made by sticking grains of sand together with spit, all the damage had already been done.

The schoolmaster started talking some more about his book dealing with the life of the white ant, then, and he said that it was well known that the termite was the greatest plague of tropic lands. Several of us were able to help the schoolmaster right. As Chris Welman made it clear to him, the Marico was not in the tropics at all. The tropics were quite a long way up. The tropics started beyond Mochudi, even. A land-surveyor had established that much for us, a few years ago, on a coloured map. It was loose talk about wilds and gramadoelas and tropics that gave the Marico a bad name, we said. Like with that Aunt Susann of the Sunshine Children's Club. Maybe we did have white ants here – lots of them, too – but we certainly weren't in the tropics, like some countries we knew, and that we could mention, also, if we wanted to. Maybe what had happened was that the white ants had come down here *from* the tropics, we said. From way down beyond Mochudi and other side Frik Bonthuys's farm, even. *There* was tropics for you, now, we said to the schoolmaster. Why, he should just see Frik Bonthuys's shirt. Frik Bonthuys wore his shirt outside of his trousers, and the back part of it hung down almost on to the ground.

The schoolmaster said that he thought we were being perhaps just a little too sensitive about this sort of thing. He was interested himself in the white ant, he explained, mainly from the scientific point of view. The white ant belonged to the insect world, that was very highly civilised, he said. All the insect world didn't have was haemoglobin. The insect had the same blood in his veins as a white man, the schoolmaster said, except for haemoglobin.

Gysbert van Tonder said that whatever that thing was, it was enough. Gysbert said it quite hastily, too. He said that when once you started making allowances for the white ant, that way, the next thing the white ant would want would be to vote. And *he* wouldn't go into a polling booth alongside of an ant, to vote, Gysbert van Tonder said, even if that ant *was* white.

This conversation was getting us out of our depths. The talk had taken a wrong turning, but we couldn't make out where, exactly. Consequently, we were all pleased when Oupa Bekker spoke, and made things seem sensible again.

"The worst place I ever knew for white ants, in the old days," Oupa Bekker said, "was along the Molopo, just below where it joins the Crocodile River. *There* was white ants for you. I was a transport rider in those days, when all the transport was still by ox-wagon. My partner was Jan Theron. We called him Jan Mankie because of his wooden leg, a back wheel of

71

the ox-wagon having gone over his knee-cap one day when he had been drinking mampoer. Anyway, we had camped out beside the Molopo. And next morning, when we inspanned, Jan Mankie was saying how gay and *light* he felt. He couldn't understand it. He even started thinking that it must be the drink again, that was this time affecting him in quite a new way. We didn't know, of course, that it was because the white ants had hollowed out all of his wooden leg while he had lain asleep.

"And what was still more queer was that the wagon, when he in-spanned it, also seemed surprisingly light. It didn't strike us what the reason for that was, either, just then. Maybe we were not in a guessing frame of mind, that morning. But when our trek got through the Paradys Poort, into a stiff wind that was blowing across the vlakte, it all became very clear to us. For the sudden cloud of dust that went up was not just dust from the road. Our wagon and its load of planed Oregon pine were carried away in the finest kind of powder you can imagine, and all our oxen were left pulling was the trek-chain. And Jan Mankie Theron was standing on one leg. His other trouser leg, that was of a greyish coloured moleskin, was flapping empty in the wind."

Thus, Oupa Bekker's factual account of a straightforward Marico incident of long ago, presenting the ways and characteristics of the termite in a positive light, restored us to a sense of current realities.

"But what are you supposed to do about white ants, anyway?" Johnny Coen asked after a while. "Cooper's dip helps, of course. But there should be a more permanent way of getting rid of them, I'd imagine."

It was then that we all turned to the schoolmaster, again. What did it say in that book of his about the white ant, we asked him.

Well, there was a chapter in his book on the destruction of termites, the schoolmaster said. At least, there had been a chapter. It was the last chapter in the book. But he had unfortunately left the book lying on his desk in the schoolroom over one weekend. And when he had got back on Monday morning there was a little tunnel running up his desk. And the pages dealing with how to exterminate the white ant had been eaten away.

Piet Siener

JURIE STEYN jerked his thumb over his shoulder at the square crate in the corner of the voorkamer. "That is for Piet Siener," he announced. "Funny he hasn't come to fetch it. Maybe he doesn't know it has arrived."

We realised that this was a joke of Jurie Steyn's, of course. As though there was anything Piet Siener, living away at the back of Kalkbult, didn't know...

I mean, that was why we called him Piet Siener. He not only knew everything that happened, but he also knew it before it happened. Some of his more fervent admirers in the Groot Marico even went so far as to say that Piet Siener also knew about things that didn't happen at all.

So when Jurie Steyn said that maybe Piet Siener didn't *know* that that square box had come for him on the Government lorry, and was waiting to be fetched – well, we understood right away that Jurie Steyn was being playful.

"Piet Siener doesn't go about much these days," Gysbert van Tonder said. "There's nearly always somebody at his house, wanting to know from him about the future. They say he gets it out of the ground. That's why you always see him walking about his farm with his eyes down, like that. It's a great gift, knowing everything, the way he does. And he won't take money for telling you what you want to know. All he'll take is just a little present, perhaps."

Then Johnny Coen told us about the last time he went to Kalkbult about something he was keen on getting enlightenment on.

"I came across Piet Siener on his lands," Johnny Coen said. "He was walking about with his eyes cast down, just like Gysbert said. Piet Siener was walking over uneven ground to try out a new pair of shop boots that his last visitor had made him a little present of."

But Piet Siener was actually looking more at his feet than at the ground, Johnny Coen added. It seemed that it was a pair of somewhat tight shop boots.

"And what did Piet Siener say?" At Naudé asked. "Did he tell you when Minnie Nienaber would be coming back from Johannesburg?"

Johnny Coen looked mildly surprised.

"Well, I did, as a matter of fact, mention something along those lines to Piet Siener," he said. "I'm sure I don't know how you guessed, though. You don't seem too bad yourself at being a seer."

But Gysbert van Tonder said that there was nobody in the Groot Marico north of Sephton's Nek who wouldn't have been able to guess, just immediately, what it was that Johnny Coen would want to go and see Piet Siener about.

"And, of course, Piet Siener guessed it, too," Johnny Coen explained. "But in his case, naturally, he didn't guess it so much as that he *divined* it. It gave me quite a turn, too, the way he was standing there on the veld with his black beard flowing in the wind and his eyes fixed on his feet divining, because all I said to him was that I had come to see him about a girl, and he asked me her name. And I said Minnie Nienaber. And he said, oh, that must be the daughter of Koos Nienaber. And I said, yes. And he asked me wasn't she in Johannesburg, or something. He asked it just like that, with his eyes down and seeming as though his gaze would pierce right into the middle of the earth, if it wasn't that his feet were in the way."

And we all admitted then that Piet Siener did indeed have very great gifts. And he was so very modest about it, too, we said. It was almost because it was so easy for him to be a seer that he didn't value it. And so we were not surprised when Johnny Coen told us that when he offered Piet Siener his watch and chain, he wouldn't take it.

"Piet Siener was quite cross about it, too," Johnny Coen proceeded. "He said that what he had told me was nothing – just nothing at all. And he said he already had over two dozen watches and chains, and what he would do with any more he just didn't know. I felt that was one of the few things that Piet Siener really *didn't* know. And he said that if I had no more use for my new guitar with the picture of gold angels on it, and if I was determined to give him a little present... "

So we said that that was Piet Siener all over. He would never accept from you anything that you thought something *of.* If you did give him a present, then it had to be something that you were finished with.

"Like the time I went to see Piet Siener about a cure for my wife's asthma," Gysbert van Tonder said. "It was just after I had bought that mealie-planter with the green wheels. I did not say anything to Piet Siener about my wife's asthma. There was no need for me to. In fact, before I could tell him what I had come about, he told me something quite different. That's how great a seer he is. He said he could see a most awful disaster hanging over my head. No, he wouldn't tell me what that disaster was, because if he *did* tell me it would turn my hair grey overnight, having that size of calamity hanging over my head. It was more than flesh and blood could stand.

"But there was still time to turn that misfortune aside from me on to someone else. So I asked him would he turn it aside on to the market master in Zeerust, and I wouldn't care how much of a disaster it was then, I said. And Piet Siener said all right. And he said that if I had to give him a little present, well, if I had perhaps thought of throwing away my mealie-planter with the green wheels, then I mustn't do any such thing. *He* would take it, he said."

After that Jurie Steyn told us about the last time Piet Siener came to his post office, and about how there was in the post bag for Jurie Steyn a new kind of hair clipper he had ordered from Johannesburg, having seen a picture of it in the *Kerkbode*. "I told Piet Siener what was in the parcel," Jurie continued. "And do you know what, before I had unwrapped it, even, Piet Siener said I mustn't throw it away on the rubbish heap, or give it to the first Bechuana I saw."

"Well, can you beat that?" At Naudé asked, and in his tone there was real admiration.

It was while we were still talking about how wonderful he was that Piet Siener himself came into the post office. He walked with a quick step, his black beard flapping. You could see he was excited.

Then he walked straight up to the counter and said to Jurie Steyn: "There's something come for me in a small packing case. It was sent free on rail."

We nudged each other when we heard that. We felt that there was just nothing you could keep from the seer.

"I got the rail note yesterday," Piet Siener said, producing a piece of paper from his pocket. "Weight 98lb., it says on the consignment. I'll take it with me."

Jurie Steyn pointed to the crate in the corner.

"I could have guessed as much," Piet Siener said when he lifted the crate and then turned it round. "Look, it says 'This side up, with care.' Instead of that you've got it standing on its end. I could have guessed that would happen."

"You mean you could have *divined* it," At Naudé said. But we didn't laugh. The moment seemed too solemn, somehow.

Jurie Steyn apologised and said there was no doubt something very precious inside. And we realised that Jurie spoke those words as though he meant them. It wasn't the way he usually apologised to people in his post office, that made you feel sorry you had brought the matter up at all.

Piet Siener said that it was all right, then. But he said that what was inside that crate was something of such importance that you couldn't be careful enough with it. He had ordered it from America, he said. And it was the latest invention in electro-biology and some kind of rays that he hadn't quite got the hang of yet, but that he was still studying the pamphlet. By means of that instrument you could tell if there was gold or diamonds under the ground.

"You can stand it on a tripod anywhere you like," Piet Siener explained. "And it will tell you what minerals there are in the crust of the earth under your feet up to a depth of two miles. Think of that – two miles."

We did think of it, after Piet Siener had gone out with the crate. And we said he couldn't be much of a siener if he didn't know what was two miles under the ground without having to look through an electric instrument that he had to order from America. And we thought nothing of his gift any more.

He could throw his seer's mantle away on the rubbish heap, now, for all we cared. Or he could make a present of it to the first down-and-out Bechuana passing along the road.

Potchefstroom Willow

"THE TROUBLE," At Naudé said, "about getting the latest war news over the wireless, is that Klaas Smit and his Boeremusiek orchestra start up right away after it, playing 'Die Nooi van Potchefstroom.' Now, it isn't that I don't like that song – "

So we said that it wasn't as though we didn't like it, either. Gysbert van Tonder began to hum the tune. Johnny Coen joined in, singing the words softly – "Vertel my neef, vertel my oom, Is hierdie die pad na Potchefstroom?" In a little while we were all singing. Not very loudly, of course. For Jurie Steyn was conscious of the fact that his post office was a public place, and he frowned on any sort of out of the way behaviour in it. We still remembered the manner in which Jurie Steyn spoke to Chris Welman the time Chris was mending a pair of his wife's veldskoens in the post office, using the corner of the counter as a last.

"I can't object to your sitting in my post office, waiting for the Government lorry," Jurie Steyn said, "as long as you're white. You're entitled to sit here. You're also entitled to drink the coffee that my wife is soft-hearted enough to bring round to you on a tray. I'm sure I don't know why she does it. I was in the post office in Johannesburg, once, and I didn't see anybody coming around *there*, with cups of coffee on a tray. If you wanted coffee in the Johannesburg post office you would have to go round to the kitchen door for it, I suppose. And I feel that's what my wife should do, also. But she doesn't. All right – she's soft-hearted. But I won't let any man come and mend boots on my post office counter and right next to the official brass scales, too, I won't. If I allow that, the next thing a man will do is he'll come in here and sit down on my rusbank and read a book. We all know my voorkamer is a public place, but I will not let anybody take liberties in it."

For that reason we did not raise our voices very much when we sang "Die Nooi van Potchefstroom." But it was a catchy song, and Jurie Steyn joined in a little, too, afterwards. Not that he let himself go in any way, of course. He sang in a reserved and dignified fashion, that made you feel he would yet go far. You felt that even the Postmaster-General in Pretoria, on the occasion of a member of the public coming to him to complain about a registered letter that had got lost, say – well, even the Postmaster-General would not have been able to sit back in his chair and sing "Die Nooi van Potchefstroom" in as elevated a manner as what Jurie Steyn was doing at that very moment.

Before the singing had quite died down, Oupa Bekker was saying that he knew Potchefstroom when he was still a child. It was in the very old days, Oupa Bekker said, and the far side foundations of the church on Kerkplein had not sunk nearly as deep as they had done today. He said he remembered the first time that there was a split in the Church. It was between the Doppers and the Hervormdes, he said. And it was quite a serious split. And because he was young, then, he thought it had to do with the way the brickwork on the wall nearest the street had to be constantly plastered up, from top to bottom, the more the foundations sank.

"I remember showing my father that piece of church wall," Oupa Bekker continued, "and I asked my father if the Doppers had done it. And my father said, well, he had never thought about it like that, until then. But all the same, he wouldn't be surprised if it was so. Not that anybody would ever *see* the Doppers kneeling down there on the sidewalk, loosening the bricks with a crowbar, my father added. The Doppers were too cunning for that. Whatever they did was under the cover of darkness."

At Naudé started talking again about the news of the war in Korea, that he had heard over the wireless. But because so much had been spoken in between, he had to explain right from the beginning again.

"It's the way the war news gets *crowded* by Klaas Smit and his orchestra," At Naudé said. "You're listening to what the announcer is making clear about what part of that country General MacArthur is fighting in now – and it's hard to follow all that, because it seems to me that sometimes General MacArthur himself is not too clear as to what part of the country he is in – and then, suddenly, while you're still listening, up strikes Klaas Smit's orchestra with 'Die Nooi van Potchefstroom.' It makes it all very difficult, you know. They don't give that General MacArthur a chance at all. 'Die Nooi van Potchefstroom' seems to be crowding him even worse than the Communists are doing – and that seems to be bad enough, the Lord knows."

This time we did not start singing again. We had, after all, taken the song to the end, and even if it wasn't for Jurie Steyn's feelings we ourselves knew enough about the right way of conducting ourselves in a post office. You can't go and sing the same song in a post office twice, just as though it's the quarterly meeting of the Mealie Control Board. We were glad, therefore, when Oupa Bekker started talking once more.

"This song, now," Oupa Bekker was saying, "well, as you know, I remember the early days of Potchefstroom. The very early days, that is. But I would never have imagined that some day a poet would come along and make up a song about the place. Potchefstroom was the first capital of the Transvaal, of course. Long before Pretoria was thought of, even. And there's an old willow tree in Potchefstroom that must have measured I don't know how many feet around the trunk where it goes into the ground. It measured that much only a little while ago, I mean. I am talking about the last time I was in Potchefstroom. But I never imagined anybody would ever write a poem about the town. It seemed such a hard name to make verses about. But I suppose it's a lot different today. People are so much more clever, I expect."

Johnny Coen, who had worked on the railways at Ottoshoop and knew a good deal about culture, assured Oupa Bekker that that was indeed the case. For a poet that wanted to write poetry today, Johnny Coen said, there was no word that would put him off. In fact, the harder the word, the better the poet would like it. Not that he knew anything about poetry himself, Johnny Coen acknowledged, but he had been round the world a bit, and he kept his eyes open, and he had seen a thing or two.

"If you saw the way they concreted up the buffers for the shunting engine on the goods line," Johnny Coen said, "then you would know what I am talking about. It was five-eighths steel reinforcements right through. After that, for a poet to make up a poem with the name of Potchefstroom in it, why, man, if you saw how they built up that extra platform in all box sections, you'll understand how it is that people have got the brains today to deal with problems that were a bit beyond them, no doubt, in Oupa Bekker's time."

Oupa Bekker nodded his head several times. He would have gone on nodding it a good deal longer, maybe, if it wasn't that Jurie Steyn's wife came in just about then with the coffee. Consequently, Oupa Bekker had to sit up properly and stir the sugar round in his cup.

"I heard that song you were singing, just now," Jurie Steyn's wife remarked to all of us. "I thought it was – well, I *liked* it. I didn't catch the words, quite."

Nobody answered. We knew that it was school holidays, of course. And we knew that young Vermaak, the schoolmaster, had gone to his parents in Potchefstroom for the holidays. Because we knew that Potchefstroom was young Vermaak's home town, we kept silent. There was no telling what Jurie Steyn's reactions would be.

Oupa Bekker went on talking, however.

"All the same, I would like to know how many feet around the trunk of that willow tree it is today," Oupa Bekker said. "And they won't chop it down either. That willow tree is right on the edge of the graveyard. You can almost say that it's *inside* the graveyard. And so they won't chop it down. But what beats me is to think that somebody could actually write a song about Potchefstroom. I would never have thought it possible."

Oupa Bekker's sigh seemed to come from far away.

From somewhere a good deal further away than the rusbank he was sitting on. We understood then why that Potchefstroom willow tree meant so much to him.

And the result was that when Gysbert van Tonder started up the chorus of that song again we all found ourselves joining in – no matter what Jurie Steyn might say about it. "En in my droom," we sang, "is die vaalhaar nooi by die wilgerboom."

Sea-colonels All

THE PASSENGER on the motor-lorry from Bekkersdal that afternoon was Japie Maasdyk, Oom 'Rooi' Maasdyk's son. We knew that Japie would be coming back to his parents' farm in the Dwarsberge on leave. We were somewhat disappointed that he came back dressed in a sports jacket and grey flannel trousers.

"We were looking forward to your return," Jurie Steyn said, "all rigged out in the blue sea-army suit that we thought you would be wearing at that college for sea-soldiers."

Japie said that if Jurie meant his naval uniform, well, it was in his luggage all neatly folded up.

"You know," At Naudé said, "I've been reading in the papers that they are going to call the different ranks in the South African Navy by a lot of new names. Has it reached to you boys in the training ship yet, Japie? I believe they are going to call the man that is in charge of your ship a sea-colonel, or something. Have you heard of it at all?"

So Japie said that he couldn't call to mind that particular name. But there were lots of other names that the young sea-cadets called the captain of the training ship. Not loud enough for him to hear, of course. He couldn't remember if sea-colonel was one of them, Japie said. But one name he could recall was son of a sea-cook.

"Anyway, they're making quite a lot of jokes about it in the papers,"At Naudé went on. "But I can't see anything funny about it. I mean, if a man *is* a sea-colonel, what else could you call him, really?"

Young Japie Maasdyk was just opening his mouth to say the word, when Chris Welman signalled to him to be careful not to use bad language, at the same time pointing in the direction of the kitchen, where Jurie Steyn's wife was. From the quick way in which Japie picked up the signal, we could see that he had learnt a thing or two during the time he was at the naval college.

Gysbert van Tonder started telling us about a sea-soldier that he met, once, in Zeerust. And so he knew the sort, Gysbert van Tonder said. Only, of course, he didn't want young Japie Maasdyk to think that he intended any personal reflection on himself. Thereupon Japie Maasdyk said Good Lord, no.

"Why, to come back here and listen to all of you talking," Japie said, "it's almost as though I've never been away. You were talking exactly the same things when I left. And I feel just as though I have missed nothing in between. Nothing worthwhile, that is."

We said that it was most friendly of Japie Maasdyk to talk like that. It was good to think that his having been on the high seas, and all, hadn't changed him from the little Bushveld boy with a freckled face and sore toes that we had seen growing up in front of us, we said. At Naudé was even able to remember the time when the new ouderling went to call at the Maasdyk farmhouse. And the only member of the family that the ouderling found at home was little Japie.

"And you stood under a camel-thorn tree, talking to the ouderling," At Naudé went on, laughing so much that the tears ran down his cheeks. "And you stood on one foot. On your left foot. You stood with your right foot resting on your left knee. Every little Bushveld boy stands that way when he's shy. And because the ouderling had much wisdom, he knew what you meant when you said that your parents weren't at home. The ouderling knew that your mother was in the kitchen and that your father had run away into the bush to hide. Like we all do in these parts when we see a stranger driving up to the front door. Ha, ha, ha."

We all laughed at that, of course. And it seemed as though Japie Maasdyk was gratified to think that we felt that he was still one of us, and that the time he had spent aboard the training ship had not changed him in any way. From the way he kept his eyes fixed straight on the floor in front of him, the while his face turned red as a beetroot, we could see just how gratified Japie Maasdyk was.

Gysbert van Tonder went on with his story about the sailor he encountered in Zeerust. And although we knew that in the story he wasn't making even an indirect sort of reference to Japie Maasdyk – since he had given us his personal assurance on that point – nevertheless, as Gysbert went on talking, more than one of us sitting in that voorkamer on that afternoon found his thoughts going, in spite of himself, to that little hand trunk in which Japie Maasdyk's blue uniform was all neatly parcelled up.

"That sea-trooper now," Gysbert van Tonder was saying, "well, I know the *sort* of man. He was swaying from side to side as he walked along that Zeerust pavement. And when he went into the bar he missed the first step. It would seem, from what he told me, that at sea all ship-soldiers walk like that. And when I saw what he had to drink – and it was before midday, too – I understood why. He tried to explain to me, of course, that the reason he walked that way was because the submarine he was employed on was so unsteady on its keel. All the same, it gave me a pretty good idea why that submarine was so unsteady. If the other under-water infantrymen were like him, I mean. He told me that he hadn't found his land-legs yet."

When Gysbert van Tonder spoke about land-legs, it gave Jurie Steyn an idea. In that way, Jurie Steyn was enabled to say a few words derived from his personal knowledge of the lore of the seafarer.

Jurie Steyn dealt with the answer that our Volksraad member had given a questioner at a meeting some years ago. The questioner had asked our Volksraad member if it wasn't a waste of money, and all that, keeping up a South African Navy, with the sea so far away. And with the Molopo River having been dry for the past four years because of the drought, the questioner added.

"The Volksraad member spoke very beautiful things, then," Jurie

Steyn said. "He explained about how our forefathers that came over with Jan van Riebeeck were all ship-military men. They were common sea-soldiers who, with their trusty sea-pots filled with common boiling lead, kept the Spaniards at arm's length for eighty years. Arm's length did not, perhaps, amount to very much, our Volksraad member said, but eighty years did count for something, and we all cheered."

Chris Welman said "Hear, hear," then, and several of us clapped. We knew that Jurie Steyn had allowed his name to go forward as a candidate for the next school committee elections, and from the way he spoke now, it seemed that he was likely to get in. A strong stand in the war against Spain was still a better bet than parallel-medium education.

"I remember that our Volksraad member said that the call of the sea was in our blood," Jurie Steyn continued. "He said that, when he first got elected, and he got a free pass to Cape Town, and he alighted from the train at the docks, by mistake, and he saw all that blue water for the first time in his life – he said how very moved he was. He said that he wanted to climb up to the top of one of those cranes, there, and empty a sea-pot full of boiling lead – or whatever was in that sea-pot – on to anybody passing within throwing distance and speaking out of his turn. That had been a hard-fought election, our Volksraad member said, just like the war against Spain had also been hard-fought, and his Sea Beggar blood was up."

It was after we had cheered Jurie Steyn for the second time that we realised how strange a thing it was to be a politician. For Jurie Steyn, who had never been to sea, received all our applause, while young Japie Maasdyk, with his blue uniform no doubt getting more and more crumpled in the hand baggage, the longer Jurie Steyn spoke, got no kind of recognition at all as a ship-private, in spite of the fact that he had been trained for the work. Whereas, if we had been told that in addition to being postmaster for the area Jurie Steyn had also been appointed sea-colonel for the whole of the Dwarsberge we would not have been at all surprised. There was something about Jurie Steyn that made you *think*, somehow, of a sea-colonel.

Oupa Bekker tried to say something, just about then. But we shut him up, the moment he sought to raise a skinny hand. We wouldn't stand for him stopping one of three, with his long grey beard and glittering eye. In the Dwarsberge there was no room for an ancient sea-private talking about an albatross. Quite rightly, we did not wish to hear about a sadder and a wiser man rising the morrow morn.

Shortly afterwards, Jurie Steyn's wife brought in coffee. When she went out of the voorkamer again, with an empty tray, she gave one look over her shoulder at Japie Maasdyk. There really was something about a sailor, we felt then.

But it was when, there being no other form of transport at that late hour, Jurie Steyn lent Japie Maasdyk his horse, that we realised how much Japie had indeed learnt at that naval college. From the awkward way he sat on that horse you could see that they had truly made Japie Maasdyk a sea-burgher.

Idle Talk

"YOU KNOW," Jurie Steyn said, right out of nothing, sort of – since we weren't talking of his voorkamer at all, at that moment, but of the best way of crating a pig that you are sending to the market – "there is something about my post office. I can't quite explain it, but I have noticed that each time there is a small gathering of farmers here, waiting for the lorry, well, quite a lot of sense seems to be talked here, somehow. You know what I mean – sense."

Gysbert van Tonder said, then, in a dignified kind of manner, that it wasn't clear to him why Jurie Steyn should give his voorkamer all the credit for it.

"If we were sitting out on the veld, under a camel-thorn tree, say," Gysbert van Tonder said, "and we were talking sensible things, as we always do, then there would be much reason and sound judgment in whatever we had to say. You haven't got to be in the konsistorie of the church in Zeerust in order to make a judicious remark. Indeed, Jurie, with all respect to your wife's cousin, who is a deacon, I actually think that some of the things I have heard said that have been least thoughtful, have been said *in* the Zeerust konsistorie."

Chris Welman said that, in talking that way, Gysbert van Tonder was being equally unfair. There was something about the way you felt when you were in the vestry, Chris Welman said, with the walls so clean and high and whitewashed, and with a couple of elders next to you that looked – well, if not *clean*, exactly, then at least high up and whitewashed. Anyway, you couldn't be yourself, then, quite, Chris Welman said.

Yes, he ended up very lamely.

Jurie Steyn felt called on, then, to come to the defence of his wife's cousin, Deacon Kirstein. For it wasn't a happy picture, somehow, that

Chris Welman had left us with, of the deacons and elders meeting in the Zeerust konsistorie before a church service. And with Deacon Kirstein perhaps looking more whitewashed than any of them.

"I can't understand Chris Welman talking that way," Jurie Steyn said, primly. "Because if Chris Welman's name ever had to be put forward, for a deacon, I am sure that nobody would talk against him and mention a truckload of Afrikander oxen that a – "

"That a *what?*" Gysbert van Tonder demanded, his voice sounding almost fierce.

"Oh, nothing, nothing," Jurie Steyn answered. "I don't know what you are suggesting, even, Gysbert. I was just trying to say that if Chris Welman's name, now, had to be put forward as deacon, well, there would be nothing against him, if you know what I mean. Chris Welman's name would be held in great respect."

Gysbert van Tonder was on the point of replying. But we realised that he pulled himself up short. Jurie Steyn had caught him, all right. For what Gysbert van Tonder *might* have said was that maybe there was nothing at all against Chris Welman as an honourable burgher and a regular church-goer. But there was Chris Welman's son, Tobie...

It was almost as though Jurie Steyn had challenged Gysbert van Tonder to mention the name of Chris Welman's son. For then there would, indeed, have been trouble. In any case, Gysbert van Tonder sat silent for a few moments. And you could see that it was on the tip of his tongue to talk about Chris Welman's son, Tobie. And to say that Chris Welman might be a good churchgoer, and all that. But that Chris Welman's son, Tobie, was even more regular. Singing a lot of hymns and psalms every Sunday without fail, for almost three years, in the chapel of the reform school.

From his silence, it was clear that that was something Gysbert van Tonder dared not mention. So Gysbert van Tonder contented himself with explaining that whatever Jurie Steyn was hinting at, about the time the stationmaster refused to have those oxen trucked unless he knew who the owner was, well – Gysbert van Tonder said – a lot of people had already had occasion to complain about how officious that stationmaster was.

"What about the time our Volksraad member's brother-in-law himself went down to the station and spoke to the stationmaster very firmly?" Gysbert van Tonder went on. "And he asked the stationmaster if he thought that every farmer in the Groot Marico was a cattle thief. He asked him that straight out, because he had brought witnesses with him. And the stationmaster said, no, but he knew that every Marico farmer was a cattle farmer, and he knew that any cattle farmer could make a mistake."

We all said, then, that that was quite a different thing. And we said that if you weren't there to see to it yourself, and you left it to a Bechuana herd-boy to go and have a lot of cattle railed to Johannesburg, why, mistakes were almost sure to happen, we said. Thereupon At Naudé started telling us about a mistake that one of his Bechuana herd-boys had made on a certain occasion, as a result of which six of Koos Nienaber's best trek-oxen got railed to Johannesburg along with some scrub animals that At Naudé was sending to the market.

"That was the time Koos Nienaber went to Johannesburg to have his old Mauser mended," At Naudé explained. "And it just happened that because he didn't know where to get off, Koos Nienaber was shunted on to a siding, somewhere, past Johannesburg station. And what should take place but that Koos Nienaber alighted from his second-class compartment just at the same time that his six trek-oxen should be walking out of a truck on the other side of the line. That caused quite a lot of trouble, of course. And before he got his six trek-oxen back, Koos Nienaber had to explain to a magistrate what he meant by loading all the five chambers of his Mauser on a railway platform, even though the bolt action and foresight of the Mauser were in need of repair. I believe the magistrate said that there were quite enough brawls and ugly scenes that had to do with gun-play taking place in Johannesburg every day, without a farmer having to come all the way from the Marico with a rusty Mauser to add to all that unpleasantness. Naturally, I gave my Bechuana herd-boy a good straight talking-to about it afterwards, for being so ignorant."

At Naudé paused, as though inviting one of us to say something. But we had none of us any comment to make. For we had long ago heard Koos Nienaber's side of the story. And from what he had told us, it would appear that all the fault did not lie with At Naudé's herd-boy. At Naudé seemed to fit a little into the story, himself.

"Anyway," At Naudé added – smiling in a twisted sort of way – "what Koos Nienaber was most sore about, in court, was that that Johannesburg magistrate spoke of his Mauser as a rusty old fowling-piece."

Koos Nienaber didn't object to the fowling-piece part of it, so much, At Naudé said. Because he wasn't quite sure what a fowling-piece was. But it took him a long time to get over the idea of the magistrate saying that his Mauser was rusty.

There was an uncomfortable silence, once again. It was broken by young Johnny Coen. Often, in the past, when there had been some mis-understanding in Jurie Steyn's post office, Johnny Coen had said some-thing to smooth matters over.

"Maybe it's like what it says in the Good Book," Johnny Coen remarked. "Perhaps it's to do with Mammon. Perhaps if we sought the Kingdom of Heaven more, then we wouldn't have such thoughtless things happening. Like a farmer sending some of his own neighbour's cattle to the market by mistake. It's a mistake that happens with every truck-load, almost. I was working at Ottoshoop siding, and I know. It used to give the stationmaster there grey hairs. Loading a lot of cattle into a truck and then not knowing how many would have to be unloaded again before the engine came to fetch that truck. And all the time it was through some mistake, of course. A mistake on the part of an ignorant Bechuana herd-boy."

It was then that some of us remembered the mistakes that the herd-boy of Deacon Kirstein had made, long ago, along those same lines. We felt not a little pained at having to mention those mistakes, consid-ering the high regard in which we held Deacon Kirstein, who was Jurie Steyn's wife's cousin. We only made mention of it because of the cir-cumstance that that mistake on the part of the deacon's herd-boy had gone on over a period of years, before it was detected. And maybe the mistake would never have been found out, either, if it wasn't that, along with a truck full of Deacon Kirstein's Large White pigs, there was also loaded a span of mules belonging to a near neighbour of Deacon Kirstein's.

And because he was already a deacon, we all felt very sorry for Deacon Kirstein, to think that his herd-boy should be so ignorant. And we winked at each other a good deal, too, in those days, one Marico farmer winking at another. And we said that it was just too bad that Deacon Kirstein should have so uneducated a herd-boy, who couldn't tell the difference between a Large White and a mule. And we would wink a lot more.

That was the line that the conversation suddenly took, in Jurie Steyn's voorkamer. We were just recalling the old days, we said to each other.

And we were enjoying this talk about the past. And we could see that Jurie Steyn was enjoying it also. And then Johnny Coen tried to spoil everything. Johnny Coen, without anybody asking him, began to talk about the Sermon on the Mount. And let any of us that was without sin, Johnny Coen added, cast the first stone.

Jurie Steyn summed it all up.

"Maybe a lot of sense gets talked here in my post office," Jurie Steyn said, "but a lot of —— , also."

Jurie Steyn said that word softly, because he didn't want his wife to hear.

Birth Certificate

IT WAS when At Naudé told us what he had read in the newspaper about a man who had thought all his life that he was white, and had then discovered that he was coloured, that the story of Flippus Biljon was called to mind. I mean, we all knew the story of Flippus Biljon. But because it was still early afternoon we did not immediately make mention of Flippus. Instead, we discussed, at considerable length, other instances that were within our knowledge of people who had grown up as one sort of person and had discovered in later life that they were in actual fact quite a different sort of person.

Many of these stories that we recalled in Jurie Steyn's voorkamer as the shadows of the thorn-trees lengthened were based only on hearsay. It was the kind of story that you had heard, as a child, at your grandmother's knee. But your grandmother would never admit, of course, that she had heard that story at *her* grandmother's knee. Oh, no. She could remember very clearly how it all happened, just like it was yesterday. And she could tell you the name of the farm. And the name of the landdrost who was summoned to take note of the extraordinary occurrence, when it had to do with a more unusual sort of changeling, that is. And she would recall the solemn manner in which the landdrost took off his hat when he said that there were many things that were beyond human understanding.

Similarly now, in the voorkamer, when we recalled stories of white children that had been carried off by a Bushman or a baboon or a were-wolf, even, and had been brought up in the wilds and without any proper religious instruction, then we also did not think it necessary to explain where we had first heard those stories. We spoke as though we had been actually present at some stage of the affair – more usually at the last scene, where the child, now grown to manhood and needing trousers and a pair of braces and a hat, gets restored to his parents and the magistrate after studying the birth certificate says that there are things in this world that baffle the human mind.

And while the shadows under the thorn-trees grew longer, the stories we told in Jurie Steyn's voorkamer grew, if not longer, then, at least, taller.

"But this isn't the point of what I have been trying to explain," At Naudé interrupted a story of Gysbert van Tonder's that was getting a bit confused in parts, through Gysbert van Tonder not being quite clear as to what a werewolf was. "When I read that bit in the newspaper I started wondering how must a man *feel*, after he has grown up with adopted parents and he discovers, quite late in life, through seeing his birth certificate for the first time, that he isn't white, after all. That is what I am trying to get at. Supposing Gysbert were to find out suddenly – "

At Naudé pulled himself up short. Maybe there were one or two things about a werewolf that Gysbert van Tonder wasn't too sure about, and he would allow himself to be corrected by Oupa Bekker on such points. But there were certain things he wouldn't stand for.

"All right," At Naudé said hastily, "I don't mean Gysbert van Tonder, specially. What I am trying to get at is, how would any one of us feel? How would any white man feel, if he has passed as white all his life, and he sees for the first time, from his birth certificate, that his grandfather was coloured? I mean, how would he *feel*? Think of that awful moment when he looks at the palms of his hands and he sees – "

"He can have that awful moment," Gysbert van Tonder said. "I've looked at the palm of my hand. It's a white man's palm. And my finger-nails have also got proper half-moons."

At Naudé said he had never doubted that. No, there was no need for Gysbert van Tonder to come any closer and show him. He could see quite well enough just from where he was sitting. After Chris Welman had pulled Gysbert van Tonder back on to the rusbank by his jacket, coun-selling him not to do anything foolish, since At Naudé did not mean *him*, Oupa Bekker started talking about a white child in Schweizer-Reneke that had been stolen out of its cradle by a family of baboons.

"I haven't seen that cradle myself," Oupa Bekker acknowledged, mod-estly. "But I met many people who have. After the child had been stolen, neighbours from as far as the Orange River came to look at that cradle. And when they looked at it they admired the particular way that Heilart Nortjé – that was the child's father – had set about making his household furniture, with glued klinkpenne in the joints, and all. But the real inter-est about the cradle was that it was empty, proving that the child had been stolen by baboons. I remember how one neighbour, who was not on very good terms with Heilart Nortjé, went about the district saying that it could only have *been* baboons.

"But it was many years before Heilart Nortjé and his wife saw their child again. By *saw*, I mean getting near enough to be able to talk to him and ask him how he was getting on. For he was always too quick, from the way the baboons had brought him up. At intervals Heilart Nortjé and his wife would see the tribe of baboons sitting on a rant, and their son, young Heilart, would be in the company of the baboons. And once, through his field-glasses, Heilart had been able to observe his son for quite a few moments. His son was then engaged in picking up a stone and laying hold of a scorpion that was underneath it. The speed with which his son pulled off the scorpion's sting and proceeded to eat up the rest of the scorpion whole filled the father's heart of Heilart Nortjé with a deep sense of pride.

"I remember how Heilart talked about it. 'Real intelligence,' Heilart announced with his chest stuck out. 'A real baboon couldn't have done it quicker or better. I called my wife, but she was a bit too late. All she could see was him looking as pleased as anything and scratching himself. And my wife and I held hands and we smiled at each other and we asked each other, where does he get it from?'

"But then there were times again when that tribe of baboons would leave the Schweizer-Reneke area and go deep into the Kalahari, and Heilart Nortjé and his wife would know nothing about what was happening to their son, except through reports from farmers near whose homesteads the baboons had passed. Those farmers had a lot to say about what happened to some of their sheep, not to talk of their mealies and watermelons. And Heilart would be very bitter about those farmers. Begrudging his son a few prickly-pears, he said.

"And it wasn't as though he hadn't made every effort to get his son back, Heilart said, so that he could go to catechism classes, since he was almost of age to be confirmed. He had set all sorts of traps for his son, Heilart said, and he had also thought of shooting the baboons, so that it would be easier, after that, to get his son back. But there was always the danger, firing into a pack like that, of his shooting his own son."

"The neighbour that I have spoken of before," Oupa Bekker continued, "who was not very well-disposed towards Heilart Nortjé, said that the real reason Heilart didn't shoot was because he didn't always know – actually *know* – which was his son and which was one of the more flat-headed kees-baboons."

It seemed that this was going to be a very long story. Several of us started getting restive… So Johnny Coen asked Oupa Bekker, in a polite sort of way, to tell us how it all ended.

"Well, Heilart Nortjé caught his son, afterwards," Oupa Bekker said.

"But I am not sure if Heilart was altogether pleased about it. His son was so hard to tame. And then the way he caught him. It was the simplest sort of baboon trap of all… Yes, *that* one. A calabash with a hole in it just big enough for you to put your hand in, empty, but that you can't get your hand out of again when you're clutching a fistful of mealies that was put at the bottom of the calabash. Heilart Nortjé never got over that, really. He felt it was a very shameful thing that had happened to him. The thought that his son, in whom he had taken so much pride, should have allowed himself to be caught in the simplest form of monkey-trap."

When Oupa Bekker paused, Jurie Steyn said that it was indeed a sad story, and was, no doubt, perfectly true. There was just a certain tone in Jurie Steyn's voice that made Oupa Bekker continue.

"True in every particular," Oupa Bekker declared, nodding his head a good number of times. "The landdrost came over to see about it, too. They sent for the landdrost so that he could make a report about it. I was there, that afternoon, in Heilart Nortjé's voorkamer, when the landdrost came. And there were a good number of other people, also. And Heilart Nortjé's son, half-tamed in some ways but still baboon-wild in others, was there also. The landdrost studied the birth certificate very carefully. Then the landdrost said that what he had just been present at surpassed ordinary human understanding. And the landdrost took off his hat in a very solemn fashion.

"We all felt very embarrassed when Heilart Nortjé's son grabbed the hat out of the landdrost's hand and started biting pieces out of the crown."

When Oupa Bekker said those words it seemed to us like the end of a story. Consequently, we were disappointed when At Naudé started making further mention of that piece of news he had read in the daily paper. So there was nothing else for it but that we had to talk about Flippus Biljon. For Flippus Biljon's case was just the opposite of the case of the man that At Naudé's newspaper wrote about.

Because he had been adopted by a coloured family, Flippus Biljon had always regarded himself as a coloured man. And then one day, quite by accident, Flippus Biljon saw his birth certificate. And from that birth certificate it was clear that Flippus Biljon was as white as you or I. You can imagine how Flippus Biljon must have felt about it. Especially after he had gone to see the magistrate at Bekkersdal, and the magistrate, after studying the birth certificate, confirmed the fact that Flippus Biljon was a white man.

"Thank you, baas," Flippus Biljon said. "Thank you very much, *my basie.*"

Play within a Play

"BUT WHAT did Jacques le Français want to put a thing like that on *for?*" Gysbert van Tonder asked.

In those words he conveyed something of what we all felt about the latest play with which the famous Afrikaans actor, Jacques le Français, was touring the platteland. A good number of us had gone over to Bekkersdal to attend the play. But – as always happens in such cases – those who hadn't actually seen the play knew just as much about it as those who had. More, even, sometimes.

"What I can't understand is how the kerkraad allowed Jacques le Français to hire the church hall for a show like that," Chris Welman said. "Especially when you think that the church hall is little more than a stone's throw from the church itself."

Naturally, Jurie Steyn could not let that statement pass. Criticism of the church council implied also a certain measure of fault-finding with Deacon Kirstein, who was a first cousin of Jurie's wife.

"You can hardly call it a stone's throw," Jurie Steyn declared. "After all, the plein is on two morgen of ground and the church hall is at the furthest end from the church itself. And there is also a row of bluegums in between. Tall, well-grown bluegums. No, you can hardly call all that a stone's throw, Chris."

So At Naudé said that what had no doubt happened was that Jacques le Français with his insinuating play-actor ways had got round the members of the kerkraad, somehow. With lies, as likely as not. Maybe he had told the deacons and elders that he was going to put on that play *Ander Man se Kind* again, which everybody approved of, seeing it was so instructive, the relentless way in which it showed up the sinful life led in the great city of Johannesburg and in which the girl in the play, Baba Haasbroek, got ensnared, because she was young and from the backveld, and didn't know any better.

"Although I don't know if that play did any good, really," At Naudé added, thoughtfully. "I mean, it was shortly after that that Drieka Basson of Enzelsberg left for Johannesburg, wasn't it? Perhaps the play *Ander Man se Kind* was a bit too – well – relentless."

Thereupon Johnny Coen took a hand in the conversation.

It seemed very long ago, the time Johnny Coen had gone to Johannesburg because of a girl that was alone there in that great city. And on his return to the Marico he had not spoken much of his visit, beyond mentioning that there were two men carved in stone holding up the doorway of a building near the station and that the pavements were so crowded that you could hardly walk on them. But for a good while after that he had looked more lonely in Jurie Steyn's voorkamer than any stranger could look in a great city.

"I don't know if you can say that that play of Jacques le Français's about the girl that went to Johannesburg really is so very instructive," Johnny Coen said. "There were certain things in it that are very true, of course. But there are also true things that could never go into one of Jacques le Français's plays – or into any play, I think."

Gysbert van Tonder started to laugh, then. It was a short sort of laugh.

"I remember what you said when you came back from Johannesburg, that time," Gysbert van Tonder said to Johnny Coen. "You said the pavements were so crowded that there was hardly room to walk. Well, in the play, *Ander Man se Kind*, it wasn't like that. The girl in the play, Baba Haasbroek, didn't seem to have trouble to walk about on the pavement, I mean, half the time, in the play, she was walking on the pavement. Or if she wasn't walking she was standing under a street-lamp."

It was then that At Naudé mentioned the girl in the new play that Jacques le Français had put on at Bekkersdal. Her name was Truida Ziemers. It was a made-up name, of course, At Naudé said. Just like Jacques le Français was a made-up name. His real name was Poggenpoel, or something. But how any Afrikaans writer could *write* a thing like that…

"It wasn't written by an Afrikaans dramatist," young Vermaak, the school-teacher, explained. "It is a translation from – "

"To think that any Afrikaner should fall so low as to *translate* a thing like that, then," Gysbert van Tonder interrupted him. "And what's more, Jacques le Français or Jacobus Poggenpoel, or whatever his name is, is coloured. I could see he was coloured. No matter how he tried to make himself up, and all, to look white, it was a coloured man walking about there on the stage. How I didn't notice it in the play *Ander Man se Kind* I don't know. Maybe I sat too near the back, that time."

Young Vermaak did not know, of course, to what extent we were pulling his leg. He shook his head sadly. Then he started to explain, in a patient sort of way, that Jacques le Français was actually *playing* the role of a coloured man. He wasn't supposed to be white. It was an important part of the unfolding of the drama that Jacques le Français wasn't a white man. It told you all that in the title of the play, the schoolmaster said.

"What's he then, a Frenchman?" Jurie Steyn asked. "Why didn't they say so, straight out?"

Several of us said after that, each in turn, that there was something you couldn't understand, now. That a pretty girl like Truida Ziemers, with a blue flower in her hat, should fall in love with a coloured man, and even marry him. Because that was what happened in the play.

"And it wasn't as though she didn't know," Chris Welman remarked. "Meneer Vermaak has just told us that it says it in the title of the play, and all. Of course, I didn't see the play myself. I meant to go, but at the last moment one of my mules took sick. But I saw Truida Ziemers on the stage, once. And even now, as I am talking about her again, I can remember how pretty she was. And to think that she went and married a coloured man when all the time she *knew*. And it wasn't as though he could tell her that it was just sunburn, seeing that she could read it for herself on the posters. If the schoolmaster could read it, so could Truida."

Anyway, that was only to be expected, Gysbert van Tonder said. That Jacques le Français would murder Truida Ziemers in the end, he meant. After all, what else could you expect from a marriage like that? Maybe from that point of view the play could be taken as a warning to every respectable white girl in the country.

"But that isn't the *point* of the play," young Vermaak insisted, once more. "Actually it *is* a good play. And it is a play with real educational value. But not that kind of educational value. If I tell you that this play is a translation – and a pretty poor translation too: I wouldn't be surprised if Jacques le Français translated it himself – of the work of the great – "

This time the interruption came from Johnny Coen.

"It's all very well talking like they have been doing about a girl going wrong," Johnny Coen said. "But a great deal depends on circumstances. That is something I have learnt, now. Take the case now of a girl that… "

We all sat up to listen, then. And Gysbert van Tonder nudged Chris Welman in the ribs for coughing. We did not wish to miss a word.

"A girl that… ?" At Naudé repeated in a tone of deep understanding, to encourage Johnny Coen to continue.

"Well, take a girl like that girl Baba Haasbroek in the play *Ander Man se Kind*," Johnny Coen said. Jurie Steyn groaned. We didn't want to hear all *that* over again.

"Well, anyway, if that girl *did* go wrong," Johnny Coen proceeded – pretty diffidently, now, as though he could sense our feelings of being balked – "then there might be reasons for it. Reasons that didn't come out in the play, maybe. And reasons that we sitting here in Jurie Steyn's voor-kamer would perhaps not have the right to judge about, either."

Gysbert van Tonder started clearing his throat as though for another short laugh. But he seemed to change his mind halfway through.

"And in this last play, now," Johnny Coen added, "if Jacques le Français had really loved the girl, he wouldn't have been so jealous."

"Yes, it's a pity that Truida Ziemers got murdered in the end, like that," At Naudé remarked. "Her friends in the play should have seen what Jacques le Français was up to, and have put the police on to him, in time."

He said that with a wink, to draw young Vermaak, of course.

Thereupon the schoolmaster explained with much seriousness that such an ending would defeat the whole purpose of the drama. But by that time we had lost all interest in the subject. And when the Government lorry came soon afterwards and blew a lot of dust in at the door we made haste to collect our letters and milk-cans.

Consequently, nobody took much notice of what young Vermaak went on to tell us about the man who wrote the play. Not the man who trans-lated it into Afrikaans but the man who wrote it in the first place. He was a writer who used to hold horses' heads in front of a theatre, the school-master said, and when he died he left his second-best bed to his wife, or something.

Springtime in Marico

"IT WILL soon be spring," Gysbert van Tonder observed, looking out of the door of Jurie Steyn's voorkamer to where the bush began.

"I don't know what spring is," Jurie Steyn replied, gruffly. "But if you mean that it's near the end of the winter, well, there I suppose you are right. You have not got such a thing as what you could call the springtime in the Groot Marico. All you get here is the end of the winter. Now, that's where the Cape is different."

We all knew that Jurie Steyn had been born in the Western Province and had lived there for the first years of his young manhood.

"The old Boland," Jurie Steyn went on, "there you do, indeed, have spring. I remember that at school in the Cape we learnt a recitation to say for the inspector, about 'viooltjies in die voorhuis.' That was in Standard Three. What recitation they learnt for the inspector the next year, I don't know. I wasn't there to find out. All the same, I expect I am better edu-

94

cated than most. If you don't count just book learning, I mean."

And so we all said, no, of course, we didn't count just such a thing as book learning, either. We knew that education – *real* education, that was – consisted in far more than what you learnt sitting at a school desk. In fact, there was not one of us in Jurie Steyn's voorkamer at that very moment that had had much book learning to speak of, we said. And yet look at us. Not that we gave ourselves *airs*, on that account, we said. It was just that we were privileged, perhaps.

Thereupon At Naudé turned to young Vermaak, the schoolmaster, and explained that we naturally did not mean him. We were all friends together, At Naudé made it clear to young Vermaak, and so young Vermaak must not get hold of the idea that we thought any the less of him, just on account of his having passed a couple of school-teacher's exams, and so on.

"Oh, no," young Vermaak answered. "You mustn't misunderstand me, either. As a matter of fact – ha-ha – nobody has got more contempt for just book learning than what I have. No, I am one hundred percent in agreement with what Jurie Steyn has been saying."

Gysbert van Tonder looked somewhat surprised.

"You know," he said, "isn't that putting it rather high? One hundred percent, I mean. We all know, of course, that a school-teacher doesn't get *much* of an education. We know that a school-teacher doesn't go as high as a doctor or a lawyer, say. Or even as high as a foreman shunter and station accounts that you study through the correspondence college. But when you say you are one hundred percent ignorant – why, surely, you don't mean to say you're as ignorant as a na–?"

Johnny Coen interrupted Gysbert van Tonder to say that he would be surprised if he knew how ignorant a school-teacher was, really. It was in connection with that same matter of railway promotion examinations that Gysbert had just mentioned.

"It was when I was on the railways at Ottoshoop and I was studying electric unit working by correspondence," Johnny Coen said, "and I asked a school-teacher about how the flanged wheels operate for points and crossings and the school-teacher said he hadn't learnt so far. Another time I asked the teacher when do you have an overhead conductor and when do you electrify the line with a third rail, and the teacher said search him. Just like that, he said. Well, if that isn't plain ignorance, I'd like to know what *is*."

At Naudé nodded his head solemnly.

"That's just what I've been thinking, also," he said. "It's all very well for Meneer Vermaak here to say that he despises book learning – meaning that he hasn't got any book learning, I suppose – but then I don't see what right he has got to be educating our children. You can see that the education department don't care what sort of people they appoint these days. When I went to school you never heard a school-teacher saying he had a contempt for education – meaning thereby that he hasn't got any."

So Jurie Steyn said that that was a scandal. What was worse, he said, was that a lot of people, including women, didn't know those things about schoolmasters, and had a silly sort of admiration for them, thinking they had book learning. Maybe they would think different about it if they knew that a school-teacher was as ignorant as a –

"But all the same," At Naudé remarked, bringing us back to what we had started off discussing. "I do not think that Gysbert van Tonder is right. We are just about at the end of the winter. Jurie Steyn says it's not the beginning of the spring. I don't quite know what he means by that. But you haven't simply got to go and look at a mopane tree to know if the winter is nearly over. You can *feel* it. You can feel it in the wind, as much as anything else. Jurie Steyn had been talking about the Western Province, seeing that I was brought up at Rooigrond. But if you were to go to Rooigrond right now, I know just what you'll find. You'll find that it's the beginning of the springtime at Rooigrond. I know it, even though I haven't been there for years. There will be a soft wind blowing over the bult at Rooigrond, at this very moment. And under the peppercorn trees the yellow soil will be streaked with white dust. And if that isn't spring-time in the Transvaal – in that part of the Transvaal – I should like to know what is."

Jurie Steyn shook his head.

"End of the winter," he announced, "that's all it is. End of the winter. Spring is something quite different. In the Boland I've known the spring. It's been a real springtime, and no nonsense. You can tell it, man. After the last loose showers have fallen, and the raindrops hang on the under part of the leaves, and a fresh smell hangs over the lands – over the wheat-lands and over the watermelon lands. You've just got to breathe it in, and you know straight away that it's not just the end of winter, it isn't. You know clear in your heart that it is the *spring*."

If At Naudé was surprised at the way Jurie Steyn spoke, that was nothing compared with how surprised the rest of us were. It certainly was most peculiar to hear Jurie Steyn talking about the heart. You would almost be led to think, from that, that he had such a thing himself as a human heart. Only, of course, we knew better.

"It must be because you were young then, Jurie," Gysbert van Tonder said. "You know, it is when you were young that you were in the Boland, and so I suppose that the Cape has all sorts of memories for you, and so on. You have got more feeling for the spring when you are young than when you are – well – perhaps not quite so young."

Gysbert van Tonder framed that remark with a certain measure of diplomatic skill. And we understood why. Gysbert van Tonder was no chicken himself, for that matter.

"I think I understand what Gysbert means," At Naudé said, winking. "Your youth is also like the springtime. When I was a young man – Lord, what wouldn't I give to be a young man again and to know what I know now. If I was young today, and I was so low as to be a bywoner on a farm, say, and I knew what I know now and the farmer came and said to me he didn't like the way I was slopping the pigs' swill all over the place instead of pouring it into the middle of the troughs – Lord, I'd turn that swill upside down over the farmer's head, trough and all. And when I was young I didn't know these things."

We didn't know whether At Naudé had started life as a bywoner. But we did know that today At Naudé did have a young bywoner working for him. And that young bywoner seemed quite content to walk about in broken trousers and with a battered khaki hat pulled down flat over his ears.

From all the wise things we were saying, it seemed as though we were just about as old as Oupa Bekker, the lot of us. Especially when Jurie Steyn went on to say that the only way he ever knew it was spring was by the dust.

"When the front door is open," Jurie Steyn said, "and a lot of dust blows into the voorkamer – red dust – then I know either that it's the Government lorry from Bekkersdal or the spring. What you *call* the spring, I mean."

But Johnny Coen said that he had that very day, on his way to Jurie Steyn's post office, seen a strange bird with long black legs by the spruit.

"I could see by his wings that that bird was very tired," Johnny Coen said. "I could see that he had come from far. And so I knew that spring was near at hand."

Shortly afterwards Jurie Steyn's wife came in from the kitchen, carrying a tray. She usually brought us our coffee at about that time. But we saw at once that Jurie Steyn's wife looked different. Only afterwards we realised that it was because of the blue ribbon that she had wreathed in her hair.

"Without any book learning," the young school-teacher said with a laugh, as he helped himself to sugar, "I can tell that it's spring. How do you like that, Jurie? Yes, it's springtime in the Marico."

The Coffee that Tasted like Tar

"WHEN THE coffee tastes like tar," Jurie Steyn announced sombrely, after his wife had gone round with the tray, "then I know I have got influenza."

So At Naudé said that he himself was still all right, then, since the coffee tasted to him like what it really was – that was to say, like burnt mealies.

Gysbert van Tonder made haste to sympathise with Jurie Steyn. "I know that feeling, Jurie," Gysbert van Tonder said. "And that taste, too. I remember how very bad I had the influenza when I was staying at Derdepoort, that time. For days on end the coffee tasted like roast baobab roots. And so you can imagine how I felt, one day, when I saw the farmer I was staying with digging up baobab roots and roasting them for coffee."

Jurie Steyn looked at Gysbert van Tonder steadily for a few moments. But Gysbert went on stirring the spoon round in his cup, very calmly.

"I really don't know what you are trying to suggest with that story, Gysbert," Jurie said after a pause. "But my head feels too thick for me to try and work it out. It's the influenza, of course."

Jurie Steyn made that explanation rather quickly. You could see he wasn't in a mood to provide Gysbert van Tonder with an opening for any low innuendoes.

Speaking to Jurie Steyn for his own good, Gysbert van Tonder thereupon advised him to take things very easily, and not to let trifles upset him.

"Actually, you ought to be in bed, Jurie," Gysbert van Tonder went on in soothing tones. "You really do look terrible. We can all see you're not normal, you know."

Jurie Steyn admitted that he wasn't feeling himself. He made this acknowledgment several times. "With this influenza I am just not myself," Jurie Steyn said, "and that's the truth."

Gysbert van Tonder said that he wouldn't like to go so far as to say that Jurie Steyn wasn't *himself*. That was a matter on which he would rather not offer an opinion, Gysbert continued. Maybe Jurie Steyn was himself, and maybe he wasn't. But what nobody could deny was that at that moment there was something very queer about Jurie Steyn. Like he was funny in the head, sort of, Gysbert van Tonder added. Winking at At Naudé, Gysbert van Tonder said that he was not prepared to say that it *wasn't* the influenza, of course –

"Oh, no," Jurie Steyn interrupted him hastily. "I know it's the influenza, all right. That you don't need to worry about. I felt it coming on for some time."

"A pretty long time, I should think," At Naudé said, taking his cue from Gysbert van Tonder and speaking in a voice that was full of kindliness. "Yes, I should say you must have been feeling it coming on for a longish time, Jurie."

It was clear that, influenza and all, Jurie Steyn was trapped. Leaning forward on his counter he looked from one to the other of us. All he saw was a row of Bushveld farmers sitting with straight faces.

"Well, they do say that the influenza is sort of – well, more *severe* this year," Jurie Steyn informed us, as though hoping that that word would explain a great deal. "That is no doubt the reason why I may of late have seemed to you somewhat – well, queer."

"Queerer than usual, even," Gysbert van Tonder said, trying hard not to choke. "That's what we've all been feeling about you for a little while, Jurie, that you have been queerer even than *usual*."

At Naudé coughed several times before he spoke. That alarmed us. For just one titter from At Naudé would set us all off laughing, and then Jurie Steyn would realise that it had all been a leg-pull. But At Naudé didn't let us down.

"It's how you look, Jurie," he said, still speaking in that unnaturally courteous sort of way, and taking trouble to say each word very clearly, "it's how you *look* more than how you act, even, that has made us – us farmers here on this side of the Dwarsberge – anyway, Jurie, old friend, you don't know how happy we all are to know that it is only the influenza. And you are quite right about saying that it is a very severe form of influenza, Jurie. Perhaps you don't even know how right you are, Jurie. Indeed – indeed, I hope you'll *never* know."

At Naudé did not say very much. But he did talk very distinctly. And at the end his voice grew quite hushed. He did it so well that even we, who knew what At Naudé was up to, began almost to believe that there was some sort of dark underneath meaning in that piece of nonsense that he had just seen fit to utter.

As for Jurie Steyn, the effect on him was most pronounced. The part

99

of his face between his eyes and his ears turned a kind of greenish colour, and when we saw that he was standing with both hands pressed heavily on the counter, we knew that it was quite different from the old days, when he had stood like that to show that he was master in his own post office. He leant in that fashion on the counter now, for support. It was almost as though he realised that he wasn't getting any support from us.

After a while Jurie Steyn said something. And his voice was a good deal softer even than Gysbert van Tonder's or At Naudé's had been.

"I think," Jurie Steyn said, infirmly, "I think I'll go and have a bit of a lie down. My head *has* been funny lately, I know. But I am sure it is only the influenza. At least, I am almost sure."

Before we had quite realised what had happened, Jurie Steyn had left his place behind the counter and had gone out through the kitchen door, on his way to bed. On the threshold of the kitchen he had paused, however. "It *must* be the influenza," Jurie Steyn had said, as if to reassure both himself and us. "Because, you know, that coffee *did* taste like tar."

The moment Jurie had gone out we could permit ourselves to laugh. We didn't overdo it, naturally. After all, there was no point in making Jurie Steyn's wife suspicious. Or in laughing so loudly that Jurie would hear us in the bedroom.

"Anyway," Gysbert van Tonder said, after a little while, "it's not so very unhealthy that the coffee his wife makes for him should taste to Jurie Steyn like tar. It could taste a lot worse. It could taste like Cooper's dip, or like that weed-killer arsenic, for instance."

We did not laugh, this time, at Gysbert van Tonder's remark. There seemed to be too much in it that was near the truth. Maybe there wasn't actually any weed-killer arsenic in the words that Gysbert van Tonder spoke. But we wouldn't swear to it that in what he said there wasn't something very near to rat poison.

More than one of us took a sideways glance at young Vermaak, the school-teacher, then. But he sat straight up on the riempies bench, with his dark hair slicked back, trying to look as unconcerned as you please.

"It's funny," Chris Welman said a little later, "that Jurie Steyn should have fallen for our little bit of fun in the way he did. I mean, we got him so easily. That's not quite like Jurie. Or is it?"

So we said, no, there quite clearly did seem to be something preying on his mind.

Maybe it was the influenza, after all, Johnny Coen suggested.

We couldn't quite accept it that way, however. For that matter, we were, the majority of us, married men. And it suddenly appeared to us that what could happen to one man might just as likely as not befall another. And although we would always be willing to admit that there were certain peculiarities in Jurie Steyn's nature that made him unpopular with us, we nevertheless found ourselves looking at the young schoolmaster with a certain measure of disfavour. It seemed as though he could almost sense what we were thinking.

"Ah, well, Jurie will get over it," young Vermaak said. "We all do, I mean. The influenza isn't as serious as all that."

There seemed quite a lot of sense in the schoolmaster's statement, too. And also in the comment that At Naudé made.

"We all," At Naudé said, "we all get it sooner or later."

Afterwards it seemed to us that Oupa Bekker's remark was pretty profound, also.

"I don't quite follow what you are getting at," Oupa Bekker said. "As you know, I am a bit deaf. But all this talk of influenza, and so on… Well, all I can say is that Jurie Steyn was looking for it."

From then onwards the conversation took a somewhat desultory turn. And when the lorry arrived from Bekkersdal we started wondering as to whether we really had been so very clever, in the way we had pulled Jurie Steyn's leg. For while he was lying in bed at ease and snoring, no doubt, we were falling about all over the place, trying on our own to sort out our letters and milk-cans and parcels, and thoughts.

Stars in their Courses

"IT SAID over the wireless," At Naudé announced, "that the American astronomers are moving out of Johannesburg. They are taking the telescopes and things they have been studying the stars with, to Australia. There is too much smoke in Johannesburg for them to be able to see the stars properly."

He paused, as though inviting comment. But none of us had anything to say. We weren't interested in the Americans and their stars. Or in Australia, either, much.

" The American astronomers have been in Johannesburg for many years," At Naudé went on, wistfully, as though the impending removal of the astronomical research station was a matter of personal regret to him.

"They have been here for years and now they are going, because of the smoke. It gets into their eyes just when they have *nearly* seen a new star in their telescopes, I suppose. Well, smoke is like that, of course. It gets into your eyes just at the wrong time."

What At Naudé said now was something that we could all understand. It was something of which we had all had experience. It was different from what he had been saying before about eyepieces and refracting telescopes, that he had heard of over the wireless, and that he had got all wrong, no doubt. Whereas getting smoke in your eyes at an inconvenient moment was something everybody in the Marico understood.

Immediately, Chris Welman started telling us about the time he was asked by Koos Nienaber, as a favour, to stand on a rant of the Dwarsberge from where he was able to see the Derdepoort police post very clearly. Koos Nienaber, it would seem, had private business with a chief near Ramoutsa, which had to do with bringing a somewhat large herd of cattle with long horns across the border.

"I could see the police post very well from there," Chris Welman said. "I was standing near a Mtosa hut. When the Mtosa woman lifted a petrol tin on to her head and went down in the direction of the spruit, for water, I moved over to an iron pot that a fire had been burning underneath all afternoon. All afternoon it had smelt to me like sheep's insides and kaboemealies. And when Koos Nienaber had asked me to do that small favour for him, of standing on the rant and watching if the two policemen just went on dealing out cards to each other and taking turns to drink out of a black bottle, Koos Nienaber had forgotten to give me something to take along that I could eat."

He could still see those two policemen quite distinctly, Chris Welman said, when he lifted the lid off the iron pot. He wasn't in the least worried about those two policemen, then. Actually, he admitted that he was, if anything, more concerned lest that Mtosa woman should suddenly come back to the hut, with the petrol tin on her head, having forgotten something. And it had to be at that moment, just when he was lifting the lid, that smoke from the fire crackling underneath the pot got into his eyes. It was the most awful kind of *stabbing* smoke that you could ever imagine, Chris Welman said. What the Mtosa woman had made that fire with, he just had no idea. Cow-dung and bitterbessie he knew. That was a kind of fuel that received some countenance, still, in the less frequented areas along the Molopo. And it made a kind of smoke which, if it got into your eyes, could blind you temporarily for up to at least quarter of an hour.

Chris Welman went on to say that he was also not unfamiliar with the effects of the smoke from the renosterbos, in view of the fact that he retained many childhood memories of a farm in the Eastern Province, where it was still quite usual to find a house with an old-fashioned abba-kitchen.

It was obvious that Chris Welman was beginning to yield to a gentle mood of reminiscence. The next thing he would be telling us some of the clever things that he was able to say at the age of four. Several of us pulled him up short, then.

"All right," Chris Welman proceeded, "I think I know how you feel. Well, to get back to that rant where I was standing on – well, I don't know what kind of fuel it was under that iron pot. What I will never forget is the moment when that smoke got into my eyes. It was a kind of smart that you couldn't rub out with the back of your sleeve or with the tail of your shirt pulled up, even. I don't think that even one of those white handkerchiefs that you see in the shop windows in Zeerust would have helped much. All I know is that when some of the pain started going, and I was able to see a little bit, again, I was lying under a mdubu tree, halfway down that rant. I had been running around in circles for I don't know how long. And it might give you some sort of an idea of the state I was in, if I tell you that I discovered, then, that I had been carrying that pot lid around with me all the time. I have often wondered if the Mtosa woman ever found that lid, lying there under the mdubu. And if she did, what she thought."

Chris Welman sighed deeply. Partly, we felt, that that sigh had its roots in a nostalgia for the past. His next words showed, however, that it was linked with a grimmer sort of reality.

"When I got back to the top of that rant," Chris Welman declared simply, "the two policemen weren't there at the post any more. And Koos Nienaber had been fined so often before that this time the magistrate would not let him off with a fine. Koos Nienaber took it like a man, though, when the magistrate gave him six months."

More than one of us, sitting in Jurie Steyn's voorkamer, sighed, too, then. We also knew what it was to get smoke in your eyes, at the wrong moment. We also knew what it was to hold sudden and unexpected converse with a policeman on border control, the while you were nervously shifting a pair of wire-cutters from one hand to the other.

Gysbert van Tonder brought the discussion back to the subject of the stars.

"If the American astronomers are leaving South Africa because they

103

can't stand our sort of smoke," Gysbert van Tonder declared, "well, I suppose there's nothing we can do about it. Maybe they haven't got smoke in America. I don't know, of course. But I didn't think that an astronomer, watching the stars at night through a telescope, would worry very much about smoke – or about cinders from looking out of a train window, either – getting into his eyes. I imagined that an astrono- mer would be above that sort of thing."

Young Vermaak, the school-teacher, was able to put Gysbert van Tonder right then. In general, of course, we never had much respect for the school-teacher, seeing that all he had was book learning and didn't know, for instance, a simple thing like that an ystervark won't roll him- self up when he's tame.

"It isn't the smoke that gets into their eyes," the school-teacher explained. "It's the smoke in the atmosphere that interferes with the ob- servations and mathematical calculations that the astronomers have to make to get a knowledge of the movements of the heavenly bodies. There's Tycho Brahe and Galileo, for one thing, and there's Newton and the mass of the sun in tons. And there's Betelgeuse in the constellation of Orion and the circumference of the moon's orbit. The weight of a terres- trial pound on the moon is two-and-a-half ounces and the speed of Uranus round the sun is I forget how many hundred thousand miles a day – *hun- dred* thousand miles, mind you."

We looked at each other, then, with feelings of awe. We were not so much impressed with the actual *figures*, of course, that the schoolmaster quoted. We could listen to all that and not as much as turn a hair. Like when the schoolmaster spoke about the density of the sun, reckoning the earth as 1.25, we were not at all overwhelmed. We were only surprised that it was not a lot more. Or when the schoolmaster said that the period of the sun's rotation on its axis was twenty-five days and something – that didn't flatten us out in the least. It could be millions of years, for all we cared; millions *and* millions of years – that couldn't shake us. But what did give us pause for reflection was the thought that just in his brain – just inside his head that didn't seem very much different from any one of our heads – the young schoolmaster should have so much knowledge.

When the schoolmaster had gone on to speak about curved shapes and about the amount of heat and light received by the other planets being as follows, we were rendered pretty well speechless. Only Jurie Steyn was not taken out of his depth.

"It's like that book my wife used to study a great deal before we got married," Jurie Steyn said. "I have told you about it before. It's called Napoleon's dream-book. Well, that's a lot like what young Vermaak has been talking about now. At the back of the Napoleon dream-book it's got 'What the Stars Foretell' for every day of the year. It says that on Wednesday you must wear green, and on some other day you must write a letter to a relative that you haven't seen since I don't know when. The dream-book doesn't know, either, mostly. Anyway, I suppose that's why those American stargazers are leaving Johannesburg. It's something they saw in the stars, I expect."

Chris Welman said he wondered if what the American astronomers saw through their telescope said that the star of the American nation was going up, or if it was going down.

"Perhaps Jurie Steyn's wife can work it out from the dream-book," Gysbert van Tonder said.

Green-eyed Monster

IT WAS again something At Naudé had read in the papers that started off the conversation in Jurie Steyn's voorkamer. At Naudé had read something about a man who, committing suicide, left behind somewhat detailed instructions for the ultimate disposition of his cremated ashes. We soon found that this was a subject that lent itself readily to discussion of a sprightly sort.

"Well, if ever I commit suicide," Chris Welman said, "I'll have my cremated ashes sent to the president of the Land Bank. Because, if I do commit suicide – and I've thought of it once or twice, lately – it will be his fault. The Land Bank seems to think that just because the price of wool has gone up, every farmer in the Groot Marico must be in a good way. Not that I *envy* the Eastern Province and Karoo sheep farmers, of course... "

So we all said that we of the Marico, who were cattle farmers, naturally did not begrudge the sheep farmers the big money they were making. They were welcome to their fat motor cars and the parquet blocks on their floors. *We* were quite content to blacken our floors with just olieblaar, we said. We cattle farmers of the Marico simply did not believe in giving ourselves airs with long shiny pianos that took up half of the voorhuis. Although we acknowledged, of course, that our womenfolk felt quite different about such things. Not that we took much notice of our womenfolk, indeed, seeing that this was a man's world, but all the same, well, it wasn't that we *begrudged* those sheep farmers their good fortune. They were welcome to everything, we said, and *more*, even.

Nevertheless, there was something about those Cape sheep farmers, taken in conjunction with certain communications of a somewhat unreasonable nature that several of us Marico farmers had been receiving from the Land Bank lately, that – very well, let us be truthful about it – that *rankled*.

"Let the Land Bank come and try to breed sheep here in the Marico," Gysbert van Tonder said – in those few words summing up what we all felt – "let the Land Bank come along and try to shear a sheep after that sheep has been through a patch of wag-'n-bietjie bush… "

"Or a clump of haak-en-steek," Jurie Steyn said, with much feeling.

"Or young soetdorings," At Naudé added. "I'd like to know how many years a soetdoring takes to grow more than sheep-high. I've never tried to work it out. But, offhand, I should say a lifetime. Not a sheep's lifetime but a human being's, I mean. Just let the Land Bank come and try it here for a little while, that's all. And I am not even talking about blue-tongue." (And we all said, no, of course not, we were not one of us even talking about blue-tongue.) "And then I would like to see the Land Bank go back to Pretoria. I'd like to see the Land Bank, then, that's all. Or, rather, I *wouldn't* like to see the Land Bank, then. With its ceiling coming all down, I mean. And with cracks in its plaster the size of a – the size of a – "

At Naudé paused. He wasn't able to think of something quite suitable to serve as a figure for conveying the size of the cracks in the Land Bank's facade.

Then Chris Welman started talking about how stupid a sheep was. A flock of sheep couldn't go anywhere at all unless they had a goat to lead them. And as for a goat… We spent quite a while in detailing sundry authentic anecdotes that had to do with a more unintelligent sort of goat that we had at various times come across.

But, all the same, we didn't envy the sheep farmers their prosperity, Gysbert van Tonder ended up by saying. And we all agreed with Gysbert van Tonder. The last thing in the world we wanted, we said, was to grow rich through just standing by the side of a stile and counting sheep jumping over it.

"Buying blue serge shop suits with wide, rolled lapels, and the pockets high up, and double-breasted," Johnny Coen said, a trifle wistfully.

"Or a trek-klavier," Gysbert van Tonder said, "with silver stars on the

106

band that goes over your shoulders. Who wants a thing like *that* – just for counting sheep, that is?"

And so we all said again, just to make it quite clear, that we weren't in any way jealous of the sheep farmers. Jealous? Why, the whole idea was so ridiculous that we didn't have to discuss it, even.

"Counting a lot of sheep jumping over a stile," At Naudé said. "Why, that's not work at all. If I had to do that, I'd be asleep before I knew where I was. Fifteen, sixteen, eighteen, twenty-two – and two crept through underneath, that's twenty-four – twenty-five, twenty-seven – chase back that goat there – twenty-eight… and so on. I could do that lying right in bed, and I'd be asleep before I knew where I was. And that's what I've found about almost every sheep farmer I've come across. He's fast asleep. He's like in a dream. And he's more like in a dream than ever when he opens the letter from the Port Elizabeth market and he studies the size of the wool cheque he's got. He holds on to the cheque very tight with one hand and then pinches himself with the other, to make sure it's real. He still thinks he's dreaming and that he's back at that stile, there, saying, 'Chase that goat away.'"

All this talk had carried us rather a long way from the subject we had started off by discussing, which was about the man who had committed suicide and had left instructions about what they had to do with his cremated ashes. It was only after Oupa Bekker had started off on a rambling account of the circumstances attendant on the suicide and subsequent cremation of his friend, Hans Potgieter, in the old days, that we were recalled to some sort of realisation of what was going on around us. The truth was that we had got into something of a dreamy state ourselves, in the course of which we were each of us imagining what *we* would do with a wool cheque – not that we envied the wool farmers in the least, of course.

We were able to catch up with Oupa Bekker's story quite easily, however. In the first place, Oupa Bekker had invested his recital of past events with a good deal of circumstantial detail. And, in the second place, the young schoolmaster, Vermaak, had pulled Oupa Bekker up several times for talking about "cremated ashes." According to the schoolmaster, it was enough to say just "ashes." The word "cremated", it would seem, meant no more than plain ashes. Moreover, the schoolmaster would make no concessions to the standpoint taken up by Oupa Bekker, which was to the effect that the words "cremated ashes" made his story *sound* much more impressive.

107

"If I've got to say just 'ashes', and not 'cremated ashes', it won't be anything like what I felt on my farm by the Molopo when the post-cart brought me that jam bottle with the screw-top and the letter from my friend, Hans Potgieter, who had hanged himself after he had been two years in Johannesburg," Oupa Bekker said. "I had been looking forward to my friend, Hans Potgieter, coming back to the Marico from Johannesburg in a new spider with green wheels and carrying a real leather portmanteau in his hand, and with a tie with stripes blowing over one shoulder, in the wind. Instead, I got just a bottle with a screw-top and a letter. From that it looked as if Hans Potgieter had not succeeded as well in the big city as he had hoped when he set out from alongside the Molopo."

Oupa Bekker paused, to allow his words to sink in. And they did – deeper than he himself knew, maybe.

"It was quite a cheap sort of jam jar, too," Oupa Bekker added. "And in his letter my friend Hans Potgieter asked me to do him a last favour. It would appear that he had grown a trifle embittered during those two years of his stay in Johannesburg, and so he had asked me would I please give his crema – I mean – his ashes, to the devil. He trusted me enough, he said, to know that I would not fail him. He said I must hand over his ashes to Beelzebub himself."

The silence that followed was of some duration.

"Did Hans Potgieter say in his letter," Jurie Steyn asked – for, of course, Jurie Steyn could not let slip this opportunity of taking the young school-teacher down a peg – "did he say his cremated ashes, or just his ashes?"

Oupa Bekker flung a triumphant look at the school-teacher. "His *cremated* ashes," Oupa Bekker announced.

"Well, of course, that was an awful one for me," Oupa Bekker went on. "There, alone by the Molopo. Perhaps you can imagine it. With nobody to talk to. And with Hans Potgieter's ashes in a kist in my bedroom. And the funny part of it is that I was all the time expecting Hans Potgieter to come back to the Marico. Wearing a stiff white collar and white cuffs on his sleeves, like I have said. And then, writing me such a letter. Well, it seemed to me, at times, that a man who could go and commit suicide belonged to the devil, in any case. He was the property of the devil, flesh and soul and bones and everything, even before they had cremated him and put his ashes in a jam pot. He already belonged to the devil, body and spirit, the moment he put that rope round his neck with his own hands. So there was no point in his asking me to hand just his cremated ashes over

108

to the devil, when everything about him already belonged to the devil."

We understood Oupa Bekker's difficulty, of course. He must have been in a pretty awkward predicament, that time. And we said so.

"There were nights when I was afraid to go to bed," Oupa Bekker continued. "I would think of the jam jar in that kist, and I would think of what Hans Potgieter had asked me to do, in his last letter, and I would wonder where I could find Beelzebub, so that I could hand over Hans Potgieter's ashes to him. But the most awful feeling of everything was when it seemed to me that Hans Potgieter *was* the devil. And that where Beelzebub really was, was inside that screw-top bottle locked up in the kist in my bedroom."

Although the incident of Hans Potgieter's suicide and his strange request and the funeral urn and the last letter written by someone about to take his own life – although all those things belonged to the distant past, we could see that Oupa Bekker was still strongly moved when he thought about it. We urged him to continue. Not in words, but through saying nothing… which is at times the most strident sort of speech.

"But I worked it all out," Oupa Bekker said, after a while. "I found the answer, alone here in the Marico. Before any of you came here. I wanted to know where I could find the devil, so that I could give the devil Hans Potgieter's ashes. And I began to fear that Hans Potgieter *was* the devil, and that the devil was in that glass bottle with the screw-top. But because I was alone, I suppose it didn't take me as long as it would otherwise to find out that Hans Potgieter hadn't made a mistake about where to send his cremated ashes to.

"That jar is still there, in my kist. And I expect the devil is still – as I found out then –inside me. Or a good deal of him is, anyway."

Casual Conversation

"IT'S AGAIN the season," Jurie Steyn announced, "when travellers with black spectacles and mosquito nets and white helmets swarm to these parts. Tourists, they call themselves."

He himself wouldn't go so far as to say *swarm* exactly, Chris Welman replied. It wasn't quite as bad as all that. Not that tourists might not become a bit of a nuisance, in time, Chris Welman added, if the authorities did not start exercising some sort of control.

But At Naudé said that that was just what those tourists would *like*, and what they could never get enough of. In fact, the surest way of having the whole of the Marico overrun with tourists, would be through making it hard for them to get here, At Naudé said.

There was that party of tourists of a couple of years back, At Naudé went on, that he came across on the other side of the Dwarsberge. It was his first tourists of the year. He spotted them through his field-glasses when he had gone on to a koppie to look for a strayed mule. And he couldn't see them too well, either, through all their mosquito netting.

"Anyway, I would have thought nothing more of it," At Naudé said. "I would just have gone back home, and I would have told my wife that I had seen my first tourists of the year, in the same way that, the week before, I had seen my first pair of yellow-tailed tinktinkies. They had grey spots on their bellies. That is, the tinktinkies had. I couldn't see the tourists as well as all *that*, of course, because of what I have told you about the mosquito nets. And they were making queer twittering sounds, and they were hopping. The tourists were, I mean. I wasn't near enough to the tinktinkies to make out what kind of sounds, if any, *they* were letting out."

He was just on the point of turning his field-glasses in the other direction, towards the kloof, At Naudé said, when something caught his attention. He had thought nothing of the way the tourists were jumping about and uttering strange cries, At Naudé explained, since he had grown to accept the fact that tourists were not quite human, so that nothing they did ever came as a surprise to you, much. Thereupon we all said no, of course, there was nothing in what a tourist did that could awaken any sort of real interest, any more. Even the most ignorant kind of Kalahari Bushman had by that time come to recognise a tourist for what he was. And it was many years since even a Koranna from the reserve had last raised an eyebrow at a tourist's foolishness.

It was just because he was well bred, At Naudé went on to say, that he started to take the field-glasses away from his eyes and to turn the screw in the middle so that he could focus on the kloof instead. But what he observed at that moment was of so extraordinary a character that he had to polish his field-glasses on his shirt-sleeve to make sure that there wasn't a mistake, somewhere.

"It wasn't that I mistrusted those field-glasses," At Naudé said. "But it was just something I couldn't believe, somehow. I mean those field-glasses – why, my uncle, Stefaans Welgemoed, used them right through the Boer War. And that was why he was never caught and sent to St. Helena. Through those field-glasses you could see an Englishman with a red neck and a Lee-Metford quicker than through any telescope anywhere in the world, my Uncle Stefaans always used to say."

It was reasonable to expect from At Naudé a plainer statement about those tourists he had seen behind the Dwarsberge. We felt that we could not just leave them there all afternoon, jumping and making noises. So Chris Welman broached the subject, and with true Bushveld straightforwardness – which is perhaps not quite the same thing as the ordinary sort of candour. After all, where would you *be*, if wherever you go you just say straight out what you think or what you *mean*, even? After all, everybody in the Marico Bushveld prides himself on his bluff frankness of speech, and all that, but that doesn't imply that you've got to be a simpleton. Consequently, because he wanted to know more from At Naudé about those tourists, Chris Welman put the question to him in a way that At Naudé would understand. Chris Welman started talking some more about those field-glasses; and he said that we all knew that those field-glasses had been in the Naudé family for many generations; and that some very strange sights must on occasion have been presented to the view of the persons who had looked through those field-glasses down the years.

That was blunt talk, all right, if you liked. But then we knew that Chris Welman always was like that. No subterfuge about his words. No fancy frills. He was inquisitive about the antics of those tourists, and so he asked At Naudé about them straight out.

"Yes," At Naudé said, beginning to sound sentimental, almost, over those field-glasses. "Yes, some pretty funny sights, I should think, down the years. Maybe, the Huguenots landing, also. You know, French. Like old Pollyvoo at the Derdepoort mission station, jumping about and waving his arms, all the time. I suppose that's how the Huguenots looked, landing at the Cape... waving their arms and jumping and calling out pollyvoo to each other. Yes, it must have been very funny. I don't suppose they could talk a word of Afrikaans, either."

Young Vermaak, the schoolmaster, was able to help At Naudé right, then. He explained that the Huguenots were French communities of the seventeenth century and that why they came to the Cape had to do with Henry of Navarre and the Edict of Nantes. It also had quite a lot to do with the Massacre of Bartholomew's Eve, the schoolmaster said. That made the Huguenots decide to go and start the cultivation of the grape-vine at the Cape. Although if it *hadn't* been for St. Bartholomew's, the schoolmaster said, there might possibly have been more passengers aboard that ship that docked at Table Bay. The schoolmaster also said that you could tell by his name that At Naudé was himself a descendant of the Huguenots. So At Naudé needn't talk.

The schoolmaster sighed a little also when he said that. It was as though he sorrowed at At Naudé's ignorance, and at At's presence in the voorkamer. It was almost as though the schoolmaster regretted the fact that the St. Bartholomew affair had not been better organised.

After that we discussed other groups – and individuals, also – that had been seen through At Naudé's field-glasses. Zulu impis, we said. And Piet Retief. And Napoleon, we said. And Dr Philip, the schoolmaster said.

"And Oupa Bekker," Jurie Steyn said, with a laugh. "More than once in the old days, somebody must have looked through those same field-glasses and seen Oupa Bekker come riding over the hill, with his long beard and all."

All this talk would have got us nowhere, if it wasn't for Johnny Coen.

"I know why you spoke like that about the Huguenots," Johnny Coen said to At Naudé. "About their jumping around and waving their arms. It's because you were thinking about those tourists behind the Dwarsberge. Forget all about your field-glasses. Why *were* those tourists acting in that way?"

But when At Naudé told us, it sounded so tame that we would rather not have heard the explanation. At Naudé reminded us that he had been out looking for his mule that had strayed. Well, it appeared that his mule had wandered down to the tourist camp. And because the tourists didn't know how a mule thinks they had tried to drive it away. As a result, the mule walked right up into their camp and started eating their mosquito netting as quick as he could get it down, which was quite a large number of square yards a minute. And why the tourists were making those twittering sounds was because they were barefooted and, in trying to chase the mule, they had landed in a patch of last season's dubbeltjie thorns.

"But why I said that it's no use making it hard for tourists if you want to keep them out of the Marico," At Naudé explained, "is this. After my mule had wandered off into the bush, there not being any more mosquito netting around for him to eat, as far as he could see, I talked to one of the tourists. And he said he had been an explorer in Tibet. And he said Tibet was averse to Western incursions. Just like that, he said it. And he was very happy about it. He had a very happy time there, he said, and he stole two prayer-wheels. Tibet was called the Forbidden Country, and so it was a pleasure for him to visit it, he said. And for that reason he was disappointed in the Marico."

What At Naudé told us, then, took a little while to sink in. There was a fairly long silence, during which we all thought pretty hard.

Jurie Steyn was the first to speak. And the words he spoke expressed all our feelings.

"Just let him wait a bit," Jurie Steyn said, "*that's all.*"

The Call of the Road

THE LATEST news that At Naudé had to communicate to us in Jurie Steyn's voorkamer was about the mayor of a highveld dorp who walked a long distance to Pretoria in order to interview a Minister about the housing shortage.

"It was as a protest," At Naudé explained, "that he set off on foot across the whole length of the Southern Transvaal, sleeping at night in the straw with a tramp who didn't have an overcoat, but only a bottle of vaaljapie wine."

Gysbert van Tonder said, then, that on a cold night, when you were sleeping in the straw, a bottle of vaaljapie could be of more use to you than an overcoat. As long as there was enough straw, Gysbert added. And enough vaaljapie.

At Naudé went on to say that the mayor had a hot flask of coffee, there in the straw, which the tramp did not wish to share with him. He never drank coffee, the tramp said.

Thereupon Johnny Coen said that he could just imagine what sort of a tramp that was – giving himself airs, and all the rest of it. He knew that sort of tramp, Johnny Coen said, since he had once been on the road himself. You came across some quite insufferable tramps, at times, Johnny Coen went on. He knew about them from his own experience – dating from the time when he himself had just suddenly felt full up to the neck with his job at the Ottoshoop siding, and had set off on foot along the road leading to the big cities of South Africa, having drawn his pay first.

"The kind of tramp that sneers at you because you forgot to tie pieces of newspaper to the bottom parts of your trousers before you left home," Johnny Coen declared, bitterly. "I know *that* sort. And I can imagine how that tramp in the straw must have sneered when the mayor pulled a hot flask of coffee out of his pocket. When the only proper pocket that the tramp had left had got its lining fastened with a safety pin, so that the bottle of vaaljapie wouldn't drop out before the tramp got into the straw.

I suppose that tramp laughed outright. Right in the mayor's face, I should imagine. And yet what brought me back to Ottoshoop, after I had run away, was also no more than a hot flask. When I had set off down the road to the south, I had left my hot flask in the wood-and-iron lean-to that the Public Works Department had erected for us workmen next to the Ottoshoop siding. And the farther I went along the road from Ottoshoop, the more I missed the hot flask, that I used to take coffee in to work. And I was too *proud* to turn back for that hot flask, if you'll understand what I mean. But in the end I overcame my pride, and I went back. And so I know just how the highveld mayor must have felt, when the tramp in the straw regarded his hot flask as... well... You see, it's not what a tramp *says*, that's important. It's the way his lip curls, without his having to use any words."

Because Johnny Coen was young, we did not feel called upon to take much notice of anything he said. We were much more interested in Gysbert van Tonder's next remark.

"To tell you the truth," Gysbert said, "I am not surprised at that mayor just taking it into his head to pack his things and walk off. I have lived in more than one highveld dorp myself. And I know what sort of things go on there. That's why I don't blame that mayor in the least. Just think what it's like to wake up in the morning and to look at the sunrise, and there's no mdubu trees or withaaks or maroelas. There's just a piece of flat veld starting right at your kitchen door, and it has rained, and you've got to start ploughing. I can quite understand a person living on the highveld putting a piece of biltong and a spare shirt into a suitcase and walking away from there, then. I mean, isn't that how quite a few of us landed here, in the Marico? And without a spare shirt, either, in some cases – in some cases that I wouldn't like to mention here in this voorkamer, I mean."

Naturally, we each of us, after that, felt it was necessary to make it clear that when we arrived in the Marico it was with more than a spare shirt in our suitcases. It was funny, and all that, what Gysbert van Tonder had said, but we weren't tramps, exactly, when we came to the Marico the first time it was thrown open to white settlement. Still, it was a good joke Gysbert van Tonder had made, we said – ha, ha.

"Who has ever heard of a tramp coming into a place with a harmonium fastened on to the middle of his wagon, just above the bok, with ox-riems?" Jurie Steyn asked. "I don't say that the top notes of the harmonium vibrated as well as you would like, perhaps. But, of course, that was just because of the way that the wagon got bumped during the long journey

114

through the Roggeveld. Still, I helped to civilise these parts with my harmonium, all right, I think."

In reply, Chris Welman said that it all depended, of course, on what you meant by civilised. He had had somewhat different thoughts himself, he confessed, on that Sunday morning when the strains of a hymn tune came floating over the vlaktes, for the first time.

"It wasn't only the top notes," Chris Welman explained. "But I could tell by the bottom notes, also, that the harmonium had trekked through some of the worst parts of the Roggeveld. I kept saying to myself that it was a pity you hadn't taken a bit of a detour."

"Well, I know that I didn't come to the Marico with just a shirt on my back," At Naudé said. "I had at least several shirts. And also my Nagmaal suit. And I have still got my Nagmaal suit. What's more, I can still wear it. I was already fat when I *came* to the Groot Marico. I didn't come to the Marico like a starved person that only starts getting fat after he has been here for some time. I *came* to the Marico fat."

After we had all explained that we were none of us tramps, or anywhere near like *some* people we knew – when we first came to live in the lowveld, it was by way of a relief when At Naudé made it clear that the mayor did not walk away from that highveld dorp because he had had enough of it, but to let the Minister know that there weren't enough houses to go round, in the dorp where he was.

So we said, couldn't he rather have gone by train?

"Or what's wrong with him writing a letter?" Jurie Steyn asked, the while his eye travelled the length of his counter, with the shiny brass scales and rubber stamps on it. "Or haven't they got a *reliable* post office there?"

But At Naudé said, no, the matter was too urgent. And when Jurie Steyn opened his mouth to say something, we all laughed.

That gave Johnny Coen his chance to tell us about the time when he himself took to the road.

"It was the Foreman," Johnny Coen said. "The Siding Foreman. Now, it doesn't matter how bad a Third Class Running Staff *Station* Foreman can get, he's nothing at all next to a *Siding* Foreman. And so, after I had been working at Ottoshoop quite a while I suddenly found I couldn't stand it any longer. The Siding Foreman had been a farmer at Rysmierbult before he went to the railways, and, as you know, there's nobody can be as inhuman to you as your own *sort*."

That statement of Johnny Coen's awakened quite a lot of memories in the consciousness of each of us, and we all nodded our agreement. In-

115

deed, the vigour with which Gysbert van Tonder inclined his head forward was so noticeable that Jurie Steyn, who was his neighbour, took it as a personal affront. We managed to stop the argument, however, before anything really unseemly happened.

"And so, when I saw that road there, winding away to the south, through the hills," Johnny Coen proceeded, "I just walked away, out of the lean-to. I didn't hand in my notice or say goodbye to the Siding Foreman, or anything. I saw only the open road, winding away amongst the hills, and I started walking. Since then, of course, I have learnt that it was wrong of me to have acted like that – running away because I found things were too hard, and being so unfriendly, as well. I am sure that the mayor that At Naudé spoke about didn't act like that. I am sure that the mayor at least went and said goodbye to the Siding Foreman, no matter what he might have thought of him privately."

Johnny Coen went on to relate to us the details of some of his adventures along the road. Mostly, his stories were of encounters with tramps, who, lying in a farmer's loft and wrapped around in the best straw, were so superior that they would hardly talk to him.

"But what brought me back, in the end, was my hot flask, that I had left behind in the lean-to," Johnny Coen said. "My hot flask had gold and green bands painted all round it, and I could picture the Siding Foreman drinking coffee out of it, and enjoying it. And wiping his beard, afterwards."

He slipped into the lean-to at an hour in the morning when he expected the Siding Foreman to be off duty.

"So you can imagine how surprised I was, when I turned round to see the Siding Foreman behind me," Johnny Coen added. "And he said he knew I would come back. He had once run away from a job, too, when he was my age. *And he could tell that I was a lot like he was,* and that I wasn't the tramp sort. And as he walked out the Siding Foreman said that I was half an hour late for work. And before I knew what I was doing, I was taking off my hat and jacket, there in the lean-to."

Lath and Plaster

THEY WERE going to do it right here, in South Africa, At Naudé declared, retailing to us what he had read in the newspapers.

It was called a sound-track, At Naudé said, meaning that part of a film which makes the glug-glug noises when an ocean liner goes down after having struck an iceberg, in a bioscope.

So we said that, while we did not know that it was called a sound-track, we were all of us familiar with that part of a movie picture that At Naudé was talking about. We were surprised that it had a name at all, we said. It seemed to us too wild a thing to be actually *called* by a name, we said.

We each of us then started remembering, from occasional visits to the bioscope in Bekkersdal, various bits of sound-track, now that At Naudé had given us the word for it.

"I remember about a white-haired clergyman," Chris Welman said. "The clergyman wore a dark suit and a round collar right through the film. It was a murder picture of course – I mean with a clergyman in it – although at the beginning it looked as though it was going to be a film just about sandbagging and forgery. But I'll never forget that sound-track piece when the handcuffs clicked on his wrists and the white-haired clergyman said, 'Y' got me, pal.' Of course, it turned out, in the end, that he wasn't a real clergyman. Or his hair wasn't really white – I forget which. But I thought then, that even one of our own predikants – and I belong to the Dopper Church myself – could not have done it so well."

In case we might perhaps misunderstand his words, Chris Welman went out of his way to say that it wasn't as though he didn't give Dominee Welthagen every credit. And so we all said, no, of course not. We all had a great respect for Dominee Welthagen, we said. And we knew just what Dominee Welthagen *was*. And if Dominee Welthagen didn't wear a round collar, he did wear a white tie and a black hat with a broad brim, we said.

Nevertheless, we felt, somehow, that if Dominee Welthagen *did* get into the kind of awkward situation that Chris Welman spoke about – well, we took leave to doubt as to whether Dominee Welthagen would have had enough sound-track experience to *know* that the game was up.

"If the clergyman had started arguing at that stage," Chris Welman said, "or if he had asked to have the handcuffs taken off, so that he could first read out a few verses from Chapter 3 of the Kolossense – why, it wouldn't have been the same thing. It would have spoilt the whole film. That is why I say that in some things, you must hand it to these sound-track ministers of religion. And I say it, even though I am a Dopper myself."

Thereupon Gysbert van Tonder stated that when he was a child growing into young manhood, he was the only kategisant in the confirmation class who could recite John Calvin's Formulier from the first word to the last without once having to draw breath. He acquired that skill through having practised swimming under water in the dam on his father's farm at Welverdiend, where there was Spanish reed and polgras, on the edge. And in an American film to do with the Church he had heard a young kategisant repeating those same words, Gysbert van Tonder said. Of course, he didn't understand the words so well, because it was in English. But he could see by the look of despair and general bewilderment on the face of that young fellow that it *must* be John Calvin's Formulier that he was reciting.

"And do you know what?" Gysbert van Tonder ended up. "He had to pause for breath *three* times. So I thought, well, they can't know much about religion in America. Either that, I thought, or else that young fellow had been studying for the catechism in a time of drought when no Spanish reeds grew on the edge of the dam on his father's farm. Maybe there wasn't any water in it, either."

Oupa Bekker coughed then. We all knew what that cough meant. We knew that Oupa Bekker was clearing his throat preparatory to embarking on a story of drought in the old days of the Marico, when the ground really *was* dry. It was fortunate for us that At Naudé was able to head Oupa Bekker off.

"Today, when you see an American film, the words the actors say and the noises they make are all in English, with the result that we can't understand it too well – the noises, especially. Anyway, I read in the newspaper that all that is going to be changed. There's a firm in South Africa is going to take those films and is going to translate the sound-tracks into Afrikaans. It's still going to be the same *film*, the people and the actions, and all that. Only, they are going to have Afrikaans actors and actresses to make the sound-track – you know, the speeches and the noises. You'll only hear these Afrikaans actors and actresses on the films. You won't see them."

Gysbert van Tonder said, straight away, that that was a very good thing. The fact that you wouldn't see them, he explained. And Chris Welman went on to say that it would be even better if you couldn't hear them, either. We did not take much notice of this remark of Chris Welman's, however, since we felt that there was a lot of jealousy in it.

We knew that Chris Welman prided himself on the way in which he could sing "Boereseun", with actions. And we also knew that Chris Welman felt that he had never received proper appreciation for it, except in the Bushveld. And he didn't count *that* sort of appreciation, Chris Welman always said. It was the applause of the wider world he wanted – even if there were a few overripe tomatoes thrown in with the wider world's applause. It didn't mean much to him, Chris Welman was in the habit of explaining, to know that a Marico audience would regularly clap its hands and stamp its feet and shout "Dagbreek toe!" and "Askoek!" every time he sang "Boereseun" with actions. And even when some of us said that, if he liked, we would bring along a packet of tomatoes and a lot of rotten eggs and a dead cat, too, if that would make him feel any better, next time he sang – it would even be a *pleasure*, we said – Chris Welman still made it clear that it wasn't quite the same thing.

"All the same, I am in favour of it," Jurie Steyn said, thoughtfully, "having these American films in Afrikaans, now."

"Why?" Oupa Bekker asked. We could sense that Oupa Bekker was in a nasty mood, because we wouldn't listen to his drought story.

"Well," Jurie Steyn said, "we'll now be able to understand everything they say in these American films."

"Why?" Oupa Bekker asked, again.

Yes, we could see that Oupa Bekker was just being difficult.

"Mind you, I don't say that these American films have always got a very good influence," Jurie Steyn went on, quickly, in case Oupa Bekker had any more questions to ask. "Especially where young people are concerned. I sometimes think that when *young* persons see an American film they may get inclined to form wrong opinions about what life is like, really. After all, if a girl smiles at you, sort of, in the moonlight, under a camel-thorn tree, when you are walking home from work and she is going to the stable for a bucket of milk to put into the stamped mealies for supper, say, well, it's downright silly to think it *means* anything. In any case what are you doing, walking home from work under a camel-thorn tree, when you should have stuck right to the Government Road, on your way home from work? There's a lot in these American films that is just foolish."

We knew that Jurie Steyn was addressing that remark to all of us who were sitting there, in his voorkamer, and not to just one person, in particular. Nevertheless, it was peculiar, the way several of us glanced swiftly in the direction of young Vermaak, the school-teacher.

And we all agreed with Jurie Steyn. Indeed, we said, the American films gave one a distorted view of life. The American films had an unhealthy effect on the minds of South African youth, we said. The American films gave you the idea that all life was just that pale kind of moonlight that you see through the thorns of a camel-thorn tree on the other side of the Dwarsberge. Some of our young people had even begun to *talk*, we said, like the men and women actors talk in a film made in America.

Johnny Coen said that that was quite true. And he told us about the way he had parted, near Vleisfontein, from a Bushveld girl who didn't want him any more. He was broken-hearted, Johnny Coen said, because that girl didn't care for him, and was going to marry a young man who would one day inherit his father's Karoo farm that had eight thousand morgen of sheep pasture.

"And although I meant every word I said, about how broken-hearted I was," Johnny Coen declared, "it was only afterwards that I realised I had actually been talking words to her that I had heard in these American films. Still, it didn't hurt any the less. 'I will say,' I said to her, 'I will away to Africa, there to seek peace for my battered spirit.' You see, the American films had got me so that I really forgot that I *was* in Africa. All the same, it didn't hurt less – any."

Do Professors Smoke Dagga?

AT NAUDÉ brought the actual cutting from the newspaper with him.

He passed the news item over to Gysbert van Tonder, who proceeded to read it out to us – reading slowly, as he explained, so that we shouldn't miss any of it. When he came to a long word, Gysbert even took the trouble to spell it out for us, to make *quite* sure that we grasped it all right, he said. And each time after he had got through a piece of spelling, like that, he paused a few moments so as to allow young Vermaak, the schoolmaster, to step in and pronounce the word.

We found out, however, that the extreme care that Gysbert van Tonder exercised in his reading – claiming that he was doing it that way because we were just ignorant farmers that he didn't want to take out of their depth, too much – was not as helpful as it should have been. Especially when he came to a particularly long word which he didn't even try to spell, but just mumbled over it.

After that, having twice failed to take the jump at quite a short word, Gysbert van Tonder suddenly thrust the cutting into the schoolmaster's hand and asked him to finish reading it. *He* had done his best with us, Gysbert said. It was too thankless a job, trying to get an understanding of fine print into the heads of people who weren't scholars, he said.

It turned out, however, that that newspaper report was, in spite of its brevity, not without a certain measure of interest.

It had to do with a student of psychology who smoked dagga – purely as an experiment, of course, just so that he could see what it was like, so as to help him in his studies.

"In his studies of what?" Jurie Steyn demanded. "That's what I keep saying about the so-called educated people we get today. I mean, when a Kalahari Bushman comes to my back door, and I can see from his eyes – with his pupils big and round, and with no whites showing, hardly – well, you all know how a Bushman looks when he's been smoking a good bit of dagga. Laughing a lot about nothing. A hollow sort of laugh."

We said yes, we knew.

"Well, how often haven't I said that about educated white people today?" Jurie Steyn asked, sounding quite aggressive. Actually, Jurie Steyn had said nothing about educated white people, so far. Nothing we could make head or tail of, that was. But we knew how he felt about young Vermaak, the school-teacher. And we also understood why, on that point, he could not perhaps always express himself as clearly as he might have liked.

"That's the next thing, I suppose, that is going to happen right here in my post office," Jurie Steyn went on. "A Bushman coming in with a bow and arrows and an ostrich egg with a hole in it under his arm, and so full of dagga that he laughs right out when I tell him that from next year the Ngami Bushman will have to pay hut tax, just like he's a Koranna. You know that dagga laugh. But the Bushman will say that why he is so full of dagga is because he's a student of psychology, and he's smoking it as an experiment, to help him through his second-year course."

"Third year," young Vermaak announced, decisively, shutting his lips in a straight line. "You only have dagga in third-year psychology."

Jurie Steyn shot a triumphant look at us with his right eye. His left eye was closed in a significant sort of way, the lid fluttering ever so lightly. There seemed something queer about it, somehow – the schoolmaster with his lips shut and Jurie Steyn with one eye closed.

"It's all right," young Vermaak proceeded. "I saw Jurie Steyn winking. But I didn't mean it that way. I meant that it's only in the third year that we really study the effect on the central nervous system of narcotic drugs like the barbiturates, or heroin, or opium, or – or – dagga, even."

"They say that dagga is habit-forming," Chris Welman declared, sententiously. "Not that I have ever thought to have seen you under the *influ-*

ence of it, Meneer Vermaak. The direct influence, that is – "

Young Vermaak said that he had never smoked dagga in his life. Nor opium, he said. He had studied the effect of a variety of drugs only in theory. The professor at the university had dictated certain notes and the students had taken the notes down.

Thereupon Gysbert van Tonder said that that explained a lot. He had often, in the joke column of the *Kerkbode*, read jokes about absent-minded professors, he said. He now understood what it was that *made* professors so absent-minded, he said. It was a pity, really, he said, because we all knew that they did have intellects, and all that. But, of course, professors said pretty silly things, too, sometimes. The schoolmaster had no doubt come across instances of that, while he was a student.

"Yes, indeed," young Vermaak acknowledged. "When I think of all the tripe I've had to listen to in the ethics class from old Van – "

"Habit-forming," Jurie Steyn interjected, swiftly. "That's what they all say about it, and I suppose it's true. Afterwards these professors get like that, they can't just take it or leave it. It *gets* them. Then they talk what Meneer Vermaak calls tripe."

The schoolmaster looked surprised. "*What* gets them?" he asked, stiffly.

And he turned really acid when At Naudé and Chris Welman both tried to explain, speaking at the same time. And he was positively scornful when Gysbert van Tonder asked if professors smoked berg-dagga or just the ordinary sort with red bearded ears.

There was silence after that. Quite a profound sort of silence, too.

"Look here," the schoolmaster said, after a while. "I know you all like a bit of fun – and so do I too, for that matter, ha, ha."

We agreed with him. Ha, ha, we said, also.

"But this talk about professors and dagga, well, it's so *silly*," the schoolmaster went on. "For one thing, professors are people with learning and knowledge. If ever you have called at a professor's house round about exam time – in the hope that over the tea table he might let slip something about what one of the questions is going to be – why, you'll understand, then, that a professor is a responsible sort of citizen. As a matter of fact, when I went to visit a professor once, around exam time, I came away with the absolute certainty that the professor didn't even *know*, then, what questions he was going to ask. What's more, after the second cup of tea, I felt that he didn't know the answers, either."

Jurie Steyn said, then, that he would like to see them dump a university professor in the middle of the Kalahari desert, with his wife and children, and leave that university professor to fend for himself, with just a hollow reed to suck water through the shell of an ostrich egg. He would *like* to see it, Jurie Steyn added. And we felt that he really would. Jurie Steyn started getting almost sentimental after that, about the hardships of the life of the Kalahari Bushman – which was something very unusual for Jurie Steyn, seeing that we all knew how Jurie felt about Bushmen.

And it was then that the schoolmaster came to the conclusion that we were having fun at his expense. He left shortly afterwards.

"Ha, ha," young Vermaak said, as he took up his hat. "I suppose I can stand a joke as well as anybody else. Ha, ha – ha, ha, ha!"

"Just as I said," Jurie Steyn remarked, winking again after the schoolmaster had gone. "Hollow laughter… I forgot to look if there was any white in his eyes."

Art Criticism

"It must be years ago since I first saw this picture hanging on your wall," Gysbert van Tonder said to Jurie Steyn, at the same time jerking his thumb over his shoulder at a painting of a farmhouse. "And there has always seemed to be something lopsided about it, somehow."

"If you think that my wife's great-uncle, Koos Schoeman, was lopsided – " Jurie Steyn began, when Gysbert van Tonder made haste to explain that he didn't mean that picture at all, but the one next to it, the one with the garden wall.

"We all admire your wife's great-uncle," Gysbert van Tonder continued, "and we venerate his memory. Koos Schoeman was as fine a burgher as ever wore a bandolier across his shoulders, and you've got no call to think I mean *him*. I'm not so stupid that I can't tell the difference between your wife's great-uncle's face and the side of a wall. Why, you can see by his portrait that he was a good-looking man. The kind of looks that they thought were good looks in those days, I mean."

"It's not the fault of the great-uncle of Jurie Steyn's wife that fashions in men's looks have changed since his time," Chris Welman declared, sententiously. "The next generation or so would find quite a lot to laugh at in a photograph of Gysbert van Tonder, say."

"Even if the fashions didn't change, they would still have a lot to laugh at," Jurie Steyn said. It was clear that Jurie Steyn was in an unpleasant mood.

123

At Naudé brought back the subject to where it had started from.

"I've also been a bit puzzled by that painting before today," he said. "I can't make out if the artist painted the front side or the back – it's the painting of the farmhouse I'm talking about, Jurie," he added hurriedly.

It seemed to make it worse, somehow, that At Naudé had to explain that.

"That door that's half open, now," At continued. "Well, it's not a proper top-and-bottom door, but a door in one piece. Now, with that door open, you wouldn't have that pig eating a piece of potato, there, next to the bucket. The pig would be in the dining room, eating the blancmange off the sideboard."

At Naudé made that remark with a certain amount of pride – to show how familiar he was with the interior of the up-to-date kind of farmhouse that had doors all in one piece.

"And the pig, at the same time that he was eating the blancmange, would be scratching himself against a cupboard with glass in front and cups and crossed foreign flags *and* plates inside," Chris Welman announced, determined not to be outdone when it came to knowing what it was like in a voorkamer where there was nothing for you to knock your pipe out against. It seemed that the picture on Jurie Steyn's wall was of *that* kind of farmhouse.

"And there's a brass clock on the wall, and it doesn't go," Gysbert van Tonder announced, triumphantly, "but they say, in that farmhouse, that the clock was in a ship that fought in a sea battle two hundred years ago. Their navy, you know."

We nodded solemnly. And we had to admit that the painting of the farmhouse on Jurie Steyn's wall did seem a little like the kind of farmhouse that we had been talking about. The kind of farm on which the farmer carried out all the instructions issued by the Department of Agriculture's experts in booklet form – and then came knocking at the door of the first Marico Boer to ask what he should do about wire-worm. In the end, of course, that kind of farmer would know better than to open the pamphlets from the Department of Agriculture, even, when they came by post. Or, if he did open them, he would yawn as he slipped the broken nail of his forefinger underneath the paper wrapping.

Jurie Steyn said that that painting was made in his father's time by a Swede or a Pole or a Turk – he forgot which now. And the artist just painted it out of his head, Jurie Steyn said. He walked about from place to place with his brushes and canvas and when he came to a suitable spot he would set up his easel and paint pictures out of his head.

"My father asked him why he didn't paint the scene in front of him," Jurie Steyn added, "but the artist said that he had never got that far, in his artistic studies. Not that he hadn't tried, he said. But each time he tried to paint a piece of Marico bush like it was, what would come out would look just like a neat row of pine trees – from which he could see that he was painting from memory. It was all out of his head."

"Seems there must have been something wrong with his head," Gysbert van Tonder remarked. "Not that this isn't a good painting, mind you, as far as I am able to tell."

So Jurie Steyn said, no, his head was all right.

"My father said that he had never come across anybody with so quick a mind as that artist," Jurie said, "when my father hinted that the milk-shed could do with a coat of whitewash. Before my father had got to mentioning the two trestles that he could put a plank over, to stand on, the artist had already packed up and was on his way through the poort, walking at a good pace. Other farmers in this area also had occasion to notice what a quick mind the artist had."

"What has struck me about this painting," Johnny Coen said, "is also about how that front door is open. It's like somebody has just come walking out of that door. Several times I have thought of it, and quite recently, too. So it's queer that Gysbert van Tonder should have started talking about that same thing. The feeling it gives me is that somebody has just come walking out of that door and has this very moment turned down that path, there. And that's why you can't see the person. I suppose it's something that the artist remembered long ago."

Chris Welman said he imagined that it must be the artist himself who had just come walking out of the door. "After they told him that the fowl-runs needed doing up, no doubt," Chris Welman continued. "That's why you can't see him by the footpath, there. He got out so quick."

But Johnny Coen could not agree. There must have been a deeper reason for the artist remembering, long afterwards and in a foreign country, just that house and that door. Some reason that had to do with longing, Johnny Coen suggested, and with regret, too, maybe.

"It couldn't be that he left that house just because he had been told that the ceiling needed fixing up," Johnny Coen said. "Because then he would have been able to paint pictures of farmhouses from outside Cape Town to the Limpopo, with an open door that he had come out of quick. No, that house there must have been an inspiration to him. He must have known that house very well. And I have heard them say that great sorrow is also an inspiration to an artist. And that is the feeling I have about that painting – that it has to do with some great sorrow in the artist's life."

Thereupon Gysbert van Tonder said that why the artist remembered that farmhouse with so much sorrow was perhaps because the farmer not only asked him to whitewash the kitchen but also to pump water for the cattle out of the borehole.

We none of us laughed at Gysbert van Tonder's words. We just felt that he didn't have the soul to understand a fine painting. And we were glad that we weren't like him.

Johnny Coen sensed that he had us interested.

"*I* believe," Johnny Coen said, then, folding his arms across his chest, "that the person that has just come out of that door is a *girl*. It's a girl that the artist was in love with. And if he's still alive – old and bent and walking out of a farmhouse where something had to be done to the pantry – then I know that he's still in love with that girl. And she has just come tripping out of that house, on her way to meet her lover – who is not the artist, of course. That is why he can never forget that open door."

Several of us got up to look more closely at the painting, then. There was something that appealed to us, somehow, in the thought that it was a picture that had to do with a sweet, sad love-story of long ago.

"And maybe that's why he didn't ever paint Marico farmhouses," At Naudé suggested. "Perhaps he couldn't get the right feeling for them. But all the same I think he could have made it clearer. He could actually have painted the girl coming out of the door, to keep her appointment with her secret lover. Unless he thought that maybe she also, in years to come, wouldn't look quite so – attractive – sort of – well, you know what we've been saying. About fashions in looks changing, and all that."

We guessed, from his remark, that At Naudé's eyes had wandered to the portrait of the burgher with the bandolier.

Jurie Steyn came from behind his post office counter and studied the painting of the farmhouse carefully.

"Maybe it *has* to do with a love-story of long ago," Jurie Steyn said at length. "Only, I don't think any girl came walking out of that door. I think that door was opened to let somebody in. With the woman's husband away at the market, as likely as not. I wouldn't be surprised if it's the artist himself who has just gone sneaking in there. That's why he can't forget about it, ever. Him with his long hair and his bright tie, the… the… "

126

Part of a Story

It WAS arising out of the impending return to the Marico of Petrus Gerber's daughter, Pauline, that At Naudé made the remark he did.

Pauline Gerber was expected back that day by the Bushveld lorry from Bekkersdal. She had been away for almost a year, having gone to a young ladies' college in the Cape in order to study free-hand drawing and how to talk Afrikaans with an English accent.

"When we sit here in Jurie Steyn's voorkamer," At Naudé said, "it's nearly always just men. And in consequence we don't talk scandal, like what happens when it's a lot of women that get together."

So Gysbert van Tonder said that perhaps we should not blame the women for it too much. We men, he said, were fortunate in that we had all sorts of interests that women didn't have, with the result that we could devote our time to better purpose than indulging in idle – and, frequently, malicious – gossip. We should be grateful that we were men, he said, and therefore free from those weaknesses of womankind that were responsible for their going in for thoughtless tittle-tattle.

"Chin-wagging," Chris Welman summed up chivalrously, clarifying his meaning by working his lower jaw up and down very fast, to the accompaniment of sundry high-pitched vocalisations allegedly illustrative of the inflections and cadences of feminine speech.

It was at that moment that Jurie Steyn's wife came in from the kitchen with our coffee.

"You men!" Jurie Steyn's wife exclaimed, staring at Chris Welman with her eyes wide. "Big strong men! And not one of you can jump up to help poor Chris Welman when he's sitting here with what looks like the heaves. How long have you had it, Chris? Drink this coffee down and see if it helps… Yes, I suppose you men have all been so busy scandal-mongering, as usual, that not one of you even *noticed* how ill poor Chris Welman has been taken. With the heaves."

We could see that Chris Welman was proud and flattered at this unexpected solicitude on the part of Jurie Steyn's wife. Indeed, he looked quite hurt, as though we had really misused him. And when he handed the empty coffee-cup back to Jurie Steyn's wife he thanked her in low and fervent tones like the way an invalid talks who has been habitually ill-treated and finds succour just when he has about given up all hope.

"I feel like a different man," Chris Welman assured Jurie Steyn's wife.

She patted him gently on the side of his head and recommended him to cheer up.

"A different *man*," Chris Welman repeated, eyeing the company in the voorkamer in a way that would have been aloof if it wasn't that he also tried to look injured, sort of, at the same time.

Gysbert van Tonder shook his head solemnly at Chris Welman after Jurie Steyn's wife had gone back to the kitchen.

"Well, of all the – " Gysbert van Tonder began, choking, "of all the – "

But Oupa Bekker held up his hand, then. It would appear that, in spite of his deafness, Oupa Bekker had followed most of our conversation, and what he hadn't heard clearly he had filled in with the knowledge of human nature that he had acquired during the many decades in which he had knocked about on this planet. Or so he claimed, anyway.

"There were bits of talk here in the post office this afternoon," Oupa Bekker said, "that I did not hear quite as unmistakably as I would have wished. Like what Chris Welman spoke just before Jurie Steyn's wife came in. Chris Welman's mouth went open and shut too quick for me to hear anything."

We winked at each other, then. For we knew that Chris Welman hadn't *said* anything. He had just been making silly shrill noises. So that showed us how deaf Oupa Bekker really was. The fact that Oupa Bekker thought he could distinguish words in that comical jargon, imitative of female conversation, that Chris Welman had produced from the top of his throat. Well, that did give you a laugh – that Oupa Bekker was so deaf.

We just about shook, then, the way we winked at each other, and nudged.

"All the same," Gysbert van Tonder went on, after a pause, "it beats me that Chris Welman can be so *low*. I can't use any other word. I mean, here were we all saying one kind of thing, and just because a woman comes in and takes a bit of notice of him, why – a man like that would sell his own grandmother. Grand*father*, I should rather say, perhaps. Where's his sense of loyalty to his own sex?"

"It's not true that men stick together," Oupa Bekker interjected. "We all know it's supposed to be that when a woman treats a man badly, then other men sympathise with that man and side with him. To his face they do, yes. But the moment he's walked out – to the bar – it's not *his* face they think of, at all. It's the face of the girl that treated him so badly that they think of – the girl that they shook their heads about while holding

128

sympathetic conversation with him. And when they think of that girl they straighten their ties – if they are wearing ties, that is."

For the first time we noticed that, contrary to established practice, Oupa Bekker was that afternoon wearing a tie. It was a stringy and faded affair, of a shade that might, a generation earlier, have been a kind of maroon. And such as his tie was, he began, with an almost unconscious gesture, to straighten it.

Several of us in Jurie Steyn's voorkamer commenced – equally unconsciously – to pattern after Oupa Bekker. Thus we made the singular discovery that, through some strange coincidence, quite a few of us were that afternoon wearing ties – threadbare and bedraggled things in most cases, maybe, but, nevertheless, ties. It was almost as though we were not in Jurie Steyn's post office at all, but in Zeerust for the Nagmaal.

And it was arising out of the impending return to the Marico of Petrus Gerber's daughter, Pauline, that At Naudé made yet a further remark: "Funny thing that Johnny Coen isn't here, isn't it?" At Naudé said. "I mean, it's a funny thing. The lorry arriving today with the post and all, that is."

But Chris Welman said that At Naudé must not jump to conclusions. Of course, we all knew that there had been talk about Johnny Coen and Pauline Gerber before she had left for the ladies' college in the Cape. We knew that he had seen a lot of her at one time, him riding through the poort to the Gerber farm, wearing a shop suit and with striped socks pulled over the bottoms of his trouser-legs. And then his visits had ceased.

"They say that was when Pauline Gerber got hold of the plan of going to that school," Chris Welman added. "But all the same, we don't know if she really was his girl. It's only what we heard. That she started getting ideas, I mean, and said that Johnny Coen wasn't good enough for her. Mind you, she always was *pretty*, all right."

And we said, yes, Pauline Gerber always was pretty, all right.

We also said that she wasn't the first girl, either, who had at one time or another made it clear to Johnny Coen that she didn't want him calling around, any more. The trouble with Johnny Coen, we said, was that he was too slow, for a young man. And we straightened our ties when we said it.

Well, with one thing and another, it was almost leering, the way we got afterwards, talking about Johnny Coen and saying to each other that we wondered what on earth got into his mind to make him think that he even stood a chance with Pauline Gerber. Because we all liked Johnny Coen, we spoke about him in the friendliest sort of spirit, too. There was none of that sly back-biting that we knew perfectly well women participated in when they got together. On the contrary, we all said that Johnny Coen had some very fine points indeed. And it was because we liked him so much that we said it was a pity that he should have gone and wasted his time in the way he did, running after Pauline Gerber, who couldn't possibly be expected to *see* anything at all in that type of admirer, we said. We were not surprised at her having sent Johnny Coen about his business, we said. We said that though we *liked* him, personally.

"In spite of her youth, you could always see that she is a knowledgeable young person," Oupa Bekker said. "What would naturally appeal to Pauline would be the more mature sort of man. The kind of man who has seen a thing or two of the world. Like who has held high office in the old Stellaland Republic, say, before it was all ruined through – "

"I wouldn't say quite so far back as the Stellaland Republic," Gysbert van Tonder interrupted Oupa Bekker. "But certainly a man who could talk about the big lung sickness that broke out in – "

Several of us interrupted Gysbert van Tonder, then, and there were a good few adjustments made to ties, and not an inconsiderable number of day-dreams about how Pauline Gerber would look today, when there was a sudden screeching of brakes and the Bekkersdal lorry drew up at the front door.

Jurie Steyn's wife got there first. Before any of us men had even seen Pauline Gerber, Jurie Steyn's wife was already talking to her. And as friendly as anything. Jurie Steyn's wife must have slipped out through the kitchen door to get there first.

"It's so nice to see you back again, Pauline," we heard Jurie Steyn's wife say. "What a pity your lovely hat got knocked all sideways in that lorry, though. And all that red on your mouth – oh, I'm sorry, I see now – I thought you had got bumped there, too, by the lorry. It's so *nice* you're back, Pauline."

Friendly as anything, Jurie Steyn's wife sounded.

Home from Finishing-school

WE KNEW, from having heard Jurie Steyn's wife talking to her, that Pauline Gerber was out there, alighting from the lorry. We men, sitting in the voorkamer, would have liked to go out and bid Pauline welcome home to the Marico. But we were restrained by a feeling of shyness. For, as Gysbert van Tonder said, she had just come back from that finishing-school where she had been learning English manners and free-hand drawing, and it would not be becoming for us to go and push ourselves forward, there at the lorry, in just our rough farm clothes, and not able to play the piano.

At Naudé, tiptoeing up to the window, did, however, venture to raise a corner of the chintz curtain. We had always known that Pauline Gerber was pretty, of course. And from the low whistle that At Naudé gave now, we were able to gather that concentration on the schedule of studies at the young ladies' academy had not spoilt her looks.

"Well, of all the pie-faced – " At Naudé said suddenly, with a pronounced sneer, "the *pie*-faced – well, I give up. Drivelling old woman, I should say."

At Naudé made further remarks that did not seem to fit in with the meaning of that first whistle. Could it be, we wondered, that on closer inspection of Pauline, the money spent by her father on her higher education would appear to have been the price of so many head of cattle down the drain?

Already Oupa Bekker was weighing in with a historically authentic account of the ruin that got visited on the Van der Sandt family through the attendance of some of its junior members at the Volksgimnasium. The Molopo Van der Sandts, Oupa Bekker added.

"It's that lorry-driver's assistant," At Naudé explained. "He comes and planks himself down right in front of her, and stands there by the radiator, talking to her as free and easy as you like. So all I can see right now is a bit of feather on her hat. He's talking, standing on one leg. Anybody would think *he's* just come out of college, where they teach you flower arrangements and higher – "

"Higher sums," Gysbert van Tonder interjected, remembering something of his own primary school curriculum and attaching to it imagined academic elevations, "and higher spelling and higher recitation and higher – "

"And now he's shifted on to his other leg," At Naudé continued. "And now he's talking… Ha, ha, ha. No, that really was funny. Ha, ha, ha. He was changing legs again. And he has just leant his one hand – as airy as you please – right on the radiator. Ha, ha, ha. He's lifting both his legs quite a bit off the ground, now, the way he's jumping. You can imagine how hot the radiator must be of a Government lorry that's come without a stop, except Post Bag Helbult, all the way from Bekkersdal, uphill."

Thereupon we all said ha, ha.

In the same moment At Naudé dropped the corner of the chintz curtain quickly and returned to his riempies chair. A little later two large but none the less trim-looking suitcases came in through the half-open door. The lorry-driver's assistant came in with them. It was our turn to whistle, then – even though, unlike At Naudé, we had not yet seen Pauline. We whistled because it was the first time we had ever seen the lorry-driver's assistant so polite to a passenger. When it came to *not* being polite to a passenger, we knew that the lorry-driver's assistant was a lot worse even than the lorry-driver himself. This was easy enough to understand, of course, seeing that the lorry-driver's assistant was trying to get promotion, and he had already learnt that the only way to get anywhere in the service was by being insulting enough to passengers.

But when Pauline Gerber came into the voorkamer we could see why the lorry-driver's assistant didn't care then about all the chances of promotion that he was sacrificing through carrying in a passenger's luggage. He could make up for it later on by losing a milk-can in a donga, maybe. Or by throwing a lighted cigarette-end among a Mtosa passenger's blankets, perhaps.

The point is that Pauline Gerber wasn't merely pretty. She brought into Jurie Steyn's voorkamer more than just good looks. And more than you could learn at just a finishing-school, for that matter. As Gysbert van Tonder said about it afterwards, Pauline Gerber's coming into the voorkamer was like the middle part of a song of which he had forgotten the words but that he could play the tune of with a comb and tissue paper. And Oupa Bekker said – also afterwards – that, far from the middle, or any other part of Pauline's entrance being forgotten, it was like something that would be ever remembered. In story and in song, Oupa Bekker added.

Anyway, there it was. The suitcases came in first, with the lorry-driver's assistant walking a little behind the handle of one of the suitcases, going a bit gingerly on that side, as though the heated radiator of the lorry hadn't done his palm much good. Then came Pauline Gerber, with Jurie Steyn's wife following in the rear.

"Not there!" Jurie Steyn's wife called out as the lorry-driver's assistant made ready to swing the suitcases on to the post office counter, nearly knocking over the brass scale and the pen-and-ink stand.

"But I can't put them on the floor," the lorry-driver's assistant mumbled, dropping the suitcases on the floor, all the same. "Wet cow-dung."

The post office floor had recently been smeared.

The sound that Jurie Steyn's wife made sounded a lot like a snort.

"Ho," Jurie Steyn's wife said, "and since when isn't cow-dung good enough for you, mister? Something seems to have turned your head, all right. Maybe you can tell us what kind of dung is good enough for you? Come on, speak up. Elephant, maybe, or – or – "

The lorry-driver's assistant looked embarrassed.

"Trouble is, I burnt myself on that verdomde radiator," he announced, studying the inside of his hand. "It's all blisters."

Jurie Steyn's wife sniffed elegantly.

In doing so she inhaled some of the aroma from the newly-smeared floor that had blended – a trifle incongruously, perhaps – with the perfume that Pauline Gerber had bought at the Cape. That much came out in her next remark.

"Something has turned your head, all right," Jurie Steyn's wife said to the lorry-driver's assistant, "something that has made you turn up your nose at my floor. The same thing that made you stand there all simpering in front of the lorry, I'm sure. And that's how you got burnt. Now, if my floor isn't good enough for those two suitcases, then what you could do, see, is to sit down on that bench, there, and hold the two suitcases in your lap. Or is there something else, rather, that you would like to hold in your lap? Not that *she'd* object very much, I should imagine."

Later on, when we discussed the matter between ourselves, in private, we said, yes, we did notice how much of the conversation in the post office that afternoon seemed to have taken on something of a low tone. That was what women's influence was on company, we said. The talk in the voorkamer had never got so low, really, we said, in all the time we could recall when there were only men. Or perhaps men and just one woman, Gysbert van Tonder said. And so we said, afterwards, that, yes, it was all right when it was just men, or just men and one woman. But when it was men and there were two women, we said, then the tone of the talk got lowered in a way that we just couldn't understand. That was what we said afterwards, in private, to each other.

Pauline Gerber took no notice of the insinuations made by Jurie Steyn's wife. You could see she had been taught that it was not ladylike to show her annoyance openly. Instead, Pauline stood straight up in the middle of the voorkamer and gazed slowly about her, at the men sitting on the chairs and benches. And a look of disappointment came over her face. It was almost as though there was something about our appearance that was distressing her. But we knew it couldn't be that, of course. We realised that we were not all as handsome as Johnny Coen, for instance – who was not there, that afternoon – but we knew that as a collection of manly-looking farmers (and not sissies) we could hold our own with any bunch of men that you could pick anywhere from between the Orange River and the Caprivi Strip. Pretty though she was, Pauline Gerber must not start giving herself airs now, we thought.

Then Jurie Steyn spoke.

"Can't one of you fat loafers," Jurie Steyn shouted from behind his counter, "get up and give the young lady a seat?"

We all jumped up then, of course. Well, if that was all it was, we knew our manners, all right, even though we hadn't been to any higher ladies' college. In a moment there were half-a-dozen chairs for Pauline Gerber to pick from. And we didn't make an issue of it with Jurie Steyn, either, for what he had said about fat loafers.

Thereupon Pauline Gerber explained, in dark sweet tones, that what worried her was that nobody of her family was there to take her home. There must have been some sort of misunderstanding, she said. It was the first time she had spoken. Her words had an extraordinary effect on Jurie Steyn.

"I'll drive you home in my mule-cart," Jurie Steyn said. "My wife can look after the post office while I'm away."

We were all much impressed with the well-bred and modest fashion in which Pauline Gerber accepted Jurie's invitation.

Some time later, however, when Jurie Steyn called out from the front of the post office to say that the mules were inspanned, we wondered if that young ladies' academy in the Cape really had changed Pauline Gerber so very much. It was when Pauline walked out of the front door, with her chin still in the air. And it wasn't what she did so much as the way she did it, that made it look as though she was at heart still very much of a Marico Bushveld girl. The way she sort of half-lifted her skirts at Jurie Steyn's wife, when she went out.

Singular Events

WHAT ACTUALLY *started* the discussion in Jurie Steyn's post office that day was afterwards not very clear. For that matter, it was not too clear, either, afterwards, as to how it all ended. At Naudé did make reference, of course, to a story that he had listened in to over the wireless. But he only brought in that wireless story to illustrate something that somebody else had already said. It had to do with a ship or a boat on which there were a lot of seamen and they were drifting about for a very long time, unable to reach land, At Naudé explained. When At Naudé explained further that it was something that had happened ever so long ago, we felt that he was taking our conversation off its course, in much the same way that the seamen he spoke about had been taken off *their* course, drifting about and all like that on the ocean.

That kind of thing naturally set Oupa Bekker off talking about another ship that couldn't make port. And even before Oupa Bekker spoke we knew what was coming. It was an established fact, as far as you liked to go north of the Dwarsberge, that Oupa Bekker on his grandmother's side was directly descended from Kapitein van der Decken, jolly skipper in the service of the Dutch East India Company's merchant navy, whose square-rigged brig, a familiar sight off the southern Cape Peninsula, had with the passing years acquired the stage name of *Flying Dutchman*.

We had heard this story so often before from Oupa Bekker that Gysbert van Tonder began heading him off the moment Oupa Bekker brought up his heel to knock out his pipe against. Gysbert van Tonder was only partially successful, however. Oupa Bekker did get so far as to acquaint us once more with some of the details of his last visit to Cape Town.

"Big white sails, just like you see in pictures," Oupa Bekker concluded. "And it gave me a lot of pleasure, you understand, to be able to be there at Camp's Bay and to wave at my ancestor. And when I thought of how old *he* was, I didn't feel so old any more, somehow, myself. And on the way back to the Transvaal I told a young man in my compartment about it. The young man was a student going home for the holidays, and he had a solemn look, and he said our nation must 'Hou koers' and he seemed older, somehow, than me, or even than Kapitein van der Decken, who is my ancestor on my grandmother's side."

Seeing that, in spite of our efforts to stop him, Oupa Bekker had actually got so far, Chris Welman, winking at us, decided to humour him.

"And what did that young student say about the Dutch East Indies ship, Oupa," Chris Welman asked, "the ship that you stood on the sand and waved at?"

"Oh, you could see that that student knew a thing or two, all right," Oupa Bekker said. "The student was very fine about it. He said that the *Flying Dutchman* was a myth. *Mities,* he said it was – just like that. And

135

so I said to him that that was just how I felt about it, too. It was a word I hadn't heard before, I told him. But that was exactly the feeling I had, standing there at Camp's Bay and waving, first with my hand and then with my hat, also. I felt it was just *mities*. And I don't care who knows it, I said to the student."

Oupa Bekker went on to say that when that student alighted at his destination, which was at a siding somewhere in the Karoo, then the student looked a good few years older, even, than when he had got into the train at Stellenbosch. Older and more solemn, Oupa Bekker remarked. And he glanced over his shoulder, too, once, cautiously, as though suspicious that Oupa Bekker might decide to get off there, also.

It was Jurie Steyn who reminded us of what we had really been discussing. He reminded us in that prim and precise tone of voice that he had started adopting ever since the post office authorities had erected a strip of brass wire-netting over half the length of his counter, thereby bringing Jurie Steyn into line with the post office at Bekkersdal. And now that, for half his length, Jurie Steyn was in line with the Bekkersdal post office counter, Jurie Steyn frequently spoke in the way that the Bekkersdal postmaster spoke when he pulled down his little green curtain behind the wire-netting and told the people waiting in the queue that that section was closed until nine o'clock next morning. Of course, Jurie Steyn didn't make use of that strip of wire-netting. For one thing, he didn't have a little green curtain behind it that he could pull down. And, for another thing, even if he did have a curtain, you could always put your head round that part of the counter where there was no wire-netting, and *see* Jurie Steyn standing there.

"Anyway, what I want to know," Jurie Steyn declared, in his new voice of higher officialdom, "is how we have come to be talking about Oupa Bekker's old ghost ship. As far as I can recall – "

"It's not a ghost ship," Oupa Bekker asserted. "If you think you know better than that student – "

"Ghost ship," Jurie Steyn continued. "And what's more – "

"Student of divinity, too" – Oupa Bekker chanced his arm – "and Kapitein van der Decken was my grandmother's great – "

"Now I remember what we were talking about," Jurie Steyn announced triumphantly. "We were talking about the meat shortage in the cities and about all the different kinds of meat that's being cut into strips and hung out on a line to dry for biltong. Baboons, I remember we said. And donkeys. They say there are lots of people in the cities can't tell the differ-

136

ence, when it's biltong. If it's some kind of taste that they haven't had before, then they think, oh, it must be ostrich. They never think it might be donkey. Isn't that what you were telling us, At?"

But At Naudé said, no, he hadn't been discussing that side of the question at all. That was what Chris Welman had been saying, At Naudé explained. He himself had been talking, he said, about that story he had heard over the wireless about those sailors ever so long ago that were adrift for months and months in a boat miles and miles away from land. That was all he said, At Naudé made clear, at the same time expressing the hope that Jurie Steyn wasn't going to get him wrong, now.

This time Oupa Bekker did lean forward, and in such a manner that, whether he wanted to or not, Jurie Steyn had to listen to him.

"Can you tell the difference by the taste, Jurie – now, just by the taste, mind," Oupa Bekker asked, "between, say, blesbok biltong and donkey biltong? Because, if you can, *it means you have tasted donkey biltong*. Perhaps you will now tell us when, and where, you *ate* donkey biltong. You know what I mean, strips of donkey hung out on a line to dry, when there's a hot sun, with naeltjies and red pepper."

Well, that was a fair enough question. All the same, we felt that Oupa Bekker need not have been so nasty about it – particularly in his going to the extent of explaining to Jurie Steyn what biltong was, as though Jurie Steyn didn't know. Well, we felt that Jurie would have been quite within his rights if he had said that Oupa Bekker looked pretty much like a long, unappetising strip of biltong himself, and without coriander spice in it.

But Jurie Steyn didn't say that. It was almost as though Jurie had sensed that Oupa Bekker wanted him to say that. Jurie was cunning, that way. Accordingly, "Have *you* eaten donkey biltong, Oupa?" was all that Jurie Steyn would reply, then.

Oupa Bekker paused, with his pipe in the air, looking thoughtful.

"I can't say for sure," he admitted at length. "I mean, when people hand you a strip of donkey biltong, they don't tell you it's donkey biltong, do they? Or that it's baboon biltong, either, for that matter – do they, now?"

We agreed that Oupa Bekker was right, there, of course. Not one of us could recall having had a statement of that description made to him just offhand, sort of.

"And so there it is," Oupa Bekker announced. "I may have – I just wouldn't know. But it's silly when people try and explain to you that they can tell by the taste what sort of biltong is what. You can try and guess, of course, but as likely as not you'll be wrong."

All the same, Oupa Bekker went on, looking doubtful, he couldn't understand how all this kind of talk had come about in the first place. It seemed a bit mixed-up to him, Oupa Bekker added.

"The sailors adrift on that ship," he said. "And donkey biltong. And Van der Decken being my ancestor on my grandmother's side – "

We could see that an idea had suddenly occurred to him.

"Oh, yes," Oupa Bekker said, "I remember now. It was the biltong we had at Chief Ndlambe's kraal, when Gert Pretorius and I were the first white men to trek into these parts. And although Chief Ndlambe asked us to guess what kind of biltong it was, Gert and I just couldn't. And afterwards Gert Pretorius and I discussed the peculiar way Chief Ndlambe had laughed when we said it was a kind of taste we hadn't really come across before, we didn't think… Well, I know now what it is that made me think of my grandmother. Because of the strange stories we heard from the Mtosas later on about Chief Ndlambe's grandmother. About the bitter kinds of disputes she had been having with her grandson, lately, and of how she had suddenly disappeared, one day, from the tribal councils. Yes, that part of it I can see quite clearly. But what have those sailors got to do with it – drifting around for months and months on that ship At Naudé has been telling us about?"

Why, it was exactly the same thing, At Naudé said.

Those sailors, At Naudé said, had to eat.

Young Man in Love

GYSBERT VAN Tonder told us, in Jurie Steyn's voorkamer, that afternoon, that Johnny Coen would be along later. He had seen Johnny Coen, Gysbert said, by the mealie-lands, and Johnny Coen was busy scraping some of the worst turf off his veldskoens with a pocket knife that had only the short blade left. Johnny Coen was also making use of various wisps of yellow grass, performing wiping movements along the side of his face. Well, we all knew that if, in the middle of the ploughing season, a man took all that trouble with his personal appearance, it must be that he was thinking of going visiting.

"Of course, it doesn't necessarily mean that he's coming *here*," At Naudé observed. "I mean, if he was busy to make himself up *so* smart, well, it might perhaps mean that he was working up the courage to go and see *her*. You know what I mean – Johnny Coen taking all the trouble to get the turf soil off his veldskoens *and* to get the turf soil off his face.

"If he was coming just here to see us, well, he wouldn't care how much black turf there was on his face. All he would be concerned about was that he didn't leave a lot of thick mud where he walked, here, in the post office, where Jurie Steyn's wife would complain about it."

Oupa Bekker shook his head.

"We know that Johnny Coen hasn't been around to the post office here, since he heard that Pauline Gerber was coming back from finishing-school," Oupa Bekker said. "And I think we can understand why. We know the kind of talk that there was about Johnny Coen and Pauline Gerber before Pauline suddenly decided to go to that ladies' school in the Cape, after all. If you remember, we said that Johnny Coen couldn't have been much of a young man if Pauline Gerber thought that going to a ladies' academy would be more exciting. Of course, we never said any of those things in Johnny Coen's presence… "

Thereupon Chris Welman remarked that since Pauline Gerber's return from the ladies' school in the Cape, we hadn't seen much of Johnny Coen's presence.

It was almost as though Johnny Coen wasn't so much shy about seeing Pauline Gerber, again, as that he was shy about seeing *us*. There was a thing now, Chris Welman remarked.

Oupa Bekker banged his tamboetie walking-stick on the floor, making small holes in the floor and sending up yellow dust. For the first time we realised that he was getting annoyed.

"You won't listen to me," Oupa Bekker said. "You'll never let me finish what I was going to say. Always, you just let me get so far. Then somebody says something foolish, and so I can't get to the important thing. Now, what I want to say is that At Naudé is quite right. And Johnny Coen *is* coming here. He's coming here this afternoon because he wants to know what *we* think. A young man in love is like that. He wants to know what we've got to say. And all the time he will be laughing to himself, secretly, about the things we're saying. A young man in love is like that, also. And his titivating himself, with the short blade of a pocket knife and a handful of dried grass – well, you've got no idea how vain a young man in love is.

"And he's not making himself all stylish for the girl's sake but for his own sake. It's himself that he thinks is so wonderful. He knows less than anybody what she is like, the girl he is in love with. And it's only the best kind of pig's fat he'll mix with soot to shine his bought boots with.

Because he's in love with the girl, he thinks *he's* something. Oh, yes, Johnny Coen will come around here this afternoon, all right. And what I want to say – "

At this point, Oupa Bekker was interrupted once more. But because it was Jurie Steyn who broke in upon his dissertation, Oupa Bekker yielded with good grace. The post office we were sitting in was, after all, Jurie Steyn's own voorkamer. There was something of the spirit of old-world courtesy in the manner of Oupa Bekker's surrender.

"——— you, then, Jurie Steyn," Oupa Bekker said. "*You* talk."

Several of us looked in the direction of the kitchen. We were relieved to see that the door was closed. That meant that Jurie Steyn's wife did not hear the low expression Oupa Bekker had used.

"What *I* would like to say," Jurie Steyn said, "is that I had the honour to drive Juffrou Pauline Gerber to her home in my mule-cart, the day she arrived here at my post office, getting off from the Government lorry and all – "

"What do you mean by 'and all'?" Gysbert van Tonder demanded.

Jurie Steyn looked around him with an air of surprise.

"But you were all here," Jurie Steyn declared. "*All* of you were here. Maybe that's what I mean by *and all*. I am sure I don't know. But you did see Pauline Gerber. You each one of you saw her. When she alighted here that day from the Zeerust lorry, on her return from the Cape finishing-school. You saw the way she walked around here in my voorkamer, picking her heels up high – and I don't blame her, her back from finishing-school and all. And her chin up in the air. And as pretty as you like. You all saw how pretty she was, now, didn't you? And the way she *smelt*. Did you smell her? You must have. It was too lovely. It just shows you the kind of perfume you can *get* in the Cape.

"And I am sure that if a church elder smelt her – even if he was an Enkel Gereformeerde Church elder from the furthest part of the Waterberg, I am sure that that Waterberg elder would have known that Pauline Gerber had class – just from smelling her, I mean. I am sure that that scent that Pauline bought at the Cape must have cost at least seven shillings and sixpence a bottle. Look at my wife, now, for instance. Well, I once bought my wife a bottle of perfume at the Indian store at Ramoutsa. And what I say is, you can *smell* the difference between my wife and – and Pauline Gerber."

Chris Welman, who had not spoken much so far, hastened to remark that there were other ways, too, in which you could tell the difference.

It was an innuendo that, fortunately enough, escaped general attention.

For it was Johnny Coen himself that came in at the front door of the post office at that moment. In one way, it was the Johnny Coen that we had always known. And yet, also, it wasn't him. In some subtle fashion Johnny Coen had changed. After greeting us, he went and found a place for himself on a riempies chair, sitting very upright.

He seemed from his manner to be almost unaware of our presence as he whittled a match-stick to a fine point and commenced scraping out the grime from under one of his fingernails.

Gysbert van Tonder, who always liked getting straight down to things, was the first to talk.

"Nice bit of rain you've been having out your way, Johnny," Gysbert van Tonder remarked. "Dams should be pretty full, I'd imagine."

"Oh, yes, indeed," Johnny Coen answered.

"Plenty of water in the spruit, too, I should think," Gysbert continued.

"Yes, that is very true," Johnny Coen replied.

"New grass must be coming along all right in the vlakte where you burnt," Gysbert van Tonder went on.

"Yes, very nicely," Johnny agreed.

Gysbert van Tonder grew impatient.

"What's the matter with you, man – why can't you talk?" Gysbert demanded. "You know all right what I am trying to say. Have you seen her at all since she's been back?"

"I saw her yesterday," Johnny Coen said, "on the road near their house. I had to go quite a long distance out of my way to be *passing* there, at the time."

Gysbert van Tonder made a quick calculation.

"Matter of just under eleven miles out of your way, counting in the short cut through the withaaks," he announced. "Did she have much to say?"

Johnny Coen shook his head.

"Please don't ask me," he almost implored of Gysbert, "because I really can't remember. We did speak, I know. But after she had gone there was nothing we said that I could recall. It was all so different, after we had met, and we had spoken there by the road, and she had gone on back home again. It was all so different after she had gone. I wish I *could* remember what we said. What I said must have all sounded very foolish to her, I am sure."

Gysbert van Tonder was not going to allow Johnny Coen to get by so easily.

"Well, how did she *look*?" Gysbert asked.

"That was what I also tried to remember, afterwards," Johnny Coen declared. "How she looked. What she did. All that. But I just couldn't remember. After she had gone it was all like it had been a dream, and there was nothing that I could remember for sure. She was picking yellow flowers there by the side of the road, she was, to stick in her hair. Or she was carrying a sack of firewood over her back for the kitchen fire, she was. And it would have been just the same *thing*, the way I felt. But I don't know. All I was able afterwards – "

"That was what I was trying to explain to them, Johnny," Oupa Bekker interjected, "but they never let me finish anything I start to say. They always – "

"Afterwards," Johnny Coen repeated, "after she had gone, that is, there was a kind of sweetness in the air. It was almost *hanging* in the air, sort of. Once I even thought that it might be a kind of scent, like what some women put on their clothes when they go to Nagmaal. But, of course, I knew that it couldn't be *that*. I mean, I knew Pauline wouldn't wear scent, I mean. She's not that kind."

"What I wanted to say earlier on, when you all interrupted me," Oupa Bekker declared, then, with an air of triumph, "is that a young man in love *is* like that."

Dreams of Rain

NOW THAT the rains had come, everything in the Groot Marico was, of course, different. It wasn't the kind of rain that starts off with swallows flying in low circles over the dam and ends abruptly just after you have got the tin bath in position in the bedroom, under the leaky place in the thatch.

On the contrary, it was the kind of rain that, beginning before daybreak, goes on, hour after hour, soaking into the Transvaal veld that doesn't seem to know how to take it, quite. Having, through long practice, got used to a condition of drought, it is only in the nature of things that the Transvaal veld should be somewhat suspicious, at the start, of all this silver balm descending out of the skies. It is only reasonable that the Transvaal veld should say, "Huh."

This is only the beginning, of course. For after it has been raining steadily for half a day, with more to come, the Transvaal veld starts giving itself no end of airs. It even begins to fancy that it's the Western

Province, the Transvaal veld does – just as though there aren't antipassaat winds and longitudinal geographical escarpments and things. Quite insufferable, the Transvaal veld gets.

The rain that had commenced a long while before dawn kept pattering on the leaf of moepel and maroela and wilde mispel. As one rainy hour succeeded the next, the farmers of the Groot Marico – who, through their proximity to the veld, shared its natural pessimism – gradually came to accept it as a fact that a drought of long standing was now, at last, broken.

More than one farmer, standing in the kitchen with his second cup of coffee in his hand and looking through the window at the wet daybreak, would employ some artless device in order to reassure himself that he wasn't dreaming… He had been caught just that way before.

"After all," as Gysbert van Tonder said in Jurie Steyn's post office that same afternoon, "what else do we dream about, mostly, during a big drought?"

As if to make sure, almost, we all of us glanced in the direction of the window. And what we saw through the panes was all right. Over the outside world there was still hung a shifting curtain of grey and white filaments. Even better proof that it really was rain, right enough, and not just a dream, was provided by the state that Jurie Steyn's post office counter was in. An appliance that consisted of a chair and an enamel basin had evidently been erected too late, and there was a suggestion of inadequacy in the absorptive resources of some spread-out newspaper and a khaki blanket. Briefly, with the rain coming in through the roof, Jurie Steyn's counter was in a mess.

"All the same," Oupa Bekker remarked, looking at the chipped areas of the enamel basin with something that came close to disrespect, "I have had rain-dreams just about as real as that. In times of long drought, mind you. The kind of drought you used to get in the old days. And we would just bear up under it, too. And there would be no newspapers to write about it in big headlines. Newspapers – "

It seemed that at that moment Jurie Steyn shared Oupa Bekker's contempt for the popular press. At all events, Jurie crumpled a number of wet sheets into a soggy ball and proceeded to replace them with fresh newspapers, the while he swore to himself in undertones.

"Well, if you must know," Chris Welman remarked, "I had exactly that same feeling, this morning. When I woke up with the rain on the roof, and I looked out into the dark and the candle shone on a puddle right at my back door – well, it was exactly like the kind of dream I have often had. I have often dreamt exactly that, and then I have woken up in the morning to see another sun pulling himself right for another scorcher – so I would again all day pump water at the borehole.

"And I've noticed that the longer a drought lasts, the more flesh and blood, sort of, a dream about rain seems to become. Why, there was one night, in a time of big drought, when I dreamt I was driving down the Government Road in my mule-cart and it was raining – I say, *that* was a cunning dream, for you, now. In my dream I started doubting if it was really raining. *I dreamt* that I said to myself, 'Well, I suppose this is just a dream.'

"And then, do you know what? In the next moment the whole Government Road was full of Mshangaans on bicycles riding back from the town to their kraal, so that they could get back home to plough while the ground was still wet. When I woke up next morning, the ground was as hard as ever, with another day of drought getting ready to bake it harder still. But how do you like that for a dream, hey? Filling the whole Government Road with Mshangaans on pushbikes just to deceive me."

We agreed with Chris Welman that it was a sad story that he had just told us. And we several of us mentioned other examples of vivid dreams we had had of rain in seasons of drought. And we acknowledged that, the more severe the drought was, the more genuine and *luminous* seemed those visions of rain that came and mocked us in the night. Came unasked, too, we said, and mocked us.

"Anyway, it's not a dream for Jurie Steyn, that it's raining now," Gysbert van Tonder remarked, eyeing Jurie's struggles with a damp stock of two-penny stamps, "although I don't say that it's not a *nightmare*, for Jurie. How does he think he'll ever get those sheets of stamps dry again? My, aren't they big, though? Must be hundreds on one sheet, and all purple. Ripe, they look to me, too, sort of. And wet. Reminds me of parstyd on a wine farm in Constantia… I say, Jurie, if you lay those sheets of stamps on the floor like that, on top of each other, they'll all stick together, man. Or do you *want* them all stuck together? You should rather separate them and hang them along the wall. Make the wall look pretty, too."

It was a sensible suggestion that Gysbert van Tonder had made, and Jurie Steyn proceeded to carry it out. But, as is always the case with good advice, Jurie Steyn was not properly grateful. First he asked Gysbert if Gysbert thought that *he* was perhaps the duly appointed postmaster for this part of the Dwarsberge section of the Groot Marico. And then, when he had had about half of one wall covered with sheets of stamps hanging on drawing-pins, Jurie said that *he* had thought of it first.

You could see that Jurie Steyn felt really proud of himself, afterwards, when all the wet sheets of postage stamps were pinned to the wall to dry. And it looked nice, too, all the greens and blues and purples and reds.

Jurie stepped back to admire his handiwork.

"Pity I haven't got any more shilling revenues," he said. "A row of them on the left, there, would make it look real smart. I wouldn't mind if the Postmaster-General came walking in here, now. No, or the new Minister of Posts *and* Telegraphs, either."

A wistful look came into Jurie Steyn's eyes as he went on gazing at the wall.

"The Postmaster-General might perhaps even have some shilling revenue stamps with him," Jurie said.

But At Naudé, who had a wireless and also read the newspapers, and was thus well up in affairs of the day, said that that sort of highly placed personage would not be coming to Jurie Steyn's post office now.

"Not now," At Naudé repeated, with a good deal of emphasis. "You see that this is a nation-wide rain – 'n landreën – and anybody as eminent as the new Minister of Posts and Telegraphs would naturally be on his way back to his farm, as quick as he can get, to plough – "

Because of Chris Welman's laughter, then, we were unable to hear the rest of At Naudé's remarks. And suddenly, one by one, it struck us, also, as to why Chris Welman was laughing. Chris Welman was thinking of his dream, we realised – his dream of the Mshangaans on their bicycles riding home as fast as they could go. And it *did* seem funny, somehow, the picture of the Minister of Posts and Telegraphs, with his head down over the handlebars, pedalling down the Government Road, ahead of those Mshangaans.

We were all laughing when the door of the voorkamer was pushed open. But it wasn't the Postmaster-General who entered, bringing in with him a flurry of rain. At the same time, we would not have been very much surprised if it *had* been the Postmaster-General. Queer things like that do happen, when you're laughing. Or when there's a big rain after a long drought.

As it turned out, however, the new arrival was only the young Johnny Coen. And he looked very miserable. It was easy to see that his courtship of Pauline Gerber was not proceeding at all smoothly. If only he would listen to the advice of men of more understanding – even though they might be a bit older than he was, maybe – he wouldn't make such a fool of himself, we felt. And the advice we had to offer him was that, seeing that she was just back from finishing-school, Pauline Gerber wouldn't be in the least interested in Johnny Coen's type. Not while there was *our* sort of man around, sitting here in the Groot Marico. Sitting on a riempies bench and chairs in Jurie Steyn's voorkamer at that moment.

"Don't you think my wall looks – er – clever," Jurie Steyn asked of Johnny Coen, pausing for the right word, "with all those different coloured stamps?"

"Yes," Johnny Coen responded, dully. He was obviously not interested. Those stamps might all just have been of one grey hue, as far as he was concerned. It was obvious that Pauline Gerber had treated him very badly. Laughed at him, we knew. With a few high notes in her laughter, too, we hoped.

"You look so dismal, Johnny," Gysbert van Tonder remarked. "Hasn't it been raining out your way?"

Chris Welman chuckled.

"Perhaps it wasn't real rain, but he just dreamt it," Chris Welman called out. "Like what we've been saying about dreams."

Thereupon Gysbert van Tonder proceeded to acquaint Johnny Coen, at considerable length, with the purport of our conversation of that afternoon.

At the end of it, Johnny Coen folded his arms and sighed deeply.

"Dreams?" he asked in a soft voice. "Dreams? That's what you've been talking about, isn't it? Well, let me tell you about a dream I had… No, there were no Mshangaans with pushbikes in it… A dream that has come to nought. Let me tell you – "

It was at that moment that the motor-lorry from Bekkersdal arrived. Not in a cloud of dust, this time, and the rain had kept the radiator cool.

We hustled around for our mail and milk-cans. We had no time to listen to stories about dreams. It was real rain that had come. Tomorrow at dawn we would be on the lands, ploughing.

Ill-informed Criticism

IT WAS some visitor from foreign parts who, just before leaving, made certain remarks to newspaper reporters about what he thought the Transvaal platteland was like. At Naudé retailed some of those remarks to us.

Primitive was one of the words that visitor had used about us, At Naudé said. And medieval, the visitor remarked. And also he had said work-shy.

Listening to all that from At Naudé in Jurie Steyn's voorkamer, that afternoon, we were, naturally enough, pained.

"Medieval?" Oupa Bekker snorted. "Well, I don't know what that word means, not having heard it more than twice or so before in my whole life, unless it was said, maybe, by somebody talking fast, so that I couldn't *catch* it. No, I don't know what that word *means*. But taken along with those other things that get said about us, from time to time, I should imagine that medieval is just about the worst of the lot."

Oupa Bekker said the word over to himself several times. Medieval – middeleeus. You could see there was something in the sound of it that, in spite of himself, Oupa Bekker liked.

"Now, just imagine a man like that visitor," Oupa Bekker continued. "He couldn't even have seen the country, properly – "

"He said he had seen enough," At Naudé interjected.

" – and then he says these things about us," Oupa Bekker went on, "and then he gets out – quick. He's away in an aeroplane before anybody can prove to him that we're not medieval. That's one way, now, where I don't hold with progress.

"For instance, in the old days, if a visitor, passing through Derdepoort, say, made a remark like that about the platteland, why, we would have caught up with him before he had got to the Molopo. And we would have *proved* to him, right there by the camel-thorns with a sjambok, how mistaken he was in saying that we were savage and unpolished and – and backward – and things like that. I can't call them all to mind, right now."

Gysbert van Tonder suggested a few words to help Oupa Bekker out. And then we all remembered one or two extra words that had also been said about us at various times. It was with a sense of pride, almost, at the end, that we realised how many words there were like that that had been said about us, by visitors from foreign parts.

But it was evident that Oupa Bekker's thoughts were still on that traveller who was now thousands of miles away, riding in an aeroplane through the sky.

"Even if they had just the train to Ottoshoop, still," Oupa Bekker declared, sounding wistful, "we would yet have been able to point out to that visitor where he went wrong. We would have been able to point it out to him with a short handkarwats on the station platform."

Anyway, what At Naudé had repeated to us from the newspaper report did awaken our interest. Chris Welman turned to the young schoolmaster.

"What does it mean, now, Meneer Vermaak, middeleeus?" Chris Welman asked. "I suppose that visitor means we's just a lot of stinking ——s, his saying we're medieval? Or a lot of pot-bellied ——s, hey, with our feet sticking out sideways, like a muscovy duck's? Is medieval as low a word as all that?"

Thereupon Jurie Steyn said that Chris Welman had no occasion to use such expressions, especially as his wife was in the kitchen, and might hear. Moreover, Chris Welman could speak for himself. Chris Welman could be as medieval as he liked, Jurie Steyn said. *He* didn't care. But he himself didn't want to be included in being called a stinking ——, thanks. He wondered where Chris Welman learnt such awful language.

"It's all right, Jurie, your wife isn't in the kitchen," Chris Welman was able to explain. "She's on the roof. I saw her when I came along. Just listen, you can hear her hammering there, now. When I came along she was sawing."

"Must be trying to fix that chimney, I suppose," Jurie Steyn observed. "It's been all over to one side since that big wind we had."

We all sat forward and Oupa Bekker put his hand up to his ear, when the schoolmaster, having cleared his throat, explained that medieval had to do in the first place with the feudal system. Chris Welman looked startled. He thought he knew all the low words there were, Chris Welman said. And what he didn't know himself he had learnt the time, long ago, when he had been a white labourer in Johannesburg digging foundations. But the word *feudal* was a new one on him. He hoped the schoolmaster wouldn't let it slip out by accident in the schoolroom, one day, in front of the children, when he lost his temper about something, Chris Welman said.

But the schoolmaster went on to explain further. And it was a long sort of explanation. And it didn't seem to lead anywhere. It seemed like it had to do with history, and in the end we were several of us yawning. There was no point to it.

From what the schoolmaster was saying, Oupa Bekker commented, it would appear that the word feudal had to do with some kind of government. And so he didn't see where the schoolmaster's explanations fitted in, at all. For that matter, he didn't accept that that kind of government was much of an improvement on what we had right here in the Groot Marico.

"Most of those things you're talking about we've already *got*," Oupa

Bekker said. "So what's the argument?"

"It seems to me that it's some more of that progress talk," Gysbert van Tonder announced.

"Well, we don't want any more of their progress, medieval or any other kind. They can go and have all the progress they want somewhere else, if they like. But they can't come and have it on my front stoep, they feudal well can't. And as for that visitor saying we're *work-shy* – well, does he know what work is, at all, I wonder? Him sitting in that aeroplane, all snooty."

For a good while after that we each of us started wondering the same thing, each of us wondering, in turn, if the visitor had ever pumped water for the cattle in the hot sun. Or if the visitor had ever chased a pig to put in a crate, in the hot sun, for several hours, with the visitor's family and the Mtosa farmhands falling over each other, all the time, and the boss-boy going to the police afterwards – the boss-boy claiming that the visitor had kicked him on the ear on purpose when the pig jumped out of the crate again.

Or if the visitor had ever got a letter from the storekeeper at Ramoutsa about what he would do unless the visitor made a big payment in three days, in the hot sun.

We all spoke about some time or other that we had worked.

The longest story of all was Chris Welman's. He had to take so long over it, not because he was working so much, but because it was the time he was in Johannesburg, digging foundations, and he had to tell us a lot of things about what Johannesburg was like, in those old days. There was a lot of labour trouble at that time on the Rand, Chris Welman said. And almost every other day they were having a general strike. He wasn't quite sure what it was all about, Chris said, but he wouldn't say it didn't suit him. It just meant that every so often he would have to put down his spade and pick and go home.

And they had a woman Labour leader that they called Miss Florence Desborough, Chris Welman said. He had never seen her, but he would have liked to, he said.

Not that she would ever have taken any notice of his sort, he knew. But he pictured what she was like from her name. And he thought of her as pretty, and having a soft, refined voice, and with an ostrich feather in her hat, and having high-up shoulders, like they wore in those days. He got all that just out of the sound of her name, he said – Miss Florence Desborough.

And then one day there was again a general strike that he and his mates, standing digging in the trench, didn't know about. How they got informed, Chris Welman said, was when one of those old-fashioned taxis that they had in those days drove up to where they were working, and a woman came dashing up to them out of the taxi, swinging a pick-handle, that was tied to her wrist with a piece of string. She was screaming, too, Chris Welman said. And he himself didn't stop running for about six blocks. Anyway, he himself was a bit disappointed, afterwards, when he learnt that that woman was Miss Florence Desborough, and that she had the nickname of Pickhandle Flo.

Jurie Steyn's wife, coming in at that moment with our coffee, didn't sound very different from Miss Florence Desborough, we thought. Moreover, Jurie Steyn's wife had a black smudge on her forehead from the chimney.

"What do you call yourselves?" she asked indignantly. "Of all the lazy, good-for-nothing loafers – talk, talk, is all you do. Here have I had to get on to the roof myself with a hammer. And a saw. And a pick. Who's ever heard of a white woman having to swing a pick?"

Jurie Steyn's wife said a lot more. We did not answer her.

"One thing, at least," Oupa Bekker chuckled, after Jurie Steyn's wife had gone out again, "one thing at least that she didn't say is that we're middeleeus."

Toys in the Shop Window

"YOU OUGHT to see David Policansky's store," the lorry-driver's assistant said. "My, but it does look lovely. All done up for Christmas. It's worth going all the way to Bekkersdal just to see it. And the toys in the window – you've got no idea. There's a mirror with a little ship on it, and cotton-wool over it for clouds, and little trees at the side of it, so the mirror looks just like it's water. And there's a toy Chinaman that goes up and down on a ladder with baskets over his shoulder on a stick when you wind him up – "

Jurie Steyn interrupted the lorry-driver's assistant to say that he was sure to go and drive all those miles and miles to Bekkersdal, just to go and look at the toys in Policansky's window. Catch *him*, going all that way to stare at a wound-up Chinaman going up and down on a ladder with baskets, Jurie Steyn said.

Thereupon, speaking earnestly to him because this was no time for foolishness, Gysbert van Tonder said to the lorry-driver's assistant that he hoped he hadn't been talking about those same toys at every Bushveld farmhouse and post office that the lorry had stopped at on the way north from Bekkersdal. Because if he *had*, why, the children would make their parents' lives impossible between now and Christmas. He himself had several children that were still of school-going age, Gysbert van Tonder said. And so he knew.

The lorry-driver's assistant looked embarrassed.

"Well, I did talk a little," he admitted. "But I didn't say too much, I don't think. Except maybe at Post Bag Laatgevonden. Yes, now I come to think of it, I did, perhaps, say one or two things I shouldn't have, at Post Bag Laatgevonden. You see, the driver had trouble with a spark-plug, there, and so in between handing the driver a spanner or a file, maybe, I *might* have said a few things more than just about the ship and the Chinaman.

"Yes, now I come to think of it, I did, at Post Bag Laatgevonden, make some mention of the train that goes underneath tunnels and then waits at a siding for the signal to go up before it goes rushing on again through the vlakte, past railwaymen cottages and windmills and Mtosa huts, and then it gets switched on to another line – but I'm sorry, kêrels.

"Yes, I'm really sorry. I know, now, that I talked too much, there. But Laatgevonden was the only place where I mentioned the train. At the other Post Bags where we stopped we didn't stop long enough – having just to hand over the mailbag and unload the milk-cans – and so I didn't say anything at those places about the train. You see, that train in Policansky's window goes such a long distance, round and round and round, and taking up water supplies, too, at one spot, that you can't talk about it, unless you've got a long *time* to talk – as I did have at Post Bag Laatgevonden, where the lorry-driver was trying to fix a sparking plug, and shouting that I was handing him the wrong tools as often as not."

In making that remark, the lorry-driver's assistant grinned.

"All the same," he added, "you've got no idea what that train is like. It's so real that you almost expect to see a gang of plate-layers running away and the passengers throwing empty bottles at them out of the windows."

We could see from this that there must have been a good deal of realism about the clockwork railway in Policansky's store. We could also see in which way the lorry-driver's assistant and his friends amused themselves, whenever they went on a train ride from Ottoshoop.

Meanwhile, Johnny Coen, who had once worked on the South African

Railways, was asking the lorry-driver's assistant if the toy train in Policansky's window was one of the new kind of toy train, such as he had heard about. Did it have bogie wheels, he asked. And did it have a miniature injector steam pipe. But when he asked if it also had miniature super-heater flue tubes, the lorry-driver's assistant said that was something Johnny Coen should perhaps rather go and ask David Policansky. He himself only thought that it looked like a train. And it looked a lot like a train, to him, the lorry-driver's assistant said. But maybe there were parts missing. He wouldn't be able to tell. It *went* all right, though, he added.

The lorry-driver's assistant was in the middle of telling us about something else that Policansky was arranging to have in the toy department of his store, for Christmas, when the lorry-driver called through the door and asked did the assistant think they could waste all day at a third-rate Dwarsberg post office where the coffee they got was nearly all roast kremetart root.

By the time Jurie Steyn walked round from behind his counter to the front door, the lorry was already driving off, so that most of the long and suitable reply that Jurie Steyn gave was lost on the driver.

Before that, with his foot on the clutch, the lorry-driver had been able to explain that his main grievance wasn't the coffee, which he was not by law compelled to drink. But he did have to handle Jurie Steyn's mailbag, the lorry-driver said. And although he was pressing down the accelerator at the time, we could still hear clearly what it was that the lorry-driver took exception to about Jurie Steyn's mailbag.

By the time Jurie Steyn had finished talking to the driver the lorry was already halfway through the poort.

"What do you think of that for cheek?" Jurie Steyn asked of us, on his way back to the counter. "He's just a paid servant of the Government, and he talks to me like I'm a Mtosa. I mean, he's no different from me, that lorry-driver isn't. I mean, I am after all the postmaster for this part of the Dwarsberge. I also get paid to serve the public. And that lorry-driver talks to me just like I talk to any Mtosa that comes in here to buy stamps."

We felt it was a pity that this unhappy note should have crept into what had until then been quite a pleasant summer afternoon's talk. What made it all the more regrettable, we felt, was because it was only another few weeks to Christmas. The way Jurie Steyn and the lorry-driver spoke to each other didn't fit in with the friendly spirit of Christmas, we felt. Nor did it fit in, either, with the even more friendly spirit that there should be at the New Year.

"And did you hear what he said about my mailbag?" Jurie Steyn demanded, indignantly. We confessed that we had. Indeed, we would have to have been more deaf yet than Oupa Bekker if we had missed any of the lorry-driver's remarks about the mailbag. Even though the engine of the lorry was running at the time, we could hear every word he said. The driver spoke so clearly. And what made what he said even more distinct was that kind of hurt tone in his voice. When a lorry-driver talks like he's injured, why, you can hear him from a long way off.

"What he said about my fowls," Jurie Steyn burst out. "That's what I can't get over. When he spoke about the mailbag that my fowls had – had been on."

Well, Jurie Steyn was expressing it more politely than the lorry-driver had done, we thought.

"And that he said afterwards that he had to handle that mailbag," Jurie Steyn continued.

Several of us spluttered, then, remembering the *way* in which the lorry-driver had said it.

"And that he declared they were a lot of speckled, mongrel, dispirited Hottentot hoenders," Jurie Steyn finished up, "with sickly, hanging-down combs. Well, that *got* me all right. There isn't a hen or a rooster on my farm that isn't a pure-bred Buff Orpington. Look at that hen pecking there, next to At Naudé's foot, now. Could you *call* it a speckled – "

Words failed Jurie Steyn, and he stopped talking.

Nevertheless, we all felt that it was unfortunate that Jurie Steyn should have had that misunderstanding with the lorry-driver. Because, what the lorry-driver's assistant had told us about the toy train in Policansky's window, at Bekkersdal, was something quite interesting. And we would have liked to talk about it some more. We felt that, in spite of Bekkersdal being so many miles away, it might perhaps be worthwhile to take our children to go and have a look at that shop window, all the same. It would be instructive for the children, we felt. But as a result of what had happened since, we weren't quite in the mood for that any more.

It was only Gysbert van Tonder who did not seem to have his feelings completely quenched.

"When that young lorry-driver's assistant spoke about the toy train in Policansky's window," Gysbert van Tonder remarked, "well, you know how it is, a toy train, with tunnels and all. I thought right away how my children would enjoy it. I even thought of driving over to Bekkersdal in my mule-cart next week, taking Oupa Bekker with me. And then we could come back and tell my children all about it, I thought. We could also tell the children all about that Chinaman that climbs up and down a ladder with baskets. We could get Policansky to wind up that Chinaman several times, I thought, so that we could explain exactly to the children how it works.

"But I haven't got quite that feeling for it, any more, if you know how it is. So my children will have to go without. And it would have been such fun for them, having me and Oupa Bekker telling them all about what makes that train work. What does make it work, I wonder? It might help them with their exams, to know."

But it was then that Chris Welman remembered what the lorry-driver's assistant was saying just before the lorry-driver shouted to him to get going. And it was as though that cloud that had come over us had never been.

For David Policansky had said that he was going to get a Father Christmas at his store again, this year. He said he had to have a Father Christmas. The toy trade was no good without a Father Christmas with a red cap and overcoat and white whiskers shaking hands with the children in the toy department, Policansky said. And we laughed and said that we would have thought that the toy trade was no good *with* a Father Christmas. And we also said that we hoped, for his own sake, that this year Policansky wouldn't get old Doors Perske to be Father Christmas, again, the same as he did last year.

We went on discussing last year's Father Christmas at Policansky's store for quite a long time.

As far as looks went, Doors Perske should have made a very good Santa Claus. He was fat and he had a red face. The circumstance of his face being on some occasions more red than on others would as likely as not escape the innocent observation of childhood.

But where Doors Perske went wrong was in his being essentially an odd-job man. For years he had contrived to exist in the small town of Bekkersdal by getting a contract to erect a sty, or to chop wood, or to dig a well. And that was how he had learnt to sub.

And so, when he was Santa Claus in Policansky's store, Doors Perske would every so often go and get a small advance against his pay from the bookkeeper. After a bit, the sight of Santa Claus entering the local public bar for a quick one no longer excited comment. The bartender no longer thought it funny to ask if he'd come down the chimney. No scoffing customers asked any more could he go and hold his reindeer.

In Policansky's store, too, everything was, at first, all right. If, in shaking hands with Doors Perske, a small child detected his beery breath, the small child would not think much of it. Since he had a father – or, maybe, a stepfather – of his own, the small child would not see anything incongruous in Father Christmas having had a few.

One day Doors Perske's wife had come charging into the toy department, swearing at Father Christmas and loudly accusing him of subbing on his wages, on the sly. And Doors Perske had called his wife an old —— , and had ungraciously clouted her one on the ear before bundling her out of the store. But even that incident did not have a disillusioning effect on the minds of David Policansky's juvenile clientele.

For the altercation had taken place at the counter where there were prams and doll's-houses and little crockery sets, and the children thronging that part of the shop were familiar with domestic scenes of the sort they had just witnessed. All they thought was that Father Christmas had just had a fight with Mother Christmas.

But it was the day before Christmas Eve that Doors Perske got the sack. He had just come back from the bar, again. And the first thing he had to do was to stumble over the shilling dips. Then, to save himself, he grabbed at an assortment of glassware stacked halfway up to the ceiling. This was foolish – as he realised next moment. The glassware offered him no sort of purchase at all. All that happened was that the whole shop shook when it fell. The next thing that went was the counter with the toy soldiers. And there didn't seem anything very martial in the way the little leaden soldiers – no longer in their neat toy-rows – were scattered around, lying in heaps and with pieces broken off them: it looked too much like the real thing. Grim, it looked.

When Policansky came rushing in, it was to find Doors Perske sitting in a wash-tub, with a teddy-bear in his arm. His red cap had come off and his Father Christmas beard was halfway round his neck. And from the position of his beard the children in the shop knew that he wasn't Father Christmas but just a dressed-up drunk.

"I couldn't get a proper grip on those glasses," Doors Perske explained. "That's how I fell."

Policansky got a proper grip on Santa Claus, all right. And he ran him out of his shop and when he got to the pavement he kicked Father Christmas, and told him not to come back again.

"Go on, there *isn't* any Father Christmas," Doors Perske jeered, suddenly recovering himself, when he got to the corner. "It's just a lie that you make up for kids."

David Policansky's face twisted into a half-smile.

"I wish I could believe you," he said, surveying the wreckage of his shop through the door. "I wish I could believe there *wasn't* a Father Christmas."

... At this Time of Year

IT WAS always about now, Jurie Steyn said, with the year drawing to an end, that he got all sorts of queer feelings. He didn't know how to say them, quite. But one feeling he did get, and that he had no difficulty in explaining, he said, was a homesickness to be back again in the Western Province where he had spent his early childhood.

Jurie Steyn heaved a medium-length sigh, then, thinking back on the years when he was young.

"Not that I haven't got a deep love for the Transvaal," Jurie Steyn added, in case we should get him wrong. "I am, after all, a Transvaler – "

And so we said, yes, it was quite all right. We understood his feelings for the old Cape Colony. He needn't explain, we said.

"And because I've said that I passed my young years in the Cape," Jurie Steyn went on, the suggestion of a combative look coming into his eye, "that doesn't mean to say that I am old, today."

We hastened to reassure him on that point, too – but not very convincingly, it seemed. Gysbert van Tonder even coughed.

"I know what you mean, Jurie," young Johnny Coen said, quickly, hastening to forestall any unpleasantness that might ensue on Jurie Steyn demanding of Gysbert van Tonder what he meant by clearing his throat, that way. "It's the place where you were born and bred and can't ever forget. I was born in the Marico Bushveld, and you've got no idea how homesick I got the time I was working on the railway at Ottoshoop.

"But, of course, Ottoshoop is at least ninety miles from here – further even, if you don't go the road through Sephton's Nek. So I know how you feel, Jurie. No matter how kind people are to you, even, if they're not your own people you do get very lonely, sometimes. Oh, yes, I went through all that at Ottoshoop."

Johnny Coen went on to describe a wedding reception that he had attended at Ottoshoop while he was an exile in those parts.

"They had spread white tablecloths over long tables on the front stoep," Johnny Coen said. "And there was a man at the party who did balancing tricks with a chair and a wine-glass. And I got more and more sad. The only time I laughed a little was when the loose seat dropped out of the chair and caught the man on the back of his neck when he was at the same time throwing up two guavas and a fork."

Johnny Coen went on to say that, as it turned out, his neighbour at table was also a foreigner.

"How I knew," Johnny Coen said, "was when that man spoke to me. And he said I was looking pretty miserable. And he asked was it that I was in love with the bride, perhaps, and that another man had taken her away from me. And I said, no, I was from the Dwarsberge part of the Marico, and I felt most homesick for the Groot Marico when the people around me were happy, I said. And that was how I got talking to that Englishman sitting next to me at the table. And when somebody in the voorkamer starting playing 'Home Sweet Home' on the harmonium we were both of us crying on to the tablecloth. And I never used to think that an Englishman had any feelings, until then.

"Another thing I found out afterwards that I had in common with the Englishman was that he didn't like that man with the balancing tricks, either."

Thereupon Jurie Steyn said that he, too, wouldn't like it very much if somebody were to start playing "Home Sweet Home" on a harmonium at this time of year. Of course, he knew it best as a German song, Jurie Steyn said, and it was called "Heimat Süsse Heimat." But the tune was the same. He had heard the German missionaries at Kronendal sing it quite often. And they would cry on to the thick slices of that kind of red sausage that they had on their plates, Jurie said.

"Take the Cape at this time of year, now," Jurie Steyn said, "in the summer."

So we said, very well, we would take the Cape, then, if he put it like that.

"Well, when it gets towards about now, towards about Christmas time and the end of the year," Jurie Steyn proceeded, "why, I just can't help it. I think of a little Boland dorp with white houses and water furrows at the side of the streets and oak trees. Not that I haven't got all the time in the world for moepel or a maroela or a kremetart or any other kind of bushveld tree. For instance, I have often walked to the end of my farm by the poort, just to go and look at the withaaks there. No, it isn't that. After all, an oak isn't a proper South African tree, even, but just imported.

157

"All the same, when it gets towards Christmas, the thought of those oak-trees in the Cape comes into my mind just all of a sudden, sort of. And I get the feeling of how much nobler a kind of person I was in those days than what I am today. I think of how much more upright I was in my youth."

Thereupon Gysbert van Tonder said, yes, that he could well believe.

We knew that Gysbert van Tonder – who was Jurie Steyn's neighbour – was hinting about the last bit of neighbourly unpleasantness they had, which had to do with the impounding of a number of stray oxen. And we didn't want to have *that* long argument all over again. Especially not with the Christmas season drawing near, and all.

It was quite a good thing, therefore, that Oupa Bekker should have started talking then about a quite ordinary camel-thorn tree that grew on one side of Bekkersdal when it was first laid out as a dorp.

"It was because of what Jurie Steyn said about oaks that made me think of it," Oupa Bekker said. "I was there when Bekkersdal was proclaimed as a township, and the bush was cleared away and the surveyor measured out the streets and divided up the erfs. And the Kommandant-General and the Dominee had words about whether the plein in the middle of the dorp should be for the Dopper Church, with a pastorie next to it, or for the Dopper Church, with a house for the Kommandant-General's son-in-law next to it, a site to be chosen for the pastorie that would be within easy walking distance for the Dominee."

Oupa Bekker said that in the end the Dominee decided that he wouldn't mind walking a little distance. Oupa Bekker said he had no doubt that what made the Dominee come to that decision was because the Dominee did not wish to make the Kommandant-General unhappy.

For it was well known throughout the Transvaal that few things made the Kommandant-General so unhappy as when he had to take firm steps against anybody who opposed him. And Oupa Bekker said it was also known that on occasion the Kommandant-General had taken steps that you might call even unusually firm against a person who stood in his way.

"And so the Dominee agreed, in the end," Oupa Bekker continued, "that a short brisk walk from his pastorie to the church, of a Sunday morning before the sermon, would be healthy for him. And so a house for the Kommandant-General was built on the measured-out erf on the plein next to the church. But all that happened – oh, so many years ago."

Oupa Bekker's sigh would have been even more prolonged than Jurie

Steyn's had been. Only, because of his advanced years, Oupa Bekker didn't have the breath for it.

"All the same, that was a funny thing," Chris Welman commented, "for the old days, that is. And so I suppose that's the reason why – "

Oupa Bekker nodded.

For we knew where the pastorie was, today, in Bekkersdal. And we knew that the present-day minister, Dominee Welthagen, had to walk a fairish distance to the church, of a Sunday, just as his predecessor of three-quarters of a century ago had to do. But that first Dominee would no doubt have been able to take short cuts, since at that time Bekkersdal would not have been as built up as it was today.

"And that erf that was measured out for the Kommandant-General's son-in-law – " Chris Welman started to remark.

"Yes, that's the reason for all that trouble there, now," Oupa Bekker said. "But the old people always knew that the Kommandant-General's son-in-law was a bit thoughtless. All those empty bottles that used to lie in his back yard, for instance. And that back yard isn't any more tidy today. Not with all those empty jam tins and all that garbage and all those empty fruit boxes lying in it. Why, that back yard looks worse than ever, now that it has been taken over for an Indian store. And right next to the Dopper Church, and all. No wonder there's that trouble about it in Bekkersdal, now."

So we said, it was very sinful of the first Indian – who was the grandfather of the present Indian – to have gone and bought that erf right next to the Dopper Church to go and open an Indian store on.

There should really have been a pastorie there, we said.

"Bit of a pity the Kommandant-General's son drank so much," Johnny Coen observed.

In the discussion that followed about what a scandal it was that there should be an Indian store next to the Dopper Church in Bekkersdal, Oupa Bekker was able only in an edgeways fashion to tell us about the camel-thorn tree that grew at the edge of the Bekkersdal township. And we were not able to pay much attention to Oupa Bekker's story, then. Whereas it was quite a pretty story.

It appears that the streets of the newly-laid dorp were planted with jacarandas – an imported tree then coming into fashion. And at the end of one street, in exact line with the jacarandas, and at the same distance from its nearest jacaranda neighbour as the jacarandas were set apart from each other, there grew that indigenous old African camel-thorn tree.

159

And although the street ended just before it came to him, the old camel-thorn tree really imagined that he was part of that jacaranda avenue. And he was as pleased as anything about it. And he started putting on airs, there, just as though he was also an imported tree, and not just an old camel-thorn that the veld was full of. And even though the municipality didn't water him, like they watered the jacaranda, the camel-thorn remained as cheerful as ever. He knew he didn't *need* watering.

Anyway, the point of Oupa Bekker's story had to do with the first summer that the jacarandas in Bekkersdal came to flowering. And one night there was a terrible wind from the Kalahari, so that in the morning the sidewalks were thickly strewn with purple flowers, and there were more jacaranda blooms stuck on the thorns of the old camel-thorn tree than any jacaranda still had on its branches, then. And the purple blossoms lay thick about the lower part of the gnarled trunk of the camel-thorn. It was his hour, and so you couldn't tell him from an imported tree.

We didn't hear very much of what Oupa Bekker had to say, however. We were too busy thinking out the right words for a strong letter we were drafting to our Member of Parliament. It had to do with the Indian Problem.

But it was after the railway lorry from Bekkersdal had drawn up at the front door that Gysbert van Tonder really let himself go on the Indian Problem. It was when Gysbert found out that the roll of barbed wire he had ordered wasn't on the lorry.

"It's the fault of the Indian storekeeper's assistant," the lorry-driver explained – although he used a different word in referring to the young Indian who has helping the old Indian in the Bekkersdal store. "I could see that the young Indian assistant wasn't himself. The shop was all done out with Christmas stockings, and things. And that old gramophone they've got at the back of the shop was playing 'Home Sweet Home.' And that young Indian assistant was busy crying on to the counter.

"Saying that at this time of the year he always got homesick for Natal, the Indian assistant said. Well, that beats me, all right. How anybody can ever feel homesick for Natal, I just don't know."

New-year Glad Rags

"Uren, dagen, maanden, jaren,
Vliegen als een schaduw heen."

THE PARTITION had been removed between the two classrooms. Ink stains and the marks left behind by water that had leaked through the thatched roof in the last rains were now covered up with a coating of whitewash. All the blemishes on the schoolroom walls of that year and of former years were hidden away.

For the more unhappy evidences of a year of educational activity within those walls the virginal film of unslaked lime served as both a mask and an immaculate cerement.

Dominee Welthagen had come over specially from Bekkersdal to hold an end-of-year service in that little Bushveld schoolhouse that had for a night been changed over into a place of worship.

Many of the desks were of the old-fashioned kind, seating a good number of pupils in a row and with the front parts detachable, so that their temporary conversion into pews had not presented much difficulty. There was that other, more modern kind of desk, however, with an iron framework, that obstinately continued to look like nothing else but standard Transvaal Education Department equipment, no matter what you did to it.

Nor did the blackboard standing on its easel in the corner take kindly to ecclesiastical disguise. Since this was a Calvinist service – and that sixteenth-century reformer's views on idolatry were well known – you couldn't go and hang an icon, say, in front of the blackboard.

Maybe, if it had been a church service that Dominee Welthagen had come to conduct at some other time, the elders and deacons would not have been so energetic in altering the appearance of the schoolroom. But there seemed to be something about devotions arranged for the end of the year that called for a certain measure of stage-setting.

After all, during the last few days of December one does, at times, become a prey to inner questionings. And it is only someone who is without human weaknesses of his own who will view with a cynical eye the earnest efforts of a deacon engaged in making a school cupboard look like an altar from the front. What is that thing inside the deacon – the cynic would ask – that the said deacon is trying to cloak? The answer, alas, is "Many things." For there never has been a church deacon that did not have his share of frailties.

161

The young schoolmaster was, strangely enough, very helpful.

It wasn't often that the schoolroom was used for a church service. And, generally speaking, a schoolmaster was not too keen on that sort of thing. In the first place, the church authorities would obtain permission direct from the Education Department head office in Pretoria to hold their service in the schoolroom, the schoolmaster's share in the formalities being limited to handing over the key of the building when an elder presented himself at the front door with a letter and a couple of Mtosa women carrying buckets of whitewash.

For the schoolmaster there was a certain amount of indignity in this situation.

All he would be able to say, reaching for his hat, was, "Well, I hope you won't slop all that stuff over my register again. Last year the inspector asked if there had been pigs at it."

Or the schoolmaster would say, unsmilingly locking some small change away in his desk, "Very well, you can take over. I've counted all the rulers and exercise books in the cupboard, there."

It wasn't that the schoolmaster was indifferent to the blessings that got conferred on the Groot Marico north of the Dwarsberge through these religious exercises. Indeed, when he thought of some of the church ouderlings he knew, he could only wonder where they would be, were it not for the benefits derived from divine intercession. Every schoolmaster who had ever taught in the Marico knew that church services held in the schoolroom did a lot of *good*.

But the trouble is that we all have our little human vanities. And the schoolmaster likes to think that in his schoolhouse he's a king. And so when a deacon, who is just an ordinary farmer, and with some of his children at that school, perhaps, turns up with a letter signed by somebody that's higher than a school inspector, even, why, it stands to reason that that schoolmaster won't feel too bucked about it. Especially if the deacon has got a kind of a sneer on his face in the act of taking over.

But with the schoolmaster, young Vermaak, it was quite different, this year, Jurie Steyn's brother-in-law said so himself. And Jurie Steyn's brother-in-law was the deacon (an ouderling not being available at the moment, because of the ploughing) who had gone to young Vermaak with a letter signed by a high authority, requesting the use of the schoolhouse for the Almighty. We knew from that that the letter must have had a pretty high-up signature.

And Jurie Steyn's brother-in-law, the deacon, said that young Vermaak was ever so polite and friendly about it. It took away a good deal of his pleasure, at first, the deacon said. He had hoped to come into the classroom and to find the schoolmaster correcting a lot of examination papers, or filling in reports, and that the schoolmaster would have been very sarcastic about having to leave, the deacon said. He was looking forward to the schoolmaster walking out of the schoolroom in a nasty temper and asking when was he expected to do his work. And so, when the schoolmaster was, instead, helpful, he almost wished he hadn't come along with that letter, the deacon said.

The deacon went on to explain that he made the Mtosas that he had brought with him lift the schoolmaster's table off the platform that it stood on, in front of the class. And young Vermaak didn't say a word. He even went to the assistance of one of the Mtosas who, forgetting for a moment that he was on a platform, stepped backwards off the edge of it, landing with his back part in a bucket of whitewash. The schoolmaster assisted the Mtosa with his boot, the deacon said, adding that he could not have done it more neatly himself, seeing that the Mtosa was sitting *in* the bucket of whitewash, and therefore not leaving much space, really, for getting properly assisted.

The schoolmaster went up a lot in his estimation, the deacon said, when he saw the quick way in which the schoolmaster helped that Mtosa to rise.

"And then I made the Mtosas stand the platform on its edge against the wall," the deacon added. "And they did that, one of them still limping a little from the way the schoolmaster had helped him. And then I said I would cover the platform with those sheets of black drawing paper that had pictures of mealies and maps of rivers on them. I said I would turn those drawings round and pin them on to the platform stood on its edge, and so it would look more like a preekstoel, the place where Dominee Welthagen was to stand.

"Those drawings had been made by young Vermaak himself, and they were stuck all round the walls. And I said it just for a joke, of course, in order to make him wild. And do you know what he did? He went and fetched a little packet of drawing-pins, so as to help us with that, also."

We were most surprised to hear that from the deacon. We were, after all, religious people ourselves. But we knew that there were limits. And we feared that if the schoolmaster got so religious, then it must be that there was something on his mind.

Then we remembered that we hadn't seen young Vermaak at Jurie

Steyn's post office for quite a few months. Maybe, that was worrying him, we thought – the fact that during all that time he hadn't come to visit us. But we also realised that, seeing it was drawing towards the end of the year, he would be too busy, setting examination papers and correcting them, and fixing things so that his favourite pupil would come first again.

Not that we bore him any ill-will, on that account, of course. It was many years since any one of us had last been at school. And we were glad to think that we had been mellowed by the years, so that we no longer retained our childhood prejudices. We thought of a teacher's pet only as a snivelling rat that wipes his nose on his sleeve, but we had no evil feelings about him.

> "Snelt dan, jaren, snelt vrij henen
> Met uw blijdskap en verdriet – "

It was beautiful the way we sang the words of the next verse of Hymn 160 in the schoolroom that had been converted into a house of worship, we all of us singing together.

This was a Reformed Church service. But that did not prevent quite a number of us, who were Doppers, from attending, also. Moreover, we who were Doppers were not allowed by our Enkel Gereformeerde Kerk to sing hymns; we were only permitted to sing psalms. And yet there was something about Dominee Welthagen's Reformed Church service that night that we couldn't resist.

And so in the end it was actually us Doppers who, strictly speaking, were not *allowed* to sing a hymn, even, that showed those Reformers how a hymn should be *sung*. But if only Dominee Welthagen had announced a psalm, instead! If only Dominee Welthagen had said "The congregation will now sing 'Kom laat ons zamen Israel's Heer'" – why, you would have heard us as far as Vleisfontein, and it would have been only Dopper voices that you would have heard, and Dominee Welthagen's own Reform congregation would have been nowhere.

There was Jurie Steyn, there, wearing his new suit that he had bought on mail order, just sending his measurements. There was Oupa Bekker, with a collar that, if it was perhaps not quite so white, any more, as the predikant's, was certainly a good deal taller and stiffer. There was Gysbert van Tonder in a suit of formal cut, with a slit up the back of the jacket that was fashionable when Gysbert van Tonder first trekked into the Marico as a comparatively young man.

At Naudé was wearing his Sunday best, also a three-piece, that, whatever its original colour, was now, except for a few undecided areas, an almost uniform green. Young Vermaak, the schoolmaster, looked dignified in navy serge. In that light you could hardly see the places where his landlady's daughter had cleaned the jacket with paraffin.

So much for the men in their New Year apparel.

The women's dresses were, mostly, new. There was consequently little that, to the male gaze, would enable one frock to be distinguished from another. With the women themselves, of course, it was different. They had a lot to whisper, behind hymn-books, about skirt lengths and waistlines and hats – that was, if you could call a thing a hat that seemed to be a piece of cardboard with a blue handkerchief stuck on it with a brass safety pin.

But there were other words and other images, also, that some of the women, whispering behind hymn-books, used in describing Pauline Gerber's hat. But afterwards they didn't talk about her hat so much…

> "Welzalig hij, die op U bouwt,
> Geheel zijn lot aan U vertrouwt – "

We sang that at the end of the service, all of us standing up.

And it was only after the church was out that we started talking about Pauline Gerber, whom we hadn't seen much of since the time she had come back, so smart and all, from finishing-school. We said that she was looking as smart as ever, now, no matter what you thought of her hat. We also started saying things about young Vermaak, the schoolmaster, then. We spoke of his singular behaviour in going away straight after the service, instead of staying to talk, first to one little group and then to another, in the way that we all did.

But mostly we spoke of Pauline Gerber. For by that time even the men, who were naturally not so observant in such matters as were the women, had noticed that, while Pauline Gerber's striped frock was no doubt styled to accord with the latest fashion, there was something in the actual fit of her dress that was obedient to a much older decree. It was well that her dress hung down wide like that, we said. It also struck us that, like young Vermaak, Pauline Gerber, too, had not stayed around outside the schoolhouse, to talk.

Notes on the Text

AS NOTED in the introduction, this volume includes the first thirty-six Voorkamer stories, word for word and in the order in which they first appeared. Each was a discrete item of between 1600 and 2 600 words, the sole exception being "School Concert", which was longer and divided into two parts over 17 and 24 June. Each may now be read as a sequential part of a larger whole. Accordingly, the pieces have been run on here, rather than presented as separate stories each beginning on a new page, to maintain the momentum of the whole.

As regards the individual texts themselves, only the usual light copyediting was required. For a while Bosman couldn't decide whether Johnny Coen should be "Johnnie" Coen; Dominee Welthagen first appears as "Dominie Wildhagen"; and the misleading "veldlangers" in "News Story" has been corrected to "veldlanges" – the last perhaps suggesting Bosman's (or *The Forum*'s) imperfect grasp of Afrikaans.

I have also corrected "Pilansberg" (Pilanesberg), "Lobatsi" (Lobatse), "Riesmierbult" (Rysmierbult), "Zambesi" (Zambezi), "koodoo" (koedoe), "Schweizer-Reineke" (Schweizer-Reneke), "boabab" (baobab), "tintinkies" (tinktinkies) and several other minor details of this sort. The usual range of punctuation errors and inconsistencies of spelling and hyphenation has been routinely adjusted.

The fact that the stories appeared only once in Bosman's lifetime (unlike, for example, the stories of *Mafeking Road*), has meant that there were no decisions to make about which version to prefer. The stories reprinted here appeared weekly in *The Forum*, without interruption, from 15 April to 22 December 1950; these original printings provided the copy-texts for this edition. The text here is without abridgements or censorings.